Bones of Holly

ALSO BY CAROLYN HAINES

SARAH BOOTH DELANEY MYSTERIES

Lady of Bones

Independent Bones

A Garland of Bones

The Devil's Bones

Game of Bones

A Gift of Bones

Sticks and Bones

Charmed Bones

Rock-a-Bye Bones

Bone to Be Wild

Booty Bones

Smarty Bones

Bonefire of the Vanities

Bones of a Feather

Bone Appetit

Greedy Bones

Wishbones

Ham Bones

Bones to Pick

Hallowed Bones

Crossed Bones

Splintered Bones

Buried Bones

Them Bones

NOVELS

A Visitation of Angels

The Specter of Seduction

The House of Memory

The Book of Beloved

Trouble Restored

Bone-a-fied Trouble

Familiar Trouble

Revenant

Fever Moon

Penumbra

Judas Burning

Touched

Summer of the Redeemers

Summer of Fear

NONFICTION

My Mother's Witness: The Peggy Morgan Story

Bones of Holly

A Sarah Booth Delaney Mystery

CAROLYN HAINES

MINOTAUR BOOKS
NEW YORK

First published in the United States by Minotaur Books, an imprint of St. Martin's Publishing Group

BONES OF HOLLY. Copyright © 2022 by Carolyn Haines. All rights reserved. Printed in the United States of America. For information, address St. Martin's Publishing Group, 120 Broadway, New York, NY 10271.

www.minotaurbooks.com

Library of Congress Cataloging-in-Publication Data

Names: Haines, Carolyn, author.
Title: Bones of Holly : a Sarah Booth Delaney mystery / Carolyn Haines.
Description: First Edition. | New York : Minotaur Books, 2022. | Series: A Sarah Booth Delaney mystery ; 25
Identifiers: LCCN 2022023225 | ISBN 9781250833754 (hardcover) | ISBN 9781250833761 (ebook)
Subjects: LCGFT: Novels.
Classification: LCC PS3558.A329 B656 2022 | DDC 813/.54—dc23
LC record available at https://lccn.loc.gov/2022023225

Our books may be purchased in bulk for promotional, educational, or business use. Please contact your local bookseller or the Macmillan Corporate and Premium Sales Department at 1-800-221-7945, extension 5442, or by email at MacmillanSpecialMarkets@macmillan.com.

First Edition: 2022

10 9 8 7 6 5 4 3 2 1

For the many wonderful librarians and book lovers
who have enriched my life

Bones of Holly

1

"Jingle Bell Rock" pours from a local jewelry store on the Main Street of Bay St. Louis, Mississippi. I walk with my friend and business partner, Tinkie, who pushes her daughter Maylin in a super-duper stroller. We pause to admire the diamonds, emeralds, and beautiful designs on display in the storefront. The window is decorated with a real cedar and holly garland that carries the scent of so many Christmases past. No store-bought decorations can ever replace the power of the real thing.

"Oh, Sarah Booth, look at the square-cut emerald. Isn't that your birthstone?"

Tinkie loves beautiful jewelry, and I stop beside her to admire the ring. "It is beautiful, but jewelry doesn't do it for me, Tinkie."

"I know. You'd rather have a hoe or wheelbarrow. Dear goodness, you are a bad role model for all the feminine women who enjoy the finer things in life."

I laugh with her. Tinkie is the perfect society lady *and* the perfect mother, facts which also sometimes cause people to underestimate her intelligence. But we aren't here in this beautiful Mississippi coastal town for work. This trip is part of our Christmas celebrations.

Bay St. Louis, a small town on the high ground of the Bay of St. Louis, was nearly wiped from the map during Hurricane Katrina. But it has come back strong, retaining the quaint and eclectic flavor that made it such a destination spot for artists, writers, designers, and those who love the coastal way of life. Booze, gambling, and easy women, while not always legal, were always available down the entire coastline from New Orleans to Alabama. Unlike so much of the rest of Mississippi, the coast has always been a "live and let live" kind of place.

Tinkie had found us the perfect place to stay for our visit. She was a master of locating unique accommodations, and the Bay Moon Inn, operated by two eccentric and very likable sisters, Martha and Ellie, was absolutely marvelous.

We move on down the street, admiring antiques, chic dress shops, restaurants with mouthwatering menus posted on chalkboards, and bars where cleaning crews are setting up for the afternoon. Christmas decorations are everywhere— and the tradition of creating Christmas scenes in storefront windows is still alive here. I love it.

The baby's stroller has a slight creak in one wheel. It's an amusing fact to me and Maylin but one that is driving my partner in Delaney Detective Agency, Tinkie Bellcase Richmond, to a near breakdown.

"If that stroller doesn't stop creaking like that, I'm going to buy some lighter fluid and matches and put it out of its misery." Tinkie kicks the protesting wheel, though not very hard. Precious cargo rides in that stroller.

"Oil can!" I pretend to freeze in place and eke the two words out of a frozen mouth. "Oil can!" I slap my leg at the knee and take a precarious step, acting as if my joints are frozen by rust. "Oil can!" *The Wizard of Oz* is my all-time favorite movie.

"You are a wart on Satan's buttocks." Tinkie glares at me, but Maylin giggles. The baby is not even two months old but she is very advanced. Or so the wags of my home-town, Zinnia, Mississippi, tell me. Maylin, the long-awaited offspring of Zinnia's most prominent family, Oscar and Tinkie Richmond, is the darling of the town. And I, for one, couldn't be happier. Maylin is a miracle baby, coming when every doctor in the Southeast said that Tinkie could never have a child.

"Sarah Booth, stop acting like the rusted tin man and do something about that wheel."

"Like I can magically conjure up some oil?" I ask, but I had noticed a quaint hardware store on the corner we just passed. Tinkie, Maylin, Oscar, and their nanny Pauline, are all in town along with my fellow, Sheriff Coleman Peters, and me, to judge the local library's annual Christmas tree decorating contest. Later we'll be joined by friends and loved ones for what has become our annual Christmas trip to a small Mississippi town. Tinkie, Oscar, Pauline, and Maylin came down in one car, and Coleman and I traveled down in the Roadster, my mother's antique convertible, which I refuse to give up for any reason.

Coleman and Oscar nearly ran over themselves heading to

the casinos that have proliferated all down the Mississippi Gulf Coast. Legalized gambling has changed the sleepy fishing villages of Biloxi and Gulfport into major tourist destinations. Not normally gamblers, Coleman and Oscar were eager for a few games of chance, and Tinkie and I were glad to see them go. We have last-minute shopping to finish.

"I'll get some oil for that wheel." I point back to the hardware store. Then I point in the other direction. "There's a pottery place if you want to wait for me there." I grin to hide my true motive. I will get the oil, but I also want to pick up a battery-operated drill for Oscar. Tinkie has him putting together all kinds of baby stuff and Oscar has never been handy. The drill should help him out a lot.

"Pottery!" Tinkie's eyes go wide. "I need to find something for Millie. Something unique. That would be perfect."

"Meet you there in fifteen. And don't kick the stroller again. If you knock the wheel off, you'll have to papoose that baby everywhere you go."

"I wonder who'd help me carry her?" Tinkie asks, all big, blue-eyed innocence—because she knows I love toting that little dumpling around. Maylin is all smiles and curiosity. Seeing the world from what I perceive as her view gives everything a new glow.

Tinkie, Maylin, and the creaking wheel head to the pottery gallery while I dash back to the hardware emporium to grab some oil and the drill. There's a commotion in the alley between the hardware store and a boutique, and I stop to see what's what. Moving down the alley is a woman in stilettos and a midnight blue sequined gown with a matching cap on top of carefully set chestnut waves. Whoever she is, she is from another era. Or at least dressed for another time.

"Hey!" My curiosity must be fed. "Hey, hold up!"

She turns to look at me and I realize I know her. Not personally, but she's famous. She's Clara Bow. I knew about her film career that started in silent films and continued into talkies. Her early life was tragic, and film success didn't erase the hardships she'd endured, but when she was in front of a camera, she had *it*. She projected a magical life filled with joy and happiness. "Hey, wait up!" She turns right at the end of the alley and disappears.

What is a long-dead movie star doing in a Bay St. Louis alley? I take off to find out.

"Clara!" I catch up with her behind the store, and I realize I know her better than I thought. Clara is actually Jitty, my resident haint. She's followed me from Dahlia House in Zinnia down to the Gulf Coast. "What are you doing here, Jitty?" I know she won't tell me, but I ask anyway.

"Louella Parsons says I have a dangerous pair of eyes."

She does. Her eyes, highlighted with heavy kohl, are mesmerizing. And sad. "Are you okay?"

She nods. "Better than okay most days. Drink the cup of joy, Sarah Booth. Pass up the cup of misery whenever you can."

It's grand advice, but it chills me to think she's talking about something specific. She won't tell me the truth, so I ask another question. "Are you Christmas shopping for the Great Beyond?"

"No, I'm bird-dogging you to make sure you don't wreck Christmas with some of your shenanigans."

Now that is the kind of smart-ass answer that lightens my heart. "Kind of hard to be a gumshoe in stilettos."

Jitty does a little turn, cocks a hip, and strikes a pose. I see the spark of life that makes Clara Bow famous.

"I don't have time for this foolishness." I am amused,

but Tinkie has become impatient since Maylin's birth. Her hormones are all aflutter, and unless she's super-heating her credit card she will be tapping her foot waiting for me. "Go home to Dahlia House, Jitty. I'll be there soon. I have to judge the tree contest and then do a little celebrating with my friends."

"That good-lookin' lawman comin' home with you?" Clara is slowly morphing into Jitty. The beautiful ball gown disappears, replaced by tights and a bright red thermal shirt with a decorated Christmas tree on the front. Yet again, she is wearing my clothes without even a word of apology.

"Yes, he is. Coleman is here with me for some fun but we'll be home in time to celebrate Christmas at Dahlia House." Jitty adores Coleman. "Now skedaddle so I can get my chore done before Tinkie comes looking for me."

"Your wish is my command." Jitty crosses her arms and does a fast nod, à la Barbara Eden, and poof! She is gone. I hurry back to the front door, grab a salesman, and find oil and the exact drill I'd envisioned for Oscar.

With the creaky wheel oiled and the packages Tinkie purchased set to be delivered to the Bay Moon Inn where we are staying, Tinkie and I set out for the local independent bookstore, Bay Books. The town has holiday charm. Old-fashioned Christmas lights and tinsel—the multicolored kind that laced along power and telephone lines—bring back memories of Zinnia when my parents were alive. Each Christmas we'd ridden around town in the convertible, bundled under coats and blankets, to see the beautiful decorations in town and at some of the country houses. There were no blow-up cartoon characters. Just colored lights, tinsel, and greenery cut from the woods. Bay St. Louis had harkened back to those times and I loved it.

We had a map of the downtown merchants, so we knew exactly where we were going, but it didn't really matter. Each little shop we passed offered tantalizing possibilities for gifts. I had only Cece left to buy for, and I wanted something that spoke to her. I just wasn't certain what that might be yet. She was the hardest of all my friends to find the right gift for.

"Coleman is very interested in the latest Jack Reacher book," I said, pointing down the street at Bay Books. "I'll pick that up as a stocking stuffer for him."

"And there's a great book on gardening I read about that I want to get for Millie," Tinkie said. "The bookstore is a terrific idea."

"Did you read the email from the library?" I asked her. I knew she hadn't. Tinkie loved the telephone, not email. She had me to do the email reading.

"Did I miss something?"

"Only that the other two judges for the Christmas tree decorating contest are local authors. Sandra O'Day and Janet Malone."

"Janet Malone!" Tinkie virtually squealed. I'd forgotten that she could hold her own with any sorority girl squealer when she chose to. "The one who writes those scandalous, sexy thrillers?"

"That's the one. And Sandra O'Day is equally famous for nonfiction."

"And they're both always throwing hissy fits and badmouthing each other." Tinkie was thrilled. "This is going to be the cat's meow."

We crossed the road, aiming for Bay Books. The smell of

8

Carolyn Haines

fresh baking bread, though, stopped Tinkie and me in our tracks.

"Yum!" Tinkie sniffed the air like my wonderful hound dog, Sweetie Pie, who was at Dahlia House being tended by Deputy DeWayne Dattilo, along with the three horses, Chablis—Tinkie's little dust mop dog—and Pluto and Gumbo, the cats. An animal lover, DeWayne always volunteered to help with the critters if we had to travel.

"Let's get our books and we can stop in that bakery. We need a treat for when the men get back from the casino. Something to soak up the alcohol you know they're drinking," I said.

"Good idea."

We set off again just as the front door of the bookstore flew open. A pretty woman with chestnut hair stumbled backward out of the store, tripped on the curb, and fell in the street. Before she could stand up, at least seven hardcover books were hurled out the door and aimed right at her.

"You plagiarizing hussy!" The woman gained her feet and I recognized Janet Malone. Her face was white with fury. She picked up several books and threw them back in the door at whoever was chucking books at her. She put a lot of muscle behind the throws. Inside, someone cried out in pain.

"Ladies! Ladies!" The bookseller, a young man, moved to stand in the door to stop the torrent of books flying back and forth. "Please, ladies. Someone is going to get hurt."

A fat book whacked him in the back of the head, and he abandoned the doorway and his attempt to stop the mayhem.

"I'm going to kick your ass all the way to the bay," Janet said as she stomped toward the front door, dodging another half dozen books. "You've taken this too far."

"Who's inside the store?" Tinkie asked. "Do you think it's Sandra O'Day?"

"I'm afraid so."

"Let's go inside." Tinkie pushed the stroller forward. Maylin was kicking her little feet as if she, too, was excited by the fight.

"Maylin could get hurt." I restrained her with a hand on her shoulder.

"Nonsense. Maylin and I can slip in and hide in the stacks. We'll be perfectly safe." Tinkie shook me off. "Get your camera out. Video this. Cece and Millie will dance at your wedding if you get this on video."

She was right about that. I pulled out my phone and started filming as we approached the store.

"You're a has-been," yelled Sandra O'Day, who had taken a position behind a huge table filled with her books. "You can't even write a decent plot anymore. If your characters didn't jump in the sack every three minutes, your book would be only blank pages."

"And if you jumped in the sack on occasion, you might not be such a pinch-lipped spinster," Janet replied. "My characters and I know how to live life fully. You're just a dried-up, angry old prune."

"You get your characters from Jerry Springer's show," Sandra replied. "You have an affinity for sluts and harlots."

"And you can only write about dead people because the dead can't sue for libel." Janet could give as good as she took.

"What you call living is pathetic." Sandra put her hands on her hips.

"I'm surprised you haven't been charged with violating a corpse, as dead as the people in your books are."

"Holy cow," Tinkie whispered to me. "They hate each other. This feud hasn't been exaggerated."

"But Cece and Millie are going to love it." I wasn't making any secret that I was videoing the writers, who didn't seem to mind at all.

"Should we introduce ourselves as their fellow judges?" Tinkie asked.

"Not me. I don't want to be hit in the head with a flying book today. And if you go over there, leave Maylin with me."

"Get out of this store," Sandra demanded of Janet. "Leave now and I won't press charges."

"Go right ahead. You're the one who pushed me down in the street and threw books at me," Janet said. "Call the cops. Please."

"Ladies," the bookseller said, "I did call the cops. I'll be sending a bill for the damages to the books to you, Ms. O'Day. And you, Ms. Malone, please stop antagonizing Ms. O'Day. My store can't afford for someone to really be hurt here. I'd have to close the doors permanently."

"Oh, no, we'd never hold you responsible," Janet said. "But your point is taken. I'm leaving now."

"Coward!" O'Day called after her. "The cops are on the way and you know you'll be arrested so you run for the hills like the coward you are!"

Janet Malone brushed past us without even a glance. She was out the door and down the street as a local police officer pulled up to the curb. A cute young man, spiffy in his uniform, came into the store. Tinkie and I discreetly eased outside and headed away. I doubted any charges would be filed, but I didn't want to end up testifying against one or both of my fellow judges.

"Let's go back to the inn," Tinkie said. "Maylin is hungry. We can order delivery from that wonderful restaurant nearby and take a nap."

I wasn't nursing a growing baby or taking care of one, but a nap sounded delightful anyway. "We have to be at the library at four to tour the trees. There are a lot of them and we should make preliminary notes on the ones we like best. There are all kinds of categories so this is going to be challenging."

The walk back to the inn was wonderful. A mini-parade of high school kids, dressed as Santa's helpers, drove slowly down the street with Christmas music playing on the car radios as the kids tossed candy at us. Tinkie and I caught several Christmas-wrapped chocolates that we put in the stroller for later.

"I love this little town," Tinkie said. "I could live here."

"Me, too. And you're going to love the library. I was there several years ago. They have the most wonderful children's room. It's the perfect place for an imagination to grow. And the librarian, Mary Perkins, is so much fun. She has a library cat, Weezie. Maylin will adore it."

Tinkie nodded and yawned simultaneously. "Can't wait. Food and nap first though."

We turned down the tree-shaded lane that led to our rooms. I pulled my key from my pocket. Since the Cadillac wasn't in the parking lot, I figured Coleman and Oscar were still at the casino. Speaking of the devil, my phone chimed and I checked the message to find a picture of Coleman and Oscar with a pile of winnings at a twenty-one table.

"Cash it in and come take a nap with me," I wrote back after showing Tinkie the photo.

"On the way," Coleman replied.

"I'll order lunches for Oscar and Coleman, too," I told

Tinkie as I helped her get the stroller into the lovely room. "And by the time they're delivered, the boys should be here."

"A plan is conceived and born." Tinkie yawned again as she lifted Maylin from the stroller. The little baby was ready for food.

"See you in about an hour." I discreetly left them to their privacy. Tinkie was still a little shy, and I was ravenous.

2

While I waited for the food to be delivered, I sent the video I'd taken of the literary catfight to Cece. As expected, I immediately got a call from my journalist friend.

"You are a goddess, dahling!" Cece laughed. "This is the best video! And those two women are your fellow judges? They're going to want to kill you when they realize you've filmed them for publication."

"I don't think so. They don't seem to mind everyone in town knowing that they hate each other."

"The insults are just so . . . delicious!"

Cece was pleased and I was elated. "Glad I could help."

"I've done a little research on O'Day and Malone," Cece said. "Interested?"

"Always." Cece had sources in the media that I envied at times.

"O'Day grew up in Waveland, Mississippi, the oldest child of a middle-class family. She started writing for her high school newspaper, worked a few years as an investigative reporter for the *New Orleans Times Picayune*, and then got her first book contract on a book about David Duke, failed presidential candidate and Grand Wizard of the Ku Klux Klan. Critics called the book fearless and groundbreaking."

"She sounds like a serious journalist." That didn't jibe with the display I'd seen earlier that morning at the bookstore. Sandra O'Day seemed more than half a bubble off.

"She was a highly respected journalist in her twenties. And she's critically regarded in the nonfiction world. Her book on Duke and the KKK was followed two weeks later by Janet's wom-jep thriller."

"Wom-jep?" Had Cece suddenly started speaking in tongues?

"Woman in jeopardy. About a journalist that infiltrates the KKK training camps in the swamps of Louisiana and frees several young girls who have been sold into sexual slavery. Of course she falls in love with one of the Klansmen and she's in a real dilemma until she figures out that he's an undercover FBI agent and not a racist lout."

I thought about it. "Same material, very different story."

"Exactly," Cece said. "This is when the celebrated feud started. Sandra went on national television and accused Janet of tapping her phones and stealing her research. It was a big hullabaloo. Sandra and Janet both went on the David Letterman show and had a catfight."

"What did Janet say about the accusation that she was a . . . plagiarist?" I wasn't certain plagiarism was the correct charge. Stealing research sources and historical information wasn't exactly what I viewed as plagiarism.

"She denied it, of course. And she responded that Sandra was trying to whitewash, so to speak, her family's role in the KKK."

Oh, brother. "Game on."

"Exactly. From there it's only gotten worse."

"So what is Malone's background?" I was very curious.

"Born in Waveland, Mississippi, to a middle-class family. Father an accountant, mother a housewife. She was often disciplined at school for skipping class and hiding out at the library reading 'torrid potboilers,' as the school psychologist labeled the books."

"Exactly what she's writing today."

"I don't think that's fair. Malone's books are much, much better than potboilers. There's a level of character development and also social conscience. Both women are fine writers. It's just uncanny how they end up writing about the same material."

"Does Malone always copy O'Day?"

"No. That's the thing. Sometimes Malone will have a new book out about something like the mafia in New Orleans, and only a few weeks later, O'Day will publish a nonfiction about the mafia's possible role in the Kennedy assassination. It's like they share the same psychic wavelength. It's one of the more fascinating things about them. And look how they both moved to Bay St. Louis. Surely that's more than a bit odd. But each one denies knowing the other was coming here. They arrived on the same day!"

"Sandra tackled the mob connection to Kennedy's assassination?" I was still stuck on that point.

"She did. She and her assistant, Daryl Marcus, received death threats."

"What's the story on Daryl Marcus?"

"Oh, that's intriguing, too. Some say he's in love with Sandra and others say he's a family relative, like a cousin or something. His devotion to her is legendary. He helps with all of her research and manages her promotion and press matters. He also orchestrates her social media, which is brilliant. He's the one thing Sandra has that Janet can't match. He lives in the old Buntman mansion with her but both deny any romantic attraction."

Cece was an endless source of juicy gossip. I couldn't wait to see Daryl and Sandra together to see if my love detector went off.

"When Sandra was working on the New Orleans mob book, Daryl was framed for a burglary at Janet's house, arrested, and held in jail until Sandra got him out. Word on the street was that Janet filed the false accusation. But some think it was set up by the mafia to send a message to Sandra to back off."

I'd dealt with cults, killers, crazies, and crackpots, but not the mafia. "Those critics were correct about O'Day. She is fearless to tackle the mob. I've heard all kinds of stories about connected gangsters in New Orleans and how ruthless they are."

"There's also the Dixie Mafia, which once ruled the Mississippi Gulf Coast," Cece pointed out. "When the casinos came in with the big Vegas money behind them, the local guys got squeezed a lot. My sources tell me there are still

some skirmishes going on in that area. I heard a rumor Sandra was dabbling in that world. If you go poking around,
be careful."

I loved the old stories of strip bars and backroom high-
stakes poker games that were part of the Gulf Coast history. There was a type of forbidden glamour that came
with the times. Those days of showgirls and fancy yachts
had all seemed so romantic—and so distant from my ado-
lescence in Zinnia, where my dad was a respected attorney
and judge. As an adult, though, I realized how powerfully
corrupting money could be. And how dangerous. For the
women trapped in the dancing or call girl trade, it was anything but glamorous.

"Any clue as to how the writers seem to know what each
other is doing?"

Cece hesitated. "Since you told me about O'Day and
Malone judging with you, I've been researching their pasts.
Their relationship has been a hotbed of accusation and
drama. They both accused each other of setting up spy cameras and tapping phones. Sandra even went so far as to request the FBI investigate Malone, a fact that didn't endear
her to Janet."

"It's almost as if fate pits them against each other."

"Lots of writers believe that certain ideas are like energy
in the air. The same story concept will hit several people at
the same time. There's no way to tell which one will win out,
and Sandra and Janet write very different types of books. It
may start from the same source but it ends up very differ-
ently."

"I've heard the same thing about the fashion industry."
And I'd heard it from Cece, but I didn't bother to toss her

that bone. "Suddenly the concept of minidresses is on the wind and everyone starts designing and selling them. Or ripped jeans. Or crop tops."

"Or yoga pants."

I didn't say anything. Yoga pants were a particular aggravation to Cece because so many people who shouldn't, wore them in public. "Uh-huh."

"Yesterday I saw Charmaine Appleton in the tightest Lycra I've ever seen. When she walked away it was like watching two possums in a wrestling match in her pants. I thought my eyes were going to bleed."

I didn't want to laugh but I couldn't help myself. "Don't ever change, Cece."

"Oh, I have no intention of becoming polite or proper. Don't worry."

"I have to go. Food delivery is here." I'd seen the car pull into the parking lot and a young man with several large bags exit the vehicle. "If you find anything I should know, text me."

"Keep sending the videos. We'll gain another hundred thousand followers with content like that. You'll have the perfect opportunity to get another scoop at the big party tonight at Sandra O'Day's mansion. I hear it is quite the showplace. Formerly owned by the movie star Helene Buntman and built by Al Capone. Get a lot of interior photos, please."

"Will do." I hung up, paid for the food, and knocked on Tinkie's door. Just as she answered with Maylin in her arms, Coleman and Oscar pulled into the lot.

We ate lunch at a wrought iron table beside a lovely pool with frogs and mermaids squirting water in sparkling arcs.

The sound of the falling water was relaxing, and Tinkie and I filled Oscar and Coleman in on our day and the cat- fight. When we were done, we urged Tinkie and Oscar to take a nap. Coleman helped me clean up the table, and then we went to our room.

"How much did you win?" I asked.

"I got three thousand and some change, and Oscar won about four thousand."

"That's amazing," I said. I didn't like gambling—it was just tedious to me—and when I tried, I never won. I'd prob- ably enjoy it more if I ever won anything. "I'm impressed."

"If we'd stayed another hour, all of our winnings would have vanished. We'll go back while you and Tinkie are busy with your judging job and we'll spend it all. My goal is to break even."

I had to laugh. Coleman was a man of reality. "Sounds like you know the score. Let's get horizontal. I have some- thing I want to show you."

"Oh, really." He knew exactly what I was up to.

I was just about to climb in the bed when my cell phone rang.

"Don't answer it," Coleman said, his shirt already off.

I looked at the number. "I have to. It's the library."

"Why is the library calling?"

"Because a lot of people don't have a reason to go to bed at . . ." I checked my watch. "One o'clock." I had to laugh. "We didn't use to be people who went to bed in the after- noon, either."

"But we weren't planning on sleeping," he pointed out with a sigh.

I answered the phone.

"Sarah Booth?"

"Yes," I said, curious to hear why Mary Perkins was calling. "What's going on?"

"Sorry to bother you, but a reporter from a New Orleans television station just called. He saw some video you'd taken of Sandra and Janet in one of their set-tos. He wants to talk to you. Is it okay if I give him your number?"

Mary was protective of her guests. "Sure. But not until tomorrow." I didn't mind talking to other media, but Cece had an exclusive with me as far as I was concerned. My video would be "old news" by tomorrow.

"And there was a woman here asking when you'd be at the library. Someone who has a case for you."

I was always happy to have work, but this was my vacation. I'd worked the last few Christmases without intending to. This time, I just wanted to be a regular person enjoying the holiday. "If I see her, I'll take care of it."

"She said she'd be back. She was kind of pushy. Wanted to know where you were staying, but I didn't tell her."

"Thank you. I'm hoping for some R and R. Tinkie, too. That baby wears her down a lot more than she expected."

"She'll get her second wind. It just takes some adjusting. Okay, I'll set up an appointment for the WXBX reporter to call you tomorrow."

"Excellent. Did the woman looking for me leave a name or contact info?"

"No. She said she'd see you tomorrow."

I put the phone on the charger and walked into the kitchen area to get a glass of water. It was a beautiful December day. Perfect for sweaters and jeans without being cold. My room at the inn faced the bay, and I stepped out on the balcony for a view of the sun reflecting off the water. The scene was framed by live oak trees, and the leaves were the perfect fringe for the beautiful view of the bay, with sailboats and speed boats anchored at the marina. A big yacht caught my eye. Two people were on the deck, dancing to the faint sounds of a big band. It was a scene made for romance, and my man was waiting for me in the bedroom. I blew a kiss to the water and stepped back to the door. The shadows shifted beneath the biggest oak tree and I froze.

A silhouette stepped out from behind the tree and stood in the glare of the sun on the water. It seemed to be staring directly at me. It lifted a hand in greeting, as if the person knew me. Then it drew its hand across its neck in the classic gesture of throat cutting.

The message was clear as a bell.

It took me a moment to gather my wits, but when I did, I rushed to the edge of the balcony. "Stop!" I called at the figure. But it was too late. It had vanished into the deeper shadows of the trees.

"What's going on?" Coleman came outside and put his hand on my shoulder. "You're trembling."

I told him what I'd seen, pulling my punches a little since it occurred to me that it could be Jitty at work. Coleman insisted on getting a gun from the car and checking out the property, even though I tried to tell him the Peeping Tom was gone. "It was probably a kid goofing around. No one here knows me." But then I remembered the woman at the library who'd wanted to hire me for a case. Someone in Bay St. Louis knew me and what I did for a living.

I fell in behind Coleman as he walked toward the bay. As I assumed, there was no sign of anyone under the trees, but we did find some partial footprints in the damp soil of the flower bed. The sprinklers had recently been on, leaving the sandy soil damp. The prints weren't distinctive enough to get an estimated size of the person, but it was validation that I'd seen someone.

"There's no one here," I told Coleman.

"No. They're gone."

"Let's go back to the inn." I glanced behind us to see the door to our room still open. The light in the bedroom seemed safe and warm. "Come on. It was probably just a kid, like I said."

He was reluctant, but he followed me back to the room. Once inside, I took care to lock the door. I made us both a Jack, neat, to take the edge off. Soon we'd put the incident behind us and pick up where we left off. One thing about Coleman, he could redirect my focus. When he set his mind to it, there was only room to think about him.

3

Coleman and Oscar set off to investigate casinos farther down the coast in Biloxi. They had a plan to work their way from Bay St. Louis to the last casino on Biloxi Bay. Tinkie and I enjoyed a poolside snack with Maylin and Pauline before we left for the judging at the strip mall. We were supposed to meet our fellow judges and check out the massive number of decorated trees. There were more than three hundred entries, and this was the preliminary round of judging. The top fifty trees would be placed in the library proper for the big shindig party they held each year. The other trees would be put on display at city halls up and down the Gulf Coast, civic and senior centers, hospitals, and nursing homes where Christmas cheer was always welcome.

It was going to be a grueling day of elimination, but I

was eager to start. Mostly because I wanted to see if Sandra and Janet went for each other's throats again. I hated to admit that I was developing a reality TV mindset, something I had always disdained.

On the way to the judging we drove through a number of neighborhoods, enjoying the Christmas decorations. The day was so pleasant, I pushed the whole incident of the peeper out of my mind. I wasn't going to ruin the day for Tinkie by scaring her.

Mary Perkins, director at the library, had organized everything for us. The trees were numbered from one on up. They'd been arranged in an empty strip mall shopping center. Tinkie and I were the first to arrive, and Mary put us right to work. We had score sheets with each tree number and description—very helpful. Especially since Tinkie thought to take photos of each tree so we could look back on them later.

We were halfway through the trees when there was a commotion at the front door.

"You'd better steer clear of me." Sandra's voice was loud and angry.

"Or what?" Janet asked. "You're going to pick out some clothes for me and kill me with bad fashion?"

"Oh, goodness." Tinkie had had enough of this bad behavior, but she also couldn't help laughing. "This has to end or we'll never get the trees judged."

I grabbed her hand and led her toward the two women who faced off just inside the doorway. I had my phone in my hand, ready for more catfight footage, but I hadn't turned it on. "Hey, cut it out, ladies. We need to evaluate a lot of trees. Some of them are so creative and beautiful. We need to work together on this."

Like synchronized robots, they both turned to face me, mouths open in an O.

"And just who do you think you are?" Janet demanded.

"She's Sarah Booth Delaney, one of the judges. And that's Tinkie Richmond, another judge. Sarah Booth is right. Stop fighting with each other and evaluate the trees." Mary had had her fill of childish behavior, too.

Janet pointed at me. "You! You videotaped us and sold it to a damn journalist." Her eyes smoldered with anger.

"We are going to kick your ass," Sandra said.

"Bring it on!" Tinkie, no longer needing to protect little Maylin in utero, was ready to rumble.

"As if you really cared about being in a newspaper," I said, stepping forward to meet them. "You thrive on the publicity. It's exactly what you crave. I did you a favor."

Hidden among the Christmas trees, someone started clapping. We all turned to look as a handsome man stepped out from behind a huge blue spruce decorated with fishing lures. "Daryl Marcus, at your service." He extended his hand to me and then Tinkie. "And yes, that video you took earlier has gone viral. Book sales have almost doubled for Sandra's new book. Even Janet's backlist saw a jump. Please, do it again."

"Let's focus on the task at hand," Mary Perkins said. She kept glancing at her watch, aware that we had a tight time line to meet.

"Yes," I agreed. "Tinkie and I will give you our list of fifty finalists ASAP." It would be a fast turnaround, but the truth was, the trees were so wonderful we could have spent a week culling the list to fifty. It was the kind of thing where it was best to act on first impulse.

Tinkie and I went back to work. So many of the trees

reflected classic holiday themes or decorations specific to the fishing industry or coastal living. And the categories added another level of intensity: best tabletop, best use of color, most original, best traditional. I was the traditionalist, but Tinkie saw the joy and beauty in a tree made from an antebellum ball gown. All tulle and sequins. I had to admit, it was extremely creative.

"This is brutal," Tinkie said. "I thought it would be a snap. Man, did I underestimate the creativity of people who love Christmas."

"Amen."

In perfect agreement, Tinkie and I made our selections and turned in our list. Janet and Sandra had put aside their differences long enough to actually evaluate the trees. They were working toward their list of fifty when Tinkie and I headed back to the inn. She needed to feed Maylin and I needed some aspirin to calm my headache. On the way, I told her about the person who'd stopped at the library and the person under the oak tree.

"It sounds sinister," Tinkie said, "but do you have any idea who it could be?"

"No." I did have a thought about who *might be* searching for me, but if it was Jitty, I had to keep it a secret.

"We'll keep our eyes open."

Perhaps it was better if she was alert. "I should have thought to ask Mary what she looked like." I hadn't been on top of my game.

My partner held out her phone. "Call her."

"Let me drop you at the inn to take care of Maylin, and I'll run over to the library and talk to Mary privately."

"Okay." Tinkie was reluctant to let me go alone, but she

knew how hardheaded I could be and Maylin was too big a magnet to ignore.

"I'll be back in less than an hour," I promised her. "Maybe we can take Maylin for a ride along the beach." The baby loved my convertible. In fact, she loved everything I loved. Tinkie had started teasing me that she was more my child than hers.

"Oh, I just bought Maylin the cutest little hat. It will be perfect for the convertible. One day she'll be driving the Roadster, Sarah Booth. She'll be just like you."

I gave my friend a spontaneous hug. She was the most generous person I knew. "Thank you."

4

Mary Perkins ushered me into her library office where Weezie, a gray-and-white cat with the attitude and belly of a wise Buddha, sat in a window in the sun. The minute the cat saw me, she hurried over for pets and kisses. Weezie was a discerning cat—she disliked most people—but some days she seemed to cotton to me. I was convinced she remembered me from my rare library visits in Bay St. Louis.

"She remembers people she likes. Those she doesn't like, she just doesn't acknowledge they exist," Mary said, offering me a cup of coffee. "You're one of her favorites. Look at that. She's nuzzling you with her whiskers. She never does that."

After several moments of mutual admiration, I pulled my attention from Weezie and looked at Mary. "Do you remember the woman who asked about me today?" It wasn't the most subtle lead-in, but both Mary and I had lots to do.

"I do."

"Was she in her fifties or sixties, red-haired?"

Mary laughed. "Far from it. She was in her thirties and brunette."

The relief I felt was like a restricting band falling off my lungs. "She didn't give a name?"

"I didn't ask. I told her you'd be here for the big gala and announcement of the winning trees."

"A job you didn't tell me would be so difficult. There are some beautiful trees. It's going to be hard to pick the winners."

"The decorations get better every year," Mary said. "We're so lucky to have such community support for the library."

"The Christmas tree display has become a real tradition for the Gulf Coast. We hear about it every year in Zinnia. Thanks for inviting me and Tinkie to be judges this year."

"If our other judges would only behave." Mary shook her head. "They got into it again after you left. They're worse than teenagers. Even Daryl was exasperated with them."

"I wouldn't want his job."

"Nor would I. I won't make this mistake again by having two authors judge. Lordy! Tonight should be interesting. It was good of Sandra to host the event, but I sure hope she and Janet can avoid a public set-to. After the publicity of their fight at the bookstore, Sandra's books have flown off the shelf and she's having a signing tonight during the gala. Smart business move."

"It is. Sandra seems to have a head for business. I'm

looking forward to seeing the old Buntman mansion." A
couple of years back Sandra had made a big splash in the
papers when she purchased the old mansion. "Did Al Capone really build the place for a movie actress?"

"He did. I've tried to talk Sandra into opening the house
for public tours, but she won't. I do understand, but the
place is spectacular. And of course all the treasure hunters
are clamoring to get in there and look for the hidden loot
Capone allegedly left. As well as the ghost hunters. It's said
Capone's ghost still haunts the property. There have been
sightings of romantic couples dancing outside on the patio
with candles lit all over the place. But when anyone goes up
there to check, it's only candle stubs and melted wax. The
house is closed up, or it was until Sandra started renovations. Maybe she'll tell us if she's gotten any secret treasure
tips from ghosts."

"Call Geraldo," I said, referencing a calamitous television show where reputed TV journalist Geraldo Rivera
opened a vault where Capone had allegedly left a treasure.
There was nothing there, ending in a real bust for the alleged reporter.

"The only thing I remember about that debacle was how
tight Geraldo's pants were." She rolled her eyes. "I think
that's what Sandra fears, a media circus that ends in hu-
miliation. It's really better for her if the rumors are never
disproven."

"You don't think there's a hidden treasure?" I was curious. I'd heard about Al Capone and his illegal money my
entire life. Capone, who was notoriously brutal and successful, served time at Alcatraz. The feds, led by Eliot Ness,
could never catch him on robbery, extortion, or murder.
They'd finally gotten him for tax evasion. Capone and

Ness had been the subject of numerous television shows and movies.

"I do think there's hidden riches," Mary said, stroking Weezie's back as she talked. "He was fabulously wealthy, and he built the mansion for Helene with a lot of secret passages, hidden rooms, and things like that. It was said that Capone never stayed in a place that didn't have at least four different exits. He vowed never to serve time again, and he wouldn't be taken alive. It's possible he hid his fortune here with the woman he loved."

"Tell me about Helene." I had learned of her work in silent films. Her glamour was legendary, and like so many of the women who began in silent movies, she'd learned to use facial expressions and makeup to convey a world of emotions. When times changed, Helene had made the transition to talkies, too. Her melodious voice was hot stuff in the first talkie films.

"Her grandfather started as a fisherman and worked his way up to owning a fleet of boats. It was the boats that first drew Capone's eye. He needed them to bring in the liquor he was importing from Cuba, and what better device than fishing vessels. The rum distilled in Cuba and the islands was in high demand here in the States. Capone and Julius Buntman, Helene's father, built quite an empire of imported liquor during prohibition. The network ran from here to New Orleans then continued north and west. They supplied the bars, gambling dens, fancy restaurants, speakeasies, and blind tigers, as they were called, all the way to Tennessee."

"How did he meet Helene?"

"She was a girl who loved risk and adventure. When a captain for a boat loaded with liquor failed to show up, Helene sailed the hooch into the port right under the nose

of the law. Then she loaded it into a van and drove it inland
to Jackson. It was a daring risk, slipping into port, unload-
ing the rum, and then running the backroads with illegal
alcohol. The shipment weighed a lot, and the roads were
notoriously dangerous. When Capone heard about her
successful journey, he wanted to meet her. She was young,
but she impressed him with her intelligence and spirit. Her
dream was to be a movie star, and he arranged for her to
have a screen test. Clara Bow took a liking to her, and
they became fast friends. Helene ran with the Hollywood
crowd, but she was always in Bay St. Louis when Al had
time to be here."

It was a fascinating history. Even I could see the appeal
of the elements of gangster love, rum-running, Hollywood,
and prison. It was like the most perfect drama ever cooked
up. And it was real life. Sandra would have another huge
best seller on her hands when she finished writing about
this—and I had no doubt she would be telling this tale.
I just wondered if she could write off the purchase of the
mansion as research.

I had a few questions for Mary about the logistics of the
tree event. "So once the fifty trees are selected, how will
you get them to the library?"

"It's a big event. We have several flatbeds and we load
the trees, tying them securely, and drive the short distance
through neighborhoods. The people come out and yell for
their favorite tree. Some of the businesses actually let their
employees off work to champion the tree they entered. I've
heard some people even pay folks to cheer for their trees. It's
great fun."

"And the trees will be here in the library tomorrow?"

"Yes, shortly after dark. It's a special thing when the

trees are lighted for the parade. It's magical, and carolers follow them all the way here. Later on, you and the other judges will come and do the final tally. You'll be able to talk and compare notes."

"Sounds . . . challenging." I wondered if Sandra and Janet would kill each other in this process.

"It'll be fine." Mary waved away my concern. "We'll have libations and food and music."

"Great." If Janet and Sandra were that bad without alcohol, how would they be tanked up?

Mary only laughed. "The big gala is tonight at Sandra's. It gets off to a late start, but come early. You'll want a tour of the house and I'll bet she'll give it to you. As much as she complained about that video you took, her sales did skyrocket. She told me her agent called and they were all aflutter. Seems they're going back for a second printing."

That was good to know. "Always glad to help an author," I said.

"Don't worry so much about it. They've been doing this the whole time they've been in town. There were stories about some of their behavior in New Orleans, too." She laughed. "You can't make that stuff up. And if you're really lucky, you might get some video that you can sell to a national outlet."

Videoing the two battling authors was easy money, I had to agree to that.

"Look, come to the party and have fun. Bring that handsome sheriff everyone in town is talking about, and I'm eager to meet Tinkie's husband, too. You'll have a great time."

I nodded.

"Just watch out where you park. Try to get in front of the house, where the hired security watches over things."

"What's going on?" I asked.

"Probably nothing, but the owner of the Bay Moon Inn, where you're staying, said she had someone in the parking lot messing with some of the cars. No damage was done, but we're sensitive to that kind of stuff around here. We're a town that depends on tourism, and vandalism can really hurt us."

"Did they catch whoever it was?" I wondered if it could be related to the figure I'd seen under the oak tree.

"No, it's probably kids. There are certain people in town who resent the tourists. They feel like strangers come in, take over, and change the town from a sleepy little place to loud music and drinking. You know, all the things that draw tourists to a place to have fun."

"I understand that attitude. I wouldn't want to have the onslaught of strangers everywhere either."

"But local businesses rely on those strangers and the money they bring into town." She stood up. "It's an attitude we can't afford here."

I did understand. "I'll keep an eye on the vehicles and park where there is someone on patrol."

"Smart. Now I have to get to work. Book orders are due and I want to have time to get all gussied up for the party."

5

I picked up shrimp po'boys—made on crispy French bread—for Tinkie, Pauline, and me. Tinkie and I needed to eat something before we went to the big party at the Buntman/O'Day mansion. Coleman and Oscar would be fine. The casinos were dens of iniquity when it came to food. Lots of things to eat and all of them bad for you! Which was the utter appeal of such places.

Maylin was napping, so we ate our sandwiches in the kitchen in Tinkie's suite. She'd rented a large unit with three bedrooms and two baths so that Pauline could have privacy and comfort. Tinkie was a good boss, and Pauline was quickly becoming a part of the family.

Tinkie was much relieved to hear that the person inquiring about me at the library was a young brunette and not a senior redhead. Neither of us had spoken aloud about she who cannot be named, but we'd both thought of Gertrude Strom. I knew my partner well enough to see it on her face. The revelation that it wasn't Gertrude lightened the entire meal and we laughed and cut up as Tinkie brought out outfit after outfit for my inspection. "I want to look like a movie star tonight," she said with an impish wink.

"The midnight blue shantung," I said. "It's perfect with your eyes and has an air of elegance. Kind of 1940s."

"Exactly why I bought it," Tinkie said. "How I loved that era."

I told them about Helene's movie career and her romance with Capone, and had them eating out of my hand until the men got back. Coleman and Oscar arrived with packages galore. To surprise us, they'd stopped to rent tuxes. I felt a little left out since I'd brought nice clothes, but nothing as formal as Tinkie's dress and the tuxedoes.

Coleman handed me a gift-wrapped box. His slight flush tipped me off to something special. "If you don't like it, blame Oscar. If you do like it, then I picked it out for you."

I lifted the lid to reveal a jewel green party dress with drop shoulders and a flared skirt. It was the most wonderful dress I'd ever seen. Five minutes later, I could see that it fit like it had been made just for me.

"Thank you, Coleman." I gave him a big kiss, to the applause of my friends.

"You better kiss Tinkie, too," he said. "She found it and told me it would suit you to a T."

I grabbed Tinkie and gave her a big kiss on the cheek. "Thank you."

"I've never seen you so excited about a dress," Tinkie said. She snapped a photo with her phone. "I'm sending this to Cece and Millie as proof that the Christmas spirit has infected you."

"That's fine by me. But Cece should put both of us on the payroll. What would they print for news if we didn't turn in copy?"

"Excellent point," Oscar said drolly. "I'll take this up with Ed Oakes the next time I see him."

"Let's get ready for the party." Coleman checked his watch.

"Did you boys win any money today?" Tinkie asked them.

They looked at each other and it was clear they'd been plotting together. "What happens on the Gulf Coast stays on the Gulf Coast," Oscar said, fighting back a grin.

"Keep your money," I said, waving a hand in the air as I gathered up my belongings. "Tinkie and I are going to find Al Capone's secret treasure and we won't share a penny with you."

"Treasure?" Oscar and Coleman asked simultaneously.

"Yes, all of Capone's riches are allegedly hidden somewhere on the Buntman/O'Day estate, where we'll be partying tonight." I was pleased at their reaction.

"Take your sneakers and a flashlight," Oscar teased as he and Tinkie walked up the stairs to the balcony. "We may have to ditch the fancy duds and do a little treasure hunting. Coleman and I need a bigger grubstake for gambling."

I was still laughing when Coleman drew me into our room and shut the door. He pulled me into his arms and gave me a kiss that pushed every other thought right out of my head. "Let's get dressed," he said. "I'm starving and I hear there's going to be exceptional food at the party."

"Really?" I couldn't believe it. "Really? Food is what's on your mind?"

"Food and treasure," he said, going into the bathroom and turning on the shower. "But I could be convinced to let you join me for a scrub."

The man was incorrigible, but I had to admit a shower with Coleman sounded fabulous.

Clean, dry, and almost ready for the evening, I put on makeup and touched up my hair. I told Coleman about the person who'd been looking for me at the library. "It wasn't Gertrude, thank goodness."

"I had those same thoughts last night about that old harridan," he admitted. "It's a relief. Maybe she's dead."

I couldn't chastise him because I'd had the same hope. "Dead or finally living her own life."

"I don't wish her any harm as long as she leaves you alone."

He put on his tux jacket and I stopped for a moment to admire what a fine figure he cut. When he zipped me into the dress, his grin said it all.

"Thank you again. It's the most wonderful dress I've ever owned."

"No one else could wear it like you do." He offered his arm and we were off.

The night was crisp and cold, and we put the top up on the car. I told him about the vandals and he pulled onto the property to park off to the side of the driveway. Arm in arm, we walked to the dazzling stucco mansion. It was artfully lit and we paused a minute to admire the handsome architecture.

"Capone really built this place?" Coleman asked.

"With lots of hidey-holes, dead-end hallways, secret rooms, and escape hatches."

We turned to look behind us at the Bay of St. Louis gleaming in the moonlight. It was such a spectacular view. It didn't take a lot of imagination to visualize it with several large fishing boats, their holds full of dark rum, angling to the port. There was something so romantic about smuggling booze, especially in the lee of a mansion built by a gangster.

The front door opened, and a butler cleared his throat, a definite signal to enter. We walked up the steps and into the foyer, where a huge, glittering chandelier cast light prisms on the tiled floor. It was a beautiful place.

The sounds of laughter and clinking crystal danced on the wind as we found ourselves in a large room with tables of food that were works of art. Servers brought champagne flutes and continued on their rounds.

"Swanky party," Coleman said. "Being your boy toy has some benefits."

I elbowed him in the ribs. "Behave. Looks like we beat Tinkie and Oscar here, so help me find Sandra and Janet. We need to keep our eyes open to keep them from killing each other."

"Just have the camera ready."

Coleman was messing with me, but I didn't mind. I caught a glimpse of Sandra on the beautiful staircase talking to Daryl Marcus, her assistant. The conversation was intense, but not unpleasant. In a moment they both laughed and Sandra came down to join the party. She made a beeline for Coleman.

"Well, hello," she said, holding out her hand. "I'm Sandra, the host."

"And best-selling author," I supplied. She did look stunning in a gold tea-length gown with padded shoulders and a slim silhouette. The entire guest list had gotten the memo about glam, and I loved the dress Coleman had picked out for me even more.

"I hear you're a private investigator," Sandra said, turning to me.

I was shocked she'd bothered to learn anything at all about me. There wasn't room in her world for another image in the mirror besides her own. "Yes, Tinkie and I seem to have a knack for solving mysteries."

"You know the history of this house?" Sandra asked.

I couldn't believe she was opening this door for me. "Only a little, but what we learned was fascinating to me and my partner."

"Come with me. I have a portrait of Helene Buntman, the woman Capone built it for." She walked through the room where a jazz band was playing and several couples were dancing. I caught sight of Tinkie and Oscar coming in the front door and waved them over to join us.

"Sandra, you've met my partner, Tinkie, and this is her husband, Oscar."

"Come along. I have to get back to my hostess duties soon, but I want you to see this. Mary asked me to give you a little tour. She's been very good to me, and I adore Weezie, so I agreed. But I don't have long to be away from my guests and I have to prepare for the book signing."

She pushed through a double door into a huge library centered with a fireplace. Above the fireplace was an incredible portrait of a glamorous woman. She wore the flapper style that was a scandal at the time. She was posed at the door of a beautiful automobile with one leg saucily lifted to show more thigh than was proper. Her heavily made-up eyes were alive with mischief. The artist had done a spectacular job. "She's so beautiful." I just stood and gawked.

"That's the reaction most people had to her," Sandra said. "Capone was smitten the first time he met her. She was a tomboy, working on her father's fishing vessels. When Julius Buntman threw in with Capone to run illegal liquor, Helene saved a large shipment of hooch when a boat captain failed to show up to run a loaded ship up the bay and into safe harbor. Helene took it a step further and drove the hooch to Jackson, evading law officers on water and land. Capone asked to meet her and that was that."

Even hearing the story a second time, I loved it.

"Wow," Tinkie said. "She must have been very brave."

"When she asked Capone to set up a screen test for her, he did it, and the rest is history, as they say." Sandra really seemed to enjoy telling the story. This was the most pleasant I'd seen her.

"Why did you decide to buy the mansion?" Tinkie asked Sandra.

She sighed. "Part of it was the history. I'm researching Capone and the group that inherited his crime kingdom, the Dixie Mafia, for a new book. Capone was paranoid, and the house has a lot of quirky things about it, which I enjoy. To fully explore it, I felt I should own it. Plus, I feel a kinship with Helene. She was a local girl here. I was raised not so far away."

"And Janet is from here also, isn't she?" Oscar asked. "Who would believe two such extraordinary talents would come from a tiny Mississippi town. And then return to live in the same area."

"Yes." Sandra's smile was only a little brittle.

I wanted to ask if Janet was fictionalizing the same subject matter for her next book, but I knew better. Sandra was being civil and gracious, but if she chose to hurl a book at me, the library had plenty of options for her to pick from.

"Are you going to search for the Capone treasure here?" Coleman asked.

"So many people have searched and come up empty-handed." Sandra didn't mind intrusive questions from handsome men. But her assistant Daryl was on alert. He shifted so that he was standing at her side.

"We don't believe there's really a treasure. If people get the idea that we're looking for something, they won't be able to resist breaking in or digging around on the estate. That kind of behavior went on for years before Sandra purchased the property. The house has been empty for a while because the last owners got fed up with local treasure hunters helping themselves to whatever they could get to. Sandra must have her privacy to write, so please don't even hint at Capone's treasure."

"I understand," Coleman said. "There's one cemetery in Sunflower County where a famous outlaw is supposedly buried. You'd be surprised at the damage treasure hunters can do and the total lack of respect for the dead."

"Not surprised at all," Daryl said with a wry grin. "And thanks for understanding. Sandra is on a hard deadline. She needs to buckle down and put all of her efforts into her writing. It's my job to make sure she has all the solitude and quiet she needs. So far, we've humored the locals with their probing questions and curiosities, but after the holidays it's work, work, work." He put a hand on Sandra's shoulder and she rolled her eyes.

"Daryl always has his eye on the bottom line." Her words were tart but the look she gave him was amused.

"If I didn't, deadlines would be missed and book contracts canceled," Daryl said. "She's the talented writer and I'm the organizer and gofer."

Sandra sighed and hugged his arm lightly. "All too true. My hero!"

The two did seem to share a remarkable working relationship, but I didn't get even a hint of romance between them. Daryl was such a handsome man, I couldn't help but wonder if he had a girlfriend or significant other tucked away somewhere. Yet he seemed totally devoted to Sandra, and he appeared to be by her side all the time. I was glad it wasn't my problem to figure out.

"Sandra is a genius at digging up facts and asking the right questions when she's working," Daryl said, "but the practical, day-to-day things that make a life run smoothly, she just ignores."

"If I didn't have Daryl, I would be lost."

No one said the money word, but I realized that it was very likely Daryl earned a salary equal to his value. Now that would explain a whole lot.

"What's your favorite room?" Tinkie asked Sandra, turning the conversation smoothly, as all Daddy's Girls knew how to do. If I had one-tenth of her social grace I would have an easier life.

"My study, of course. Follow me."

We headed up the stairs to the third floor, leaving the chatter and laughter of the party behind us. The first floor was decorated in traditional Christmas garlands, candles, and an incredible coral Christmas tree that matched the exterior stucco of the house. Hand-painted decorative figures had been hung as ornaments. To my surprise, the third floor was bare of all decorations. It was a space for working and researching.

A noise coming from one of the rooms stopped us. Coleman instinctively stepped forward. His hand went for his gun, but of course he wasn't armed. Not at a Christmas party. "Is someone supposed to be up here?" he asked Sandra quietly.

"No one comes up here but me." Sandra was adamant and unnerved.

"Stay back." Coleman waved everyone back as he quietly approached a closed door. He turned the knob and silently pushed the door open.

Inside the room, a woman screamed, followed by, "Who the hell are you and what are you doing up here?"

"I could ask you the same," Coleman said.

Before anyone could stop her, Sandra rushed forward. I didn't have to be psychic to know what was coming next. I'd recognized Janet's voice. She was in Sandra's office doing god knew what.

"You thief! You wretched thief!" Sandra ran into the room full tilt. Tinkie, Oscar, Daryl, and I stood frozen for a split second before we all darted into the room and tried to separate the brawling women. They were tumbling around on the floor, screeching and punching at each other. Coleman had Sandra around the waist but, as strong as he was, he couldn't pull her off Janet.

The minute he got a little space between them, Janet launched herself at Sandra.

"I wasn't stealing anything," Janet panted, trying to stuff some papers back into the bodice of her dress.

"Oscar!" Coleman called out.

Tinkie's husband jumped into the melee, grabbing Janet by both wrists and tugging her away from the snarling Sandra. Once Coleman had some help, he was able to subdue both women. He and Oscar just held on until the writers got tired of struggling to get free. When they both settled down, the men released them.

"Shall I call the police?" Daryl asked.

"No." Both women spoke at the same time.

"No?" Tinkie and I spoke in unison. "Why not?" she demanded.

"I don't want cops here and I don't want a big incident made over this. Do you know how many people will believe that fool Janet was searching for Capone's treasure? They'll flock over here and dig up the gardens and sneak into the house looking for hidey-holes and secret rooms. No! No police! No media! None of that." Sandra had shaken free of Coleman. She straightened her dress, smoothed her hair, and turned to Janet. "Get out of my house right now."

"I can't leave. It's the big party. If I leave it'll draw attention. And you don't want that." Janet was quick to pick up on Sandra's weakness—a desire to stop all media attention.

"Go downstairs and stay there. I mean it. Daryl, please go with her. Make sure she doesn't explore the rest of my house."

"Aren't you even going to ask her what she was looking for?" I asked. I couldn't believe it. Sandra had her reasons, but this seemed foolish and stupid. "She has papers—"

"Leave it alone," Sandra said. "Now if everyone will just leave me here so I can go through my research and see if anything is missing." The look she gave Janet would have frosted a sunspot. "If anything is missing, I *will* call the police. I don't care what it costs me."

"Lucky for me I'm not a thief." Janet shifted her dress into the right places, found her missing shoe, and marched out of the room with Daryl hot on her heels.

"You're going to go one step too far, Janet. You really are," Daryl was calling after her as he followed her down the stairs at record speed.

"You really aren't going to prosecute her?" Tinkie said.

"She had pages stuffed in her dress," I pointed out.

"No, I'm not going to prosecute her, and I know she took something." Sandra's grin was sly. "Which is why every bit of research I left out on my desk was wrong. Totally wrong. Wrong names, wrong dates, just wrong." She almost clapped her hands with glee. "Brilliant, yes?"

I hated to admit it, but it was indeed brilliant.

For Sandra, the house tour was over, but I'd seen—and photographed—plenty of party shots. I intended to pull Sandra aside and let her know Cece wanted to do a story about the beautiful old house. I feared she wouldn't like the idea, but I had to tell her before I sent the photos to the newspaper.

We drank more champagne and enjoyed the party food, which was delicious. At last it was time for the book signing. Sandra had agreed to sign copies of her new book and everyone wanted a copy for themselves. Many had a list of names for Christmas gifts.

Daryl was Velcroed to Janet, just as Sandra had asked him to be. When the bookseller approached him and whispered something, Daryl nodded. "I'll get her." He bounded up the stairs and Tinkie and I went for a champagne refill. Coleman and Oscar were having a good time, talking with some locals about the town's history.

"Do you think both authors will live long enough to

judge those trees?" Tinkie said to me. She was only half kidding.

"They do hate each other."

There was some restlessness in the queue that had formed for the book signing. The bookseller sought out Mary Perkins, who'd come over to chat with me and Tinkie. "Where is Sandra?" the bookseller asked.

I looked around and noticed that Janet was missing also. And Daryl. What if they'd gotten into it again?

"Don't worry. It's okay. Daryl went to get Sandra," Mary told him, but I could tell she was worried, too. "Let me go check."

She hurried up the stairs as the party slowly ground to a halt. All attention was on her. It seemed like forever, but had really only been a few minutes when Mary came to the banister and looked down on us. "She's gone," she said. "Her study is wrecked and she and Daryl are just gone."

6

Mary called the local police chief, who sent a team over to investigate. The ransacked office indicated that Sandra had been forcefully removed. But how? And how much was just damage from the catfight I'd just witnessed? As far as I could tell there was no way out of her study except via the staircase and front door. There were back stairways that had been built for the help to use, but the only access to them was from the first floor. The study was something like a private suite.

"Look, there's nothing we can do here," Oscar said. He kept watching the doors as if he expected Bad Santa to jump out.

Mary Perkins had joined our group, a frown forming a deep line between her eyebrows. "You're right, Oscar. Y'all should go. I'll talk with the police and tell them all I know, but there's no need for you to stay here. I'm just worried sick."

"What about Janet Malone?" I asked.

Mary looked around, the frown lines deepening. "I haven't seen her."

"Who's looking for me?" Janet came around the corner of the hallway. "I was looking for Sandra and Daryl. No sign of them in the kitchen area, though I have to tell you the gingerbread pudding is to die for. What a shame it was never served."

"Do you know where they could have gone?" Coleman asked her.

She shook her head. "It's not like Sandra to leave before she collects all that money for her signed books. This is a real mystery!" She was almost gleeful. Almost, but she reined it in just in time.

"The police will want to talk to you," Tinkie told her.

"Oh, goody! My new book is about to drop and this will clinch the number one spot on the best-seller list. If I'd thought to have Sandra abducted from her own party, I would have done it, you know. This is just too good! I hope they videotape my police interview and I can get a copy. I can release it on TikTok and I'll be a sensation yet again."

"Do authors do TikTok?" Tinkie asked. "I thought it was all about dancing and cute pets."

"You are behind the times, aren't you?" Janet shrugged. "Now I have to go. The police can come to my house to talk to me. Or"—her eyes widened—"they can take me down to the police station. That's a much better photo op. Let me call the New Orleans TV station. They'll surely want to cover this. Must dash! Ta!"

She was almost down the driveway when the police herded her up and stopped her.

"Just let me go home and change," she said as they led her to a patrol car. "I'm perfectly willing to cooperate, but I need to refresh my wardrobe. I wore this gown for an Atlanta bash last year and I can't be seen in it again."

Somehow, I suspected this wasn't going to be the press event Janet wanted. Of course there had been no real crime. So far. Sandra and Daryl were merely missing. They might return at any moment. Still, the police had to talk to Janet. The vendetta between Sandra and Janet couldn't be ignored.

We said our goodbyes to Mary and headed out to a local blues club to finish the evening. Soon Millie, Cece, and her fella, Jaytee, would be on the coast, along with the hot and oh, so cool blues band that Jaytee played harmonica in. They were booked for a holiday gig at the Hardrock Casino. But the small club on the outskirts of Bay St. Louis where we went was perfect. Fog coming in off the bay made the twinkling Christmas lights misty and blurred. The music and dancing couldn't be beat, and we could sit outside where heaters warmed the night. We could hear the music fine, but also talk.

"Do you think something bad has happened to Sandra and Daryl?" Tinkie asked me.

"No. I think this is another publicity stunt Sandra cooked up. All of that BS about not wanting to publicize the Al Capone–Helene Buntman connection was just a lie. She bought the house to stage exactly this kind of event, and what better time than Christmas? Those two, Sandra and Janet, live to be on television."

"You're right about that."

We settled back, sipped our drinks, and listened to a guest appearance by an Italian blues band. I couldn't understand the lyrics, but the meaning of the songs came through loud and clear. Coleman offered his hand and we took to the dance floor for some belly-rubbing dancing. In so many ways, Coleman was the perfect man for me. We fell into step with each other, most of the time. No real effort. It just happened. We could, and did, compromise, but so many things, like dancing, were just natural, fluid, and easy. As the great writer Jonathan Carroll had once written about love: Coleman liked to wash the dishes and I liked to dry them. Compatibility for a lifetime.

When the set was over and a new band was taking the stage, my cell phone rang. It was nearly two o'clock in the morning, and I didn't recognize the number, but I stepped outside to answer, worried that something might have gone wrong in Zinnia with the critters.

"Delaney?" The woman's voice was sharp and strident.

"Who is this?"

"Janet Malone. I want to hire you and your partner to find Sandra. The cops think I've done something to her and Daryl."

"Have they charged you?"

"Not yet, but it's coming. They found blood in the mudroom sink. They think it's Sandra's or Daryl's or both."

"How much blood?"

"Enough to indicate someone was hurt. They're testing it now to see who it matches."

"Do you think Sandra and Daryl are in danger?"

She hesitated. "I would say no, except for the book signing. Sandra is so competitive she'd never miss an opportunity to sell several hundred books. Everyone at that party wanted a signed copy. Some had their Christmas shopping list to buy for. Sandra wouldn't walk away from that."

She had a point. "What do you think happened to Sandra and Daryl?"

"They've been abducted." Her tone let me know she
thought I was dense.

"I realize they're missing, but for what purpose?"

"Sandra is a bitch. She pisses people off all the time.
There's a long list of enemies. My first guess would be that
someone is getting even with her. Daryl is nothing more
than collateral damage. He's umbilically attached to Sandra so the kidnapper had to take him, too."

She didn't sound too upset about the possibility that
an angry person had abducted the two of them. "Do you
know something about their disappearance?"

"Not really. Right now, I'm not worried about Sandra
and Daryl. I'm worried about me. I have a new book coming out in a couple of weeks. While being charged with
kidnapping might increase book sales, if they lock me up
without bail, I won't be able to do the book signings. I've
booked a twenty-city tour. They're presold, thousands of
books, but I have to sign them. I have to be able to do my
job. I'm right at the edge. If this next book does as good as I
think it will, then I'll become a household name. A brand."

I normally admired someone who kept their eye on the
prize, but Janet and Sandra were a breed apart. "What are
you hiring me to do?"

"Find Sandra and Daryl."

"Where do you suggest I look?"

"If it's someone local that she's stepped on, she'll be
nearby."

"I don't think someone with hurt feelings would abduct
two people and hold them against their will. Kidnapping
carries a harsh prison sentence." Her logic didn't make sense.

"Then it's probably about that stupid Capone treasure. Sandra has pretended all over the place that she doesn't want to talk about it, but whenever she opens her mouth, some juicy tidbit about Capone, Buntman, rum-running, or her mansion falls out."

She was right about that. "You're assuming local treasure hunters took Sandra and Daryl?"

"Maybe." There was a pause. "Look, Sandra was digging into some things that could be dangerous, I guess."

"Clarify, please."

"Mobsters. Thugs. Criminals. The past and present. She was asking a lot of questions."

At last she was facing the reality of what could have happened. "Yeah, she said she was researching the Dixie Mafia, right?"

"Yes. I told her it was stupid to stir up that hornet's nest. They're supposed to all be dead or long retired, but I never bought that. If there's money to be made, there's always someone with criminal intentions around to make it whether they call themselves the mafia or not."

"When the big casino money came in, I heard it pushed the local guys out." Growing up in Zinnia, I'd heard about the Gulf Coast as a mythic place of sin and sensation. Alluring and dangerous. Forbidden and irresistible.

"I grew up here and left, but I know that isn't true. I don't write true crime, but I've learned enough to know it never works that way. There are private poker and dice games all over the place. Clubs where a guy can sit back in the shadows and watch strippers, or more. What if the local thugs do have her? Who knows what they would do to stop her from writing that book."

7

I returned to the patio and signaled Coleman, letting him know about Janet's request that we take her case.

"Are you going to work with her?" he asked.

"Let's see what Tinkie says." I knew it was going to be touch-and-go with Oscar. Tinkie had given birth only a few months earlier. Oscar wanted to bundle her up and keep her safe. Tinkie firmly resisted swaddling. I saw both sides of the situation and made up my mind. If Tinkie said no, then it was off. I wouldn't question or press. The truth of the matter was that neither Sandra nor Janet had left me with a warm and fuzzy feeling or the desire to protect them.

To give Tinkie and Oscar some time to talk privately, Coleman and I hit the dance floor for "Back Door Santa," made famous by Mississippi's own B. B. King. The guitarist in the band was almost as good as King, and Coleman had the moves. I let my body move with his and tried not to watch the interplay of emotions on Tinkie's face as she and Oscar hashed out their decision. When we returned to the table, it was Oscar who spoke.

"Since we're down here already, Tinkie wants to take the case. I've agreed as long as there is minimal danger."

I wasn't going to be the one who said "Mafia" to him. Tinkie didn't lie to Oscar, but sometimes it took her a while to spit out the whole truth.

"You sure?" I asked Tinkie.

She nodded. "I love Maylin and I could spend every minute of every day with her. But I have to keep one foot in the world of work and adults. Maylin is like a drug. I can't get enough time with her, and I can see trouble down the road if I don't make certain that I also have my own life. It wouldn't be healthy for any of us."

Tinkie was smarter than the average bear, and she'd hit on one thing about birthin' babies that worried me. Would I be a parent who could allow my child to grow up and away? What if I smothered them? But that was a worry for another time. "Good. Then we'll take the case."

"Good," Tinkie agreed. She reached across the table to put her hand on top of Oscar's. "Thank you for understanding that I need to work. I promise you, if the case takes a dark turn we'll quit. We will. But I honestly think Sandra and Daryl are pretending to be kidnapped."

That was a distinct possibility. But either way, we would get paid. Tinkie and Oscar had more wealth than they'd ever spend, but earning money herself had given Tinkie a sense of self-worth she'd never had before. She'd always been a daughter and a wife. Now she was a private investigator, a businesswoman. As for me, I was able to save my family home and even do some much-needed repairs. I was glad to have the work.

I finally turned to Coleman. "Are you good with this?" He tried very hard not to interfere in my work. His job as sheriff of Sunflower County was dangerous, and he knew that the sauce that was good for the goose was also good for the gander in my world.

"I like it when you have a case and I'm not working in the sheriff's office and can be around to help."

We were all okay with the job. "I'll call Janet and let her know."

Coleman and Oscar had signed up for a boat ride out to Ship Island, one of the beautiful, wild barrier islands that marked the end of the Mississippi Sound and the beginning of the Gulf of Mexico. The string of "walking" islands, meaning that each big storm shifted their geographical contours, were the source of fascinating legends and lore. When hurricanes barreled out of the Gulf, the barrier islands took the first brutal hit and often saved the mainland from the worst of the storm's fury. From Dauphin Island in Alabama to Horn, Petit Bois, and Ship in Mississippi, the islands were home to thriving communities or preserved as wilderness.

On the south side of Ship Island, the water was a beautiful aqua green with the sugar sand beaches that the Gulf was famous for. The Mississippi Sound side was murkier and calmer. Navigating the channels between the barrier islands had once been a challenge for the rum smugglers who loved the Bay of St. Louis and the many inlets and marinas where a swift boat could outrun and hide from the "revenuers" and maritime agents trying to halt the illegal liquor from coming in.

From the Gulfport marina, Tinkie and I waved the men off for their sea-loving adventure. With their profiles facing into the wind, whipping their hair, they were a noble duo.

Tinkie and I stopped at a local diner for breakfast. The day was bright, sunny, and brisk. I regretted working instead of sightseeing. I'd never been to Ship Island and I'd planned to go with Coleman for a picnic. Instead Tinkie and I returned to my room to plot our next move, which was to arrange a meeting with Janet.

Janet had been released without being charged, but the Bay St. Louis police chief pulled no punches. He told Janet that if Sandra didn't show up, and soon, she'd be back in custody as the prime suspect in her rival's disappearance. Attitude and tantrums weren't going to change her situation, and she was smart enough to twig onto that. Her verbal abuse stopped, and just as if her fairy godmother had waved a lobotomy wand over her head, she became sweet, docile, and very helpful.

We met in Janet's beachfront home, a beautiful cement-and-glass three-story on a high mound of grassy lawn. The house would look more at home in California than Mississippi, but it was still very beautiful.

She opened the door with a nod and ushered us into a comfortable sitting room where we took a seat at a beautiful tiger-oak table with an Ouija board created in the design of the wood.

"Are you into mediumship?" I asked, curious if Janet received her ideas for her stories from the dead. She was certainly able to conjure up the glamour of the past.

"I was told I had a gift, but I'd rather write than talk

with dead people." She grinned and I saw the mischief she kept so well hidden. "Writing is so much more lucrative."

"Maybe dead people help you write," I said, mostly joking.

"That's a distinct possibility. But I don't have to share royalties with them."

I had to laugh. I hadn't expected Janet to be a wit and fun. Her behavior with Sandra was atrocious, but then Sandra's was, too.

"What can I do to help find Sandra?" she asked.

"Just stay here." Tinkie was kind but direct. "This is a beautiful place. Call a friend or hire a person to be with you so you constantly have an alibi."

"That's really great advice." I was impressed with my partner. We'd had a recent case where our client was his own worst enemy, disappearing from safe places and showing up at the scene of the crimes. "If you follow Tinkie's advice, you'll certainly speed up the process."

Janet started to say something but clamped her mouth shut. I had to admire her restraint.

"What are you going to do today?" she asked. "What's the first step?"

"What do you know about Daryl?" Tinkie responded.

"He's Sandra's good-looking hand-holder. I've never met anyone so needy. She needs someone to be with her all the time. She literally can't go to the bathroom without someone standing outside the door to talk to her."

That was an interesting tidbit and might explain why Daryl was missing along with Sandra. If their disappearance was voluntary, she would want him with her. If she'd been snatched, she'd made the kidnappers take him along. Poor Daryl!

"He's a handsome man," Tinkie continued. "Does he

have a family? A home? Where did he work before he met Sandra? How did they meet?"

"Why are you asking about Daryl?" Janet asked. Her radar was up.

"We know a little about Sandra. We're developing a strategy to search for them, but we have to know the places they might go, why they'd disappear and worry everyone. Who might have a reason to harm them? It's just the basic part of the casework," I said. Which wasn't the total truth, but it was all she needed to know right now.

"Let me think about Daryl. He's been with Sandra for such a long time, it's almost like he's her family." She looked suddenly surprised. "I guess he *is* her family. I mean, there isn't anyone else. She has two brothers but they moved away and think she's nuts. Neither Sandra nor I had children, and her parents are dead. Sandra has Daryl. That's it."

"And who do you have?" Tinkie asked her.

"A cat charity." She gave a mocking grin. "My folks are alive and well taken care of but out of the country. I'm one of those rare people who can make the Earth a better place when I die. I didn't reproduce and I intend to donate everything to charity. Cats R Us."

Yet again, Janet had surprised me. She was so focused on work and competing with Sandra that I'd assumed she was into private jets, jewels, and acquisition. Always more, to pass down to her kids. She had other plans.

"All of it?" Tinkie asked. As the beneficiary of a family trust, Tinkie knew the power of inherited wealth, but she'd also talked to me about the downside of knowing the rough road so many trod was paved with gold for her. She'd never had to prove herself, until she became a PI.

"I have everything I need," Janet said. "What else does

a person need but shelter, transportation, and sustenance? I have more than enough already. It's the joy of succeeding, the thrill of besting Sandra that keeps me working."

"Do you even have cats?" Tinkie looked around. There wasn't a cat hair on anything.

"I have twenty-seven," she said. "All rescues. All loving and adorable."

I was just about to ask how she kept such a clean house with so many cats when a maid brought coffee and home-made Danish and provided us with cups, saucers, and silver service. Another came in to vacuum but smiled and left when she saw us.

"A few years ago at Christmas, I took all the strays the local shelter had. And I've arranged for my money to be used to start a spay-and-neuter center to serve southern Missis- sippi. Neutering is the only solution. Cats, dogs, and some men need it, too."

"How wonderful! And so very wicked!" Tinkie was totally won over.

"When you have money, you meet a lot of cads," Janet said. "Of course the same is true for wealthy men and gold-digging women, but I only know my experience. It's painful to care for someone and realize your value to them is a meal ticket."

"I've seen it happen more than once," Tinkie agreed.

"Lucky me, I've never had that kind of money. Now let's try out some ideas." I was ready to get to work. We only had a few days to figure this out before it would be time to return to Zinnia. While I wholeheartedly believed that Sandra and Daryl were okay, each hour that passed lessened my belief. "Tell us about the blood found at San-dra's."

"The police chief wouldn't give any details about the blood, but he told me it was Daryl's, not Sandra's." Janet frowned.

"Why did they have Daryl's DNA on record?" Tinkie asked. "I mean, they'd have to match it, right?"

"Daryl was born north of Bay St. Louis. His family ran a bait shop, diner, and liquor store on the northern portion of the bay. There was a robbery in that community and Daryl and about fifteen other young boys were suspects. He gave his DNA to clear his name."

That made perfect sense. "I would never have guessed bait shop and convenience store from looking at Daryl. He looks so cosmopolitan."

"Daryl hated the outdoors. Selling bait, filling gas tanks, that kind of stuff was something he despised. He loved books. He read everything. He met Sandra in the library years back. She was hosting a book signing and he was there to meet her. He'd read all of her books and wanted to write. Sandra realized what an asset he could be and hired him on the spot. Changed his life, and hers, too."

"They seem very close." I needed to know their exact relationship without being tacky.

"They are. Great friends and business partners. If anything else, Sandra is maternal with him. There's nothing romantic there."

"Does Daryl have a partner?"

"He was involved with a beautiful woman but she's working in Europe right now. She's a fabulous photographer and is in high demand. Their future goal is for Daryl to write a book and Lulu to take the photographs."

"It sounds like a wonderful partnership," Tinkie said. "Does Daryl's family still run the bait shop?"

"I don't know. To the best of my knowledge, they do.

Daryl doesn't communicate with his family. He's so different, and I think the fear of being trapped into his old life makes him skittish about going back to visit."

He was less than an hour away and didn't see his parents. I'd give my right arm to see my family, but he was happy to ignore his. Ah, youth.

"Or that's what he wants everyone to believe," Tinkie said. "Let's check out his family." What she was really saying was that Daryl and Sandra might be hiding out in this backwater. It was the most logical place to check first.

"Janet, when you were in Sandra's office, you stuffed some papers into your dress." I had to know what she'd taken. "Care to share?"

"It was a list of the extended families connected with the Dixie Mafia. From back in the day. Sandra really relished poking the snake, if you get my meaning. I was curious to see who was on her list."

Oh, I did see, and it was helpful Janet had taken the list. "I'll need a copy of those names." Sandra had said that she'd left incorrect information deliberately. Even so, I wanted the list. "If Sandra is playing with fire, she could easily get burned by local criminals fearing exposure. The same applies to you."

"You really think some of those thugs snatched her up?" For the first time Janet seemed worried.

"I don't know, but if they did, the quicker we find her the better off she'll be. And you, too. Now we're going by the police department and then out to find the Marcus family. Stay here with your employees. Don't go anywhere without someone who is willing to testify to what you did at what time." I wanted to tattoo that point on her forehead.

"Cheerio!" she said. "You two be careful."

Words to live by.

8

The police chief was out of his office and no one else would talk to us, so we headed north, past I-10 and up into the rural areas of Hancock County to the Beer and Bait shop. It was a beautiful drive and we rode with the top down.

"I sure miss Sweetie Pie and Chablis," Tinkie said.

"And Pluto." I'd been thinking the exact same thing. "Do you think Gumbo will ever become a detective with us?"

Tinkie laughed. "Gumbo is plenty smart. In fact, too smart to get caught up in these cases where we starve, freeze, sweat, or stomp through woods and fields where snakes and ticks can eat us alive. She's a civilized puss who adores fine food and comfy pillows in the sun."

The cat did have more sense than we did. "How long do you think it will take us to find Sandra and Daryl?" I'd had a wave of homesickness for the horses, the cats and dogs, and Dahlia House.

"I think we may resolve this today. If we do, we might consider giving Janet back half of the retainer. I mean, half a day's work? It wouldn't be fair."

She was right. "Sure." It made me happy to think of shutting the case only hours after we'd taken it on. That was the kind of statistic that made Delaney Detective Agency highly sought after. Still, I had plans for that money.

Tinkie laughed. "Your enthusiasm is contagious."

Then I had to laugh, too. "You're right. It's the Christmas thing to do. But let's find the Houdinis before we start handing money back."

We were several miles inland and the flora of the beach was giving way to pine barrens. The soil was still sandy and well drained—except where there were sloughs or creeks and springs. The pine forest was thick, the trees tall and uniform. These were crop trees, and while I knew the resulting wood-built homes and a million other things made from the pines were necessary, I hated to think of the forests cut down. Often they were clear-cut—leaving nothing left alive. It was a brutal practice for the many animals who lived in the wood-land tracts.

The trees broke open to a clearing where a clever little house on stilts had been built beside a marina near the Jour-dan River. Fishing vessels and other working ships, along with pleasure boats and sailboats, were tied up by the dock. A middle-aged man was filling the tank of one boat, talking to his customer. It could have been a Norman Rockwell painting.

"You think that's Daryl's father?" Tinkie asked, searching her purse for lipstick. No matter the occasion, Tinkie was always beautifully turned out.

"I do. He looks like Daryl." He was a handsome man, an older version of Sandra's assistant. We got out of the car and as we walked toward the house/diner/convenience store, a sign made me smile. CRICKETS, BEER, WORMS, GASOLINE—the essentials of life for a real man. There was also a tantalizing odor coming from the little house.

"Morning, ladies," the man I believed to be Mr. Marcus said. "Martha's in the diner. We have red beans and andouille made up with fresh corn bread and collards on the side."

We had eaten Danish only an hour before, but there was no reason not to eat again as far as I could see. We clunked up the stairs to the screened door. I could have gained five pounds just smelling the food cooking.

I took in the diner, which fronted on the river that opened onto the bay. A brisk wind was flapping some flags on one docked boat, and a motorboat pulled into the marina. Mr. Marcus walked out to help tie it off.

Inside, a younger woman working one section of the tables might have been Daryl's sister, but the woman who asked if she could help us was clearly his mother.

"Mrs. Marcus," I said, introducing us. "When you have a minute, we'd like to talk."

"About?" She was friendly but shrewd.

"Daryl."

Her face went expressionless. "I'm sorry, we don't know anyone by that name." She turned on her heel and walked away.

"Now just one cotton-picking minute." Tinkie stalked after her. "That's your son you're disavowing."

"And that's none of your business." The glint of tears shone in the older woman's eyes.

"Daryl is a respected man," Tinkie said, softening instantly. "He's working with a famous author and he's living in a world that he fits into."

"You don't know my son," Mrs. Marcus said. "I'm not sure anyone does."

Tinkie was taken aback, but after a split second she recovered. "I've only met him recently. You're correct about that. But the author Sandra O'Day values his work highly. We really need to find Daryl and Ms. O'Day."

"What do you mean find them? They're over in Bay St. Louis living like lords."

The hint of bitterness in her voice made Tinkie sigh. "No, they're not. They went missing last night at a party at Ms. O'Day's home. No one has seen them since."

The tightening of the skin beneath Mrs. Marcus's eyes gave her away. She was worried about her son. She might be angry with him, but she was worried. "So where is he? Why would he run away like that?"

"That's what we're trying to find out," Tinkie said. "Will you help us?"

She looked around the diner. "Let me be sure my people are served." She was gone before we could respond.

"I don't think she knows where Daryl is," Tinkie said.

"I agree. That hit her pretty hard. It's easy to be mad with your kid when you think he's living high on the hog in perfect safety. Not so easy when it's possible he's in danger."

"You sound like you'd make a pretty good mother." Tinkie grinned.

"I'm going for the title of Best Godmother Ever."

"Maylin is one lucky girl."

"Thanks, Tinkie." I nodded toward Mrs. Marcus. She was motioning us over to a table in the corner.

"Sit here," she said. "I'll get you some food. When things slow down, we can talk."

I had no intention of resisting the delicious scent coming from the kitchen. "Sure."

Almost before we could get into our seats, she was back with sweet iced tea for both of us. "Another ten minutes," she said. "Folks will clear out to get back to work." She whizzed back by and put bowls of red beans, andouille sausage, and rice in front of us with plates of turnip greens and corn bread.

"We're going to pop wide open," Tinkie said. "The good thing about being plump is that I can't see my feet so I can wear my most comfortable shoes all the time now."

Tinkie could always find the silver lining.

"We can walk on the beach later. Burn some calories." I knew we'd never do it, but it sounded good.

Before Tinkie could answer, Mrs. Marcus sat down with us. There was another waitress at the cash register, checking out the last of the customers. Lunch hour was over.

She got right to the point. "My son is missing and no one knows where he is!" Color heightened her cheeks.

"He is missing, along with Sandra O'Day."

"Tell me what happened." She rested her hands on the table. "All of it."

We told her the story of the party and how both Sandra and Marcus disappeared. No one noticed until it was time for the book signing. Then they were nowhere to be found and no one recalled seeing them leave.

Tinkie and I shared a glance. We knew each other so

well, I could read the question in her eyes. Was I going to mention the blood in the mudroom sink? Daryl's blood?

"We don't want to frighten you, Mrs. Marcus, but blood was found at the scene."

"What do you mean?"

"We didn't see it," Tinkie said, "but the police found Daryl's blood in a sink in the mudroom."

"How much blood?" she asked.

"We don't know. If we find out, we can call you if you'd like. But if there had been a lot of blood, the police would have taken a different approach to this. Right now, they're treating it as a suspicious disappearance." I was doing my best to avoid the word *kidnapping* until Janet was charged with that crime.

"Daryl was a good son. This wasn't the life for him. The boys around here, they're all about hunting and camping. Daryl loved his books. He dreamed of New York City and a life with theater and book signings. Donnie, that's his dad, told me when I started letting him spend all that time in the library that I was making a mistake. That it would make him a sissy. But I didn't make Daryl anything. He was born loving books and hating to kill anything. The boy would starve before he would shoot a deer or wring a chicken's neck." Her eyes filled but she blinked back any tears. "Donnie never understood. He never got it that the world is bigger than the hunting camp and the bay. That it was okay to want a different life. He said we had to let Daryl go. I shouldn't have listened to him."

"Did Daryl have any enemies around here?"

"Good heavens, no. Most of the boys never took notice he was alive. The girls liked him, but he wasn't interested in settling down with someone who wanted to live beside her mama and daddy right here. Daryl was friendly—he had plenty of friends—but he wasn't staying here and there was no reason to start something with a girl that he wasn't going to finish."

I liked Daryl more and more. "Mrs. Marcus, do you know anything about the treasures supposedly stashed around here by Al Capone?"

She laughed. "Oh, I loved those stories growing up. My granny grew up around here during that time, and she could truly spin a yarn. Al Capone was a criminal, but he was also a hero to some of the people because he wouldn't buckle. He fought against the law."

The South had a deep reverence for people who stood alone against authority. Sometimes it was a good thing, but most often it was not. "Did Daryl know about the tales?"

"He did his high school English term paper about Capone and the many treasure locations."

"Seriously?" Tinkie asked.

"No one has ever found the treasure, that we know about," Mrs. Marcus said, "but Daryl and I, we would talk about finding it and dream big dreams. How that would have changed our lives. Especially his. He could have gone to some of those fancy schools he yearned to attend." She wiped a tear away. "He never said anything to his daddy, but he wanted to go to Vanderbilt. He wanted it in the worst kind of way, and it was always just out of his reach. He could have gotten to the moon more easily." She paused and looked at Tinkie, then me. "I let him down by not providing that for him. I did. And it's bitter to me. So bitter that I've almost convinced myself it's better he's gone from here." She exhaled a ragged breath. "But if you see him . . . when you find him, tell him to please come home."

9

I left Tinkie to gather more info from Mrs. Marcus. My partner had a genuine sympathy for people caught in the clutches of bad situations. Donnie was no longer in sight, so I walked down to the marina, hoping to talk with him about his son's interests and friends. The sun on the water of the small marina was classic winter beauty in the Deep South. The water glittered silver and gold as the wind riffled it. An inlet to the east held the huge cypress knees that were enigmatic bayou regulars. Along the banks, moss draped the barren limbs of sycamore, water oak, wild cherry, and persimmon trees.

The water was black, an indication of the depth. The Jourdan was a black water river with high ground and marshes. Fairly large vessels could navigate these waters. Mississippi was a state blessed with lots of rivers and navigable bayous and streams. The Mighty Missi'sip was the most famous, but the Delta had the slow, sluggish rivers that fed the soil. The lower part of the state had the Pascagoula system and the beautiful Wolf and Escatawpa rivers that were favorites for canoeing and recreation.

Back in my college days I'd spent more than one summer weekend canoeing the Wolf and the Tchoutacabouffa rivers with my theater friends. Their flair for the dramatic made each camping trip a riotous adventure. I'd fallen in love with the pure white sandbars, sleeping under the stars, drinking Jack Daniel's, and listening to my talented friends play the guitar and sing.

I scouted along the marina, but Mr. Marcus was nowhere to be found. I wondered if he'd taken a boat out for a run, but then I spied what had to be a bait shed. The December day was warm, and I removed my jacket as I walked.

Someone was inside the shed. A shadow shifted in front of the window. The outline of the person was vague, which made the hair on my neck stand on end. There was something ghostly about it, and even though I lived with a very old ghost, I never grew accustomed to her visits.

I opened the door and entered, but I stopped in my tracks. A woman in a wedding dress and a long veil stood beside a wire cage of crickets. The soft whirring of the insects was the only sound, until I heard a soft sniffle. The bride was crying.

"Hello." I thought she'd seen me but I couldn't be certain. She turned to face me, and I inhaled sharply. She was beautiful. Glamorous in a way that was long gone from the world I lived in. Her wedding gown was exquisite lace, and a lace caplet woven with ribbons and flowers anchored a cascading veil that flowed about her to the floor. Her heavily kohled eyes held deep sadness.

"Who are you?" I asked. Of course it was Jitty as some early movie star, but I didn't recognize which star and I was honestly captured by the winsome beauty of the young woman.

"I was known as the Hungarian Rhapsody in the silent films." Her accent was thick.

I knew her instantly. She'd been a smash movie queen, costarring opposite such greats as Rudolph Valentino and Ronald Colman. Her expressive eyes and face had garnered her a dedicated audience across Europe and then in Hollywood. Her first Hollywood movie, produced by Samuel Goldwyn, was *The Dark Angel*—her ticket to international fame. In the era of the silent film, Vilma Bánky was hot stuff. Her thick accent ended her career when the talkies came along.

"Are you dressed for your movie role or for your own wedding?" I asked. Jitty's appearances were always oblique, but I hoped to find any relevance to my case—if there was one.

"Samuel Goldwyn discovered me in Europe and brought me to Hollywood. For a time, I was the queen of Hollywood. Twenty years later no one remembered my name."

The more she talked, the easier it was for me to understand her. I found her accent lovely, but the low technology of the early talkies would have been a challenge for her. "Do you regret leaving Europe?"

"No. Mr. Goldwyn produced my marriage to Rod La Rocque, a wonderful actor. It was the most elegant and elaborate wedding ever seen in Hollywood. Mr. DeMille was Rod's best man. We were happy for many, many years, even after we both gave up acting."

I was fascinated by Vilma, but I didn't understand why Jitty had come to me as this actress.

"I've watched many of your films," I told her. "I studied your facial expressions and movements in my theater classes at college. In one review *The New York Times* said you were 'so exquisite that one is not in the least surprised that she is never forgotten' by her lover in the film."

I knew the quote from school and also because Aunt Loulane had been a huge fan. Not to mention Millie, who loved all things Hollywood and had a special reverence for the silent movie era. "I wish my friend Millie could meet you."

The bridal veil swirled around Vilma and when it settled back into place, Jitty was staring back at me. The thick Hungarian accent was replaced by my haint's soft Southern drawl. "I wish I could hang out and talk movies with Millie, too. We're kindred spirits. We just can't risk the consequences, can we?"

"No." It was a simple answer. Jitty was my secret, the last of my family left at Dahlia House. While we technically weren't related by blood, Jitty had been with my great-great-grandmother during the Civil War. The bond forged between the women, one Black and one white, during a time of hardship, was closer than blood. They had survived together. Neither alone would have made it. Jitty now kept me connected to the rich heritage of Dahlia House and the people I'd loved and lost. I couldn't risk losing her. But that wouldn't keep me from calling Millie to reveal that I'd had "an encounter" with Vilma Bánky. I would tell her it was a dream.

I had a sudden thought about Jitty's peculiar interest in old movie stars. "Jitty, are you trying to tell me that the film actress Helene Buntman is the key to the disappearance of Sandra and Daryl?" I knew she'd never admit it even if it was true, but I liked to keep her on her toes. Jitty knew all the rules of the Great Beyond and sharing info with me was illegal.

"I'm not tellin' you a darn thing," Jitty said.

"Can I guess?"

"No, you cannot guess because I won't tell you so much as the day of the week." She grinned. "Time don't mean nothin' to a ghost."

"But if Helene is the answer, how do I use that information?"

"Sarah Booth, you got a wicked streak a mile wide. Your mama never saw it, but Aunt Loulane knew. You'd walk out the door to go somewhere with your friends and Aunt Loulane would smile until she closed the door. Then she'd just say, 'That girl is going to get herself in big trouble one of these days.' She wasn't even psychic but she had you pegged."

"Aunt Loulane did worry about me. She'd want you to help me solve this case."

Jitty only glared at me. "I'm leavin'. You're tryin' to pull me into your business and I can't do it."

I had Jitty on the run, and it felt marvelous. She deviled me all the time about my eggs drying up before I could fertilize them. She could document every single "womb disorder" ever suffered by a Delaney woman. And she wasn't shy about barking on about how Coleman deserved a wife who cooked, cleaned, had babies, or any number of things I refused to do. Now, I'd found something I could pinch her with. Like a snapping turtle, I wasn't going to let go of her until it thundered.

"Jitty, you could have been a movie star." I meant this. Jitty was beautiful. A difficult life had not hardened her full face or intelligent eyes.

"You think so?"

Her question was so childlike that I felt instantly guilty. It was cruel to play with someone's dreams. Jitty had died long before the time when movies were a reality, and the hard truth was that no matter her talent, her ethnicity would have prevented a film career up until the 1940s.

"Jitty, I think you would have wowed them. You still could today if you were corporeal." That was the honest truth. I was done messing with her. "Of all the things you could have done in this world and the next, you chose to be with me. Thank you."

"Why you all teary-eyed and sentimental?"

I had to laugh. Jitty was suspicious of the kinder, gentler me—as I would be of her. We had a pattern to our interaction, and it centered on torment, warnings, and love. "Sometimes I forget how much I rely on you and need you in my life."

Her eyebrows shot up. "You're handin' me a loaded weapon, Sarah Booth."

"I know. I'm going to regret this, I know."

"You really are." She grinned and the glint in her eyes was no longer childlike or naïve. It was the devil dancing a tango.

"Helene Buntman? How does she fit into this case?"

"Beauty is sometimes a reward all in itself." That was her final offer. She pulled the veil around her face and disappeared just as a cote of doves broke cover outside the window. Jitty did have a flair for the dramatic.

I turned and headed back to the diner to collect Tinkie and find out what she'd unearthed. Jitty wasn't going to be a bit of help, and I was tired of trying to outfox her.

10

Mr. Marcus showed up at the stairs to the diner. He came out from under the restaurant, which was built on fifteen-foot pilings to avoid floodwaters. I noticed plastic chairs and tables, canoes, and other items tied to the pilings so they couldn't float away.

I chatted with him for a moment before Tinkie came down, but he basically confirmed everything his wife had said. Mr. Marcus went about his business, and Tink and I waddled to the car to go home. We both suffered from overindulgence. Mrs. Marcus had a way with spices and flavors. The red beans were the best I'd ever had, and her corn bread—it was a work of art. I was so full, I honestly thought my pants would split. Good thing I'd chosen denim.

Drinking in the atmosphere of the diner—the jam-packed parking lot, the men talking around a picnic table where five daring seagulls waited patiently for scraps—it was apparent to me that this was the place for a home-cooked meal for the entire community. Everyone seemed to be a valued regular. I understood why Daryl couldn't stay here, but I also understood why his parents couldn't easily accept that.

"Learn anything new?" I asked Tinkie as we got in the car and pulled out of the parking lot to head back to the coast.

In her talk with Mrs. Marcus, Tinkie had observed that the Marcus family was respected and liked, but she hadn't gotten information about Daryl or where he might be. I told Tinkie about my desire to do more research on Helene Buntman. Jitty, right or wrong, had left a bee in my bonnet.

"You think Sandra and Daryl have been taken because of Capone's alleged treasure?" Tinkie stared out the front window of the Roadster.

"It's a possibility."

"Yeah, it is."

Tinkie was quiet on the ride back to Bay St. Louis. I could tell she was troubled, and I suspected it was the chasm between Daryl and his parents that nagged at her. Tinkie wasn't close with her folks, and it chafed her. She'd never felt she was the most important thing in their lives, as I had. I grew up knowing my wants and needs and development topped the list of both my parents. Spending time with me was a priority for both of them. Tinkie didn't feel that way.

"The Marcus family seems nice," I offered. "They really love Daryl. They just don't know how to show it. He's an alien in their midst."

"Maybe." Tinkie wasn't going to let them off the hook that easily.

"It's hard to be different in a small, tight community. It's hard on the kid and the parents. Daryl did it, though," I pointed out. "He had the strength of character to be himself."

"I was everything my mother wanted me to be," Tinkie said. "I led every society program, wore every scratchy, tight, uncomfortable dress she picked out, joined her sorority at Ole Miss, married the man who could take over the bank and run it the way Daddy wanted." She sighed. "I don't think my mother ever cared if I had a child or not. She still hasn't been to see Maylin."

That was a raw sore and none of my words were balm enough to soothe it. But I had to try. "You have to give your folks the room to be who they are, Tinkie. They can't think and feel like you because they've lived in different times under different circumstances. Love them as they are and believe they love you. Otherwise, they're going to continually disappoint you and make you unhappy."

She squared her shoulders in the passenger seat and nodded. "Damn good advice, Sarah Booth. I'll give it some thought. Now, do you think someone took Sandra and Daryl? Someone with an agenda?"

"With each passing hour, I think that more and more."

"I know," she agreed. "But why? And if the abductors want something, what? Money, revenge, to stop Sandra from researching her book, an old family score to be settled? Remember, she's from around here, just like Janet. Maybe this is about her background or her family or someone feels she cheated them."

Tinkie had pinpointed the most reliable reasons for an abduction. "Good list."

"If it's about money, surely there'll be a ransom note." She sounded hopeful. And at this point, a ransom note would at least point us in a particular direction.

"Unless it was someone who wants them gone. Like permanently gone. A childhood acquaintance or old boyfriend. If she's as bitchy with other writers as she is around here, maybe someone just wanted to take her out and Daryl got in the way." Having seen Sandra in action, I could see why that might be so. But then I'd been surprised by Janet Malone's likability.

"What's next on the list of things to do today?" Tinkie asked.

"We have to speak to the police chief. We'll just sit right in the station until he's willing to talk to us. He can't hide forever."

The Bay St. Louis Police Department was small but lively. The officers were friendly, and the chief, Lester Thibodeau, was a gregarious man with a Sam Elliott mustache and a voice equally wonderful. "I'll bet when he questions a suspect, they fall all over themselves to confess," I whispered to Tinkie as he went to get us some coffee.

He returned with two handmade mugs and set them down in front of us. "Ladies, what do you need from me?"

"Would it be possible to see the crime scene photos of the blood at Sandra's house?" I asked.

He scratched his chin lightly. "I guess it can't hurt. You're working for Malone, right?"

"Yes, she says she isn't involved in this."

"And we believe her," Tinkie added. "She's concerned about the blood in the mudroom, and so are Daryl Marcus's parents. We talked to them this afternoon."

Thibodeau leaned back in his chair. "I remember Daryl when he was a tot and would spend every waking hour he could at the library. Mary Perkins loved him. He told stories to the younger kids, read to them, helped arrange special events. He was a genius at the Dewey Decimal system. That boy never met a book he didn't like."

"That's what we've heard," Tinkie said. "He certainly is devoted to Sandra."

"What do you know about the O'Day family?" I asked him. "They're local, right?"

"They are. Grew up over in Waveland. Good, hardworking family. I think Sandra had two brothers who joined the military and found careers in other cities. Her folks died a few years back."

"Died?" I did the math. They were too young to die of old age.

"It was a tragic accident, about two years ago. Gas leak. The pipes in the house were old." He shook his head. "I didn't investigate, but I know the fire chief who did and he's a straight-up guy. It was a cold winter night. One of those rare, bitter nights when the temperatures drop into the twenties. The O'Days went to bed with a gas space heater lit. Just enough to take the chill off in the bedroom. Somehow the flame was extinguished and the gas kept coming out. Seems Mr. O'Day woke up and flipped a light switch in the bedroom. Boom!"

"That's terrible," Tinkie said. She put a hand on my shoulder, knowing that I felt the echo of that loss.

"They were hardworking people. Mrs. O'Day ran a day care, and her husband was a businessman. They also owned a couple of fishing vessels that they ran as a charter business. Mr. O'Day had grown up on the water and he loved it. But he couldn't raise a family on an income that fluctuated so wildly. He and the boys, though, they'd take tourists and businessmen out on weekends. He had a fine reputation as a captain and as a man."

"None of the O'Days are still in the area?" I asked.

"No. I've contacted the brothers about Sandra's disappearance. They're ready to come home if needed, but I told them to give it a day or so just in case she's off doing research and doesn't want to be disturbed." He leveled a gaze first at Tinkie and then at me. "Sandra has a reputation as a difficult person. So does the other one, Janet Malone. Half the police department thinks this is a publicity stunt."

"That thought has crossed our mind," Tinkie said.

The chief pressed a button and asked his secretary to bring copies of the crime scene photos from the O'Day house.

"You can have these. I'm giving it a few more hours before I pull my men off their regular jobs and start looking at this as an abduction. We've got two detectives on it right now. Your fellow offered to help if we need him," he said to me. "We may give him a call. Since Hurricane Katrina, we're still playing catch-up on staff and funding."

"Coleman would be happy to help. He does love a good case." And that would put us squarely on the inside of the law officers' work.

"Chief Thibodeau," Tinkie said, "do you know the Malone family?"

"Everyone along the coast knows most everyone else. Or

they used to before the New Orleans people jammed over here after Katrina. Lots of strangers living all over the county now. But the Malones are an old family. Good folks."

"Does Janet have any siblings living here?"

"No. Only child. Her folks worked hard to send her to that fancy writing school in Iowa. She sure made that pay off. She's sold millions of books."

He was accurate with that. "Are her folks still in the area?" She'd told us they were out of the country. More details would be great.

"No, she bought them some mansion in Costa Rica. From the messages they send back here, they have a wonderful life. Janet visits when she can."

"Chief, who do you think took Sandra and Daryl?" Tinkie asked.

"I don't know that they were actually taken," he answered.

"They aren't here." Tinkie wasn't shy about pointing out the facts.

"Perhaps they left on their own. It hasn't even been twenty-four hours. What if they went to New Orleans for something?"

"Sandra left her own party and a big book signing. Seems it would need to be an emergency to leave all that." Tinkie turned on the charm. "I know you've given this a lot of thought. What do you really believe?"

"I don't have enough information to have a real opinion, but I will give you this: Something isn't right. I'm just not sure it's risen to the level of a crime. Could just be Sandra's typical rudeness. I know you've seen O'Day and Malone at work. They delight in chaos, mean comments, and mayhem. And I've heard Sandra's book has jumped in sales, which will only continue to rise once this story breaks in the media." His eyebrows went up and the mustache gathered as he pursed his lips. "Which I don't want to happen right now. No media. None at all. Understand?"

"Yes, sir," we said in unison. Lester Thibodeau was a man I wanted to stay on the good side of.

11

Tinkie had some Christmas shopping to finish up and she dropped me at the library so I could do more research on Helene Buntman and the O'Day and Malone families. Mary Perkins was an excellent source of details and possible leads. She would also remember Daryl, and she might have memories or insights that would be helpful.

I was tempted to spy on Tinkie—she was being so secretive about her shopping—but instead I focused on work. We had another round of Christmas tree judging and I was curious how the library would handle Sandra's absence.

Mary took me back into her office where I fed Weezie a can of high-dollar cat food and was honored when she settled on my lap while we talked. Weezie was not a cat who liked humans, except for Mary, but sometimes I caught a glimpse of real affection in her green eyes when she head-butted me or held my hand with her little white paws. *Pet me more! Pet me more!* She could communicate as well as a child.

"Mary, tell me what you know about Daryl Marcus."

"Ah, Daryl. Hasn't he grown into such a fine, handsome man?"

"He has." He could easily have been a heartthrob if he was a little less bookish and formal.

"He spent so much time here when he was younger, and since he's been back in town with Sandra, he's volunteered again. The children love him. He's traveled with Sandra and been exposed to so many different libraries. He has such creative and wonderful ideas, and he's started doing the children's hour again. I hope he's back by Saturday morning or the children will be so disappointed."

"Do you know where he's gone?"

"No. I wish I did. I've wracked my brain trying to think of where those two might be."

"Sandra hasn't called about the tree judging this afternoon?"

Mary shook her head. "Come outside. I need a cigarette."

We settled at a table under some shade trees beside a sculpture of a child reading a book. The work of art captured the whimsy of those carefree days of stories and imagination when my world had been parents, home, and whatever my imagination cooked up.

Mary exhaled a puff of smoke and gave me a look. "I don't think Sandra is going to show up to judge the trees."

"We still have three judges. We can do it." She'd worked so hard, I didn't want to stress her.

"Okay. I'm torn between wanting to punch her in the nose and being really worried that something has happened to her."

"I think the police chief feels the same way."

Mary laughed loud and long. "Thanks, I needed that. Yes, Lester doesn't suffer a fool lightly, and he will be really mad if this is one of Sandra's harebrained publicity stunts. He'll put her in jail for sure, messing up Christmas for everyone."

The little imp on my right shoulder danced with glee. Sandra needed a few nights in the hoosegow. Daryl, too, if he was part of this plot. But Daryl was the topic I wanted to plumb.

"Do tell me all about Sandra's assistant."

Mary tapped her ash and considered. "Daryl is a good man. A lover of books and the written word. I've always hoped that one day he would write. He used to make up stories for the children's hour and he could capture those kids with the first sentence."

"Would he go along with Sandra on a publicity stunt?"

"He adores Sandra. She's the parent-slash-friend he always wanted and never had. She's an acclaimed writer, and she takes Daryl seriously for his research and writing. She listens to his interests and needs, and doesn't find him lacking because he prefers intellectual pursuits."

"I met his parents this morning. They love him, but there is a barrier between their lifestyle and his. They've judged him harshly because they don't understand his world. And I think they feel a little judged as well for not being . . . well read."

"I see it all the time," Mary said. "Good kids who want something different. Their parents fear this. Anything new or that alters their small world, it's frightening to them. The irony is that in fearing they are losing their child, they push them away. Daryl loves his folks. He's just tired of ramming his head into the brick wall of their determination that he be exactly like them."

I saw that. "Maybe when we find him we can intercede on his behalf. I truly believe his folks would welcome him if we could get them over the fear."

"Maybe. If too much damage hasn't already been done. Rejection always brings a price, Sarah Booth. But let me think whether if I can tell you anything of critical importance about Daryl. Any clues as to where he might be hiding with Sandra, if they are hiding."

Mary knew exactly what I needed. "Thanks."

"He loved the history of this region, from the days of Bienville and the pirates to the tribes of Native Americans who lived here."

It was easy to see the French influence in the architecture of the entire Gulf Coast region and New Orleans. The Native Americans left a much smaller footprint, something that I loved about their beliefs and values. "So that was his focus?"

"He did a lot of research for Sandra in that area. And on the Capone time period. You know the gangster loved Bay St. Louis. Some of the local people, they had grandparents who knew Capone. Some worked for him. They said he was generous to the local businesses and there's still a lot of loyalty to Capone's and Buntman's memories."

"So he was generous to the community? He needed goodwill or someone would turn him in to the feds?"

"There is that." Mary laughed. "But he also had charm. Or at least that's the way I heard it. And Helene Buntman, she was the most beautiful woman many of the folks around here had ever seen. She grew up here, left, and came back a celebrity known around the world. She was one of us who made good, and she came home. The town adored and protected her. And therefore they protected Capone. Not to mention that a lot of people made a lot of money selling untaxed and illegal hooch."

"Did Daryl have any special places he loved around here?"

"Ship Island. You know boys and sailing fantasies. He wanted a sailboat, but his father was more focused on charter fishing expeditions. A sailboat was for pleasure, the other was a way to provide for a family—that's how Mr. Marcus saw it. But Daryl loved the idea of sailing and he often rode the ferry over to Ship Island for his solitary explorations."

I excused myself and sent a text to Coleman, alerting him to the possibility that Daryl could be on the island. I seriously doubted Sandra was camping out on a barrier island—she was more likely camping at the Plaza in New York City. Which reminded me to ask Chief Thibodeau if he'd checked the flights out of Gulfport and New Orleans. If the missing duo was playing a prank, they could be anywhere.

"What are the chances this is a trick?" I asked.

"Fifty-fifty. Daryl was always an upright person, but if this helps book sales for Sandra, he would do it. He is totally loyal to her. You've met her; she wouldn't hesitate to pull a stunt like this."

"Anyone you know who would want to harm them?"

"Pretty much everyone in town has a grudge against Sandra. Since she's been back, she's been to city, county, school board, and state legislative meetings and offices raising hell about one thing and another. She beat up a man who kicked his dog. She flew at him like a rabid chicken, squawking and flapping. I don't know what she had in her purse but it was heavy. She hit him with it so hard he had to go to the emergency room."

"She physically assaulted him?" I didn't blame her at all. Anyone who kicked a dog deserved harsh punishment. And it was interesting that both writers were ardent animal lovers.

"She did. He didn't file a complaint because he was so afraid of what she might do next." Mary was grinning. "That one counts to her good side."

"Indeed. He got what he had coming."

"She also took his dog and found it a loving home. She told him if she ever saw him with another pet he'd spend the rest of his days in a place he really hated."

Sandra was a handful, but when she was right, she was right. "At the governmental meetings, what was her goal?"

"She's complained about everything. All the time. With the school board it was the school curriculum, even though she has never taught and doesn't have a child."

"What didn't she like about it?"

"She insisted it was inadequate and hid the truth about the history. She's also right about that. She isn't a teacher but she's done tons of research. To me, that also falls on the good side. With the city council and state, she's starting a film commission to try to draw Hollywood attention to all that the Gulf Coast offers as movie settings. On the whole, it's fifty-fifty there, too. She's done a lot of good and aggravated a lot of people doing it."

I had a revelation. "She's another person who doesn't quite fit in with the expectations of her hometown."

Mary nodded. "Excellent point. Maybe that's what she and Daryl have in common. I heard she offered to send him to any school he wanted, but he didn't go. Said he was learning more working with her, and that's probably correct. They're like siblings or mother and son."

"Are there places he might go, other than Ship Island?"

"There are wonderful little communities all north of I-10 in Hancock and Harrison County. Pearl River County, too. Honestly, if he has friends or connections there, we won't ever find them until they're ready to come out."

"And Capone's treasure. Where do you think it might be?"

"I'm not playing Geraldo Rivera for you." She chuckled. "But if I had to guess, I'd say the Buntman mansion."

"Was the mansion in use when Sandra bought it?"

"No. It had been closed for years. And partially vandalized. If the money is there, it's well hidden."

"When did Sandra buy the property?"

Mary shook her head. "The renovation was just finished a couple of months ago, and it took about a year. So sometime before that."

"Did Sandra hunt for the treasure when the house was renovated?"

"All of that work was done before she moved in. She hired a contractor who handled things. It was all kind of hush-hush. All us townsfolk knew was that the property had sold. I don't know any details, but the contractor might be able to tell you."

"Do you know the contractor's name? And can you recommend some books on Helene Buntman and her family?"

"Sure can. And I can get the name of the contractor who did the renovations on the mansion."

All in all, some very good leads came from Mary Perkins. I left the library with an armful of books about Bay St. Louis and Helene Buntman.

12

Tinkie picked me up at the library and we went back to the inn for a little Maylin time and to look over the photos Chief Thibodeau had given us. The blood in the mudroom sink didn't indicate a fatality, but someone had been injured. That someone was Daryl, according to the blood analysis.

There wasn't any way to tell how Daryl had been hurt. Nothing in the mudroom had been damaged, and it was possible Daryl had cut himself outside and simply gone there to wash up. The evidence was too flimsy to read, and the chief had noted there was no time line on when the blood got into the sink.

Mary called with the contractor's name, and Tinkie gave him a ring. Watching the expression on her face, I could tell she wasn't getting much information at all. When she hung up, she growled with frustration.

"The contractor didn't remember Sandra looking for anything. In fact, he had a rather shoddy memory all around. He did say that no structural changes had been made to the house, only cosmetic. The house has a lot of secret passages and exits, though. He did say that. We really need to examine that place. If we can figure out how Sandra and Daryl left without anyone seeing them, it may help us find where they are."

"Does the contractor have the house plans?" I asked.

"If he does, he isn't going to share them with us."

Another dead end. "Coleman and Oscar should be back soon. Maybe they've found something about Daryl and Sandra." It was the longest of long shots, but it didn't hurt to hope.

Tinkie had Christmas gifts to wrap, and I still had a few gifts to pick up. I left her with Maylin and the nanny, and I walked to the small downtown where pottery shops and boutiques were the order of the day. I found a pair of beautiful earrings for Millie and some cuff links for Harold. The holiday party season was upon us and Harold, the ultimate host, always dressed to the nines. The cuff links were embossed with the image of a dog that looked exactly like his demonic canine, Roscoe.

With my shopping concluded, I strolled to the inn to wait for the men to return. I took the library books to a table beside the pool, where an arbor of vines filtered the bright sun. As I began to read a biography of Helene Buntman, I entered another time; a world of glamour, style, and adventure.

Helene grew up working as a hand on fishing expeditions with her father, whom she adored. She became more proficient on the boats than any of the other crew, and at sixteen she was trusted to pilot the shipments of booze into the Bay of St. Louis. Her skill as a pilot—and the rescue of a boat loaded with rum—earned her the attention of Al Capone.

As much as Helene loved the water and the thrill of rum-running, she harbored a dream of being an actress. By the time she was nineteen, she was headed to New York City for a screen test. Capone had made the arrangements for her.

Her beauty and athleticism earned her starring roles in a number of films, from a pirate to Cleopatra. Her expressive eyes became her trademark. When she was twenty-five she returned to Bay St. Louis when her mother became ill, and she met and spent time with Capone.

Capone built the stucco mansion for her. It was said to be one of the finest homes along the Gulf Coast, rivaling even the dwellings of the wealthy in Natchez, Mississippi, where half the millionaires in the United States lived before the Civil War.

The book I was reading contained a number of photographs of Helene, including publicity shots from the Hollywood studios. Others were snapshots of her on the fishing boats or walking along the sandy beach of Ship Island. Some were of Helene singing in the clubs that peppered Highway 90 along the coast. Apparently she was a glamourous torch singer in great demand, though that had been overshadowed by her acting career.

Several reviews of her club performances had been included in the book. "Her voice was throaty and sensual, perfect for the blues."

When the photos continued her life story to illustrate the building of the mansion and the lavish parties held there, I sank deeper into Helene's world. To my surprise, there were no photos of her with Capone, though he lived in the mansion with her.

A photo showed a mausoleum on the estate where Helene was buried in what appeared to be a solitary grave. She had never married, never had a child, and after she said goodbye to acting, never returned to Hollywood. She lived out her days in Bay St. Louis sailing the *Wayward Wench*, her boat. The conclusion of her life seemed bittersweet, and a bit lonely. All of her family had died before her. She was alone in the crypt that had been designed for her and Capone. The gangster died in Florida of cardiac arrest and his body was later moved to a cemetery in Illinois near his family.

The final photo was the most intriguing of all. In her later years, Helene had been acknowledged as a talented medium. The photo showed her with a group of women seated around a table preparing for a séance.

I dug through the other books, but I didn't find more information on her mediumship or a reason why Capone and Buntman parted ways. As I closed the books, I was left with a pang of sadness. I had no real clue to the personalities of either Capone or Buntman, except he was smart and ruthless and she was daring and brave. But the man had built her a mansion and then disappeared from her life. He'd done a stint in Alcatraz and been diagnosed with third stage syphilis—not a pretty ending. Perhaps he'd gone to Florida to spare Helene from watching his mental and physical decline. Or perhaps I was being a romantic fool.

I checked the time, surprised to see how late it had gotten. I texted Tinkie that we had to head for the library soon, and I also texted Coleman. He and Oscar were on a special holiday voyage on the ferry to Ship Island, a place where tourists frolicked. I went online to check the time of the ferry's return and found that they should have returned an hour ago. A flicker of concern tickled my spine. I walked over to Tinkie's suite. "Have you heard from Oscar?"

She sensed my worry and checked the time. "No. They should be back."

"I know."

She clicked on the local news as she put on her earrings. WLOX out of Biloxi was all about Christmas-related stories—toy drives, angel trees, the parade schedule for the coastal cities, carol signing, and church chorales. I was relieved. And annoyed. I texted Coleman again, and got nothing. Tinkie tried Oscar with the same result.

"The one thing I know is that if there is trouble, we'll hear about it." Tinkie was ticked off. "Let's go do our job."

I tickled Maylin's tummy and got her to kick her feet before we left to do our judging. On the ride to the library, I told Tinkie what I'd found out about Helene. Not much of it was useful.

"We can ask, but it seems the world's interest in her waned before she hung out a medium's shingle. She lived out her life here quietly, sailing her boat and just doing the day-to-day thing."

"Do you think the Capone treasure is hidden in the house?"

"Tinkie, let's hope not. If Sandra and Daryl have been abducted by people on a quest for treasure, they could be in serious trouble."

She nodded. "Let's judge those trees. If Oscar and Coleman haven't returned by the time we finish . . ."

"We'll find them." I forced myself to sound upbeat. I had great faith that Coleman and Oscar were able to handle themselves, but I also couldn't stop the worry that gnawed at me. It was going to be a long evening of judging unless the two men showed up. Or answered their phones.

Once we entered the library, I stopped and drank in the changes. Like magic, the top fifty trees had been brought into the library. They were artistically displayed, creating a real magic land of Christmas beauty. Mary handed us our score cards and we were turned loose to tour the library, ranking all the incredible trees in categories. The imagination and creativity used by the entrants was breathtaking, ranging from a silver tinsel tree decorated in peacock feathers to the full skirt of a 1950s ball gown used as a tree, with ornaments of handcrafted jewelry hooked to the netting.

Some of the local businesses had theme trees showing off their goods and wares, and several trees reflected the bay and its seafood offerings. One beautiful tree, decorated with coral, turquoise, and gold, contained images and mementos depicting the Capone/Buntman mansion. I had to wonder if the civic group that had used that theme knew who the judges might be.

Speaking of which, our remaining fellow judge was late.

"Do you think she'll show up?" Tinkie asked.

"It would be really mean if she didn't." The library staff had worked so hard to make this magical display for the holidays. The big party was planned for Saturday night, where the winners of the decorating awards would be announced. I assumed we could go forward with two judges, but I also had a suggestion.

"We can offer for Millie and Cece to step in as judges," I said. "Assuming Sandra and Janet don't show up."

"Now that's an excellent idea. They can rush over here as soon as they arrive in town and rank the trees. Then there'll be time to tabulate the scores and the library can give us the list so we can pick the top winners in each category."

Before I could talk to Mary about alternate judges, Janet arrived. She'd been distressed earlier in the day, but now she was frantic. She came straight to us. "Have you found Sandra?"

"Nothing solid," I told her. "We talked to Daryl's parents. They claim they haven't seen him. The police chief is looking for both of them. The only sign of foul play is the blood in the mudroom sink and no one can say for sure that it was caused by violence or an accident or even how long it's been there."

"In other words, you've accomplished nothing." Janet impaled me with her glare.

"Not for want of trying, Janet. We're doing all we can. We need access to the mansion and we need to know more about the house. The most logical reasons for anyone abducting Sandra is to find Capone's alleged treasure or to stop her from revealing secrets from the past. We need some help with both motives."

"Help how?" Janet kept clenching her hands into fists at her sides.

"Was Sandra looking for a treasure? Had she had any threats from the people she wrote about or was researching for the next book?"

The look that passed over Janet's face told me a lot more than her words. Someone had threatened Sandra. "Tell us." I had to get her to spit out the information if we were to help her. "We don't have a direction to look in."

"Sandra didn't tell me much. She hates me," Janet said. She dabbed at her eyes with a tissue. "But she was afraid. Someone had been leaving notes for her at her front door."

"What did they say?" Tinkie asked with an impatience that I also felt. We could have used this information yesterday.

"That she should pack up and move out of the house and out of town. That her books were trash and poorly researched, and that if she didn't leave, she would be hurt."

"Where are these notes?" I asked.

Janet shrugged. "I never saw them. She just told me about them. To make me feel sorry for her, I guess. It sure didn't work."

"Did you tell this to the police chief?" Tinkie asked.

She shook her head. "I promised Sandra I wouldn't. She thought that if the person threatening her got publicity it would only get worse."

"Call Chief Thibodeau." Tinkie's voice was firm. "Now."

"As soon as I finish this judging." She waved a hand at the trees. "They are so beautiful and I can't enjoy them at all. I'm worried."

"About Sandra?" The question popped out of my mouth before I could stop it. "You despise each other."

"We've grown comfortable in our competitiveness. And I don't want her hurt. No writer would want to see another harmed."

"Call the chief." I added to Tinkie's admonition.

"Will do. Now I need to judge." She nodded to several library employees waiting to tabulate our findings so they could close and go home.

"We'll talk in the morning," she said.

Tinkie and I moved on to the children's trees that took thematic inspiration from fairy tales and beloved books. I was particularly taken with the Nancy Drew tree, which was decorated with children's drawings of covers of the many Carolyn Keene mysteries. How I had loved reading those books of my mother's. She had the entire collection. The Hardy Boys, too.

The good thing about the judging work was that it required our full attention. So much so that when I heard my name called, I turned around without expectation. Coleman and Oscar stood there, excitement on both their faces.

"Did you find something?" Tinkie demanded.

"We did. That's what took us so long," Oscar said.

Now wasn't the time to talk about it. "We'll be done in half an hour. Let's meet at that little restaurant on the corner. It's quiet and we can talk. Can it wait that long?" The men looked like they were about to pop.

"We'll meet you there. Hurry!" Coleman and Oscar slipped out as quietly as they had come in, leaving me and Tinkie champing at the bit to hear what they'd learned.

13

The men had a pitcher of margaritas waiting for us and salt-rimmed glasses. I was ready for a libation. The judging had been difficult because so many of the trees deserved to win. As soon as Coleman had poured drinks for all of us, the men launched into what had occurred on Ship Island.

"We had a hot lead on Sandra and Daryl," Oscar explained. "One of the crew on the ferry had seen them yesterday on the Gulfport docks. He didn't know if they'd gone out to Ship Island or not, but he told us of some places where visitors to the island liked to hang out. Some private places."

This sounded promising. "And what did you find?"

Coleman blew out a breath. "Not nearly what we hoped. The island is unspoiled. And it isn't a huge Christmas destination. That made it easier to check—Sandra and Daryl haven't been on the ferry. But the captain pointed out that any number of private boats can access all of the barrier islands. They could have gone out there at any time."

"Did you get a chance to look around?" Tinkie asked.

"We did." Oscar shared a glance with Coleman. "There's an old fort there. Lots of possibilities for treasure, but as to the island itself, it changes with every hurricane. The land mass physically shifts every year. Any treasure buried could easily now be underwater."

"What about Sandra and Daryl? Any sign that they made it to the island?" I felt deflated.

"One park employee thought she'd seen them on the beach yesterday, but she couldn't be certain," Oscar said.

"And we met a boat owner on the dock that said he thought they were trying to book a boat, but again he couldn't be certain. You know eyewitnesses are the least reliable testimony, in any case." Coleman didn't sound too hopeful, either.

"Why would they go out there?" Tinkie asked. "I mean is there something on the island that would draw them at this particular time?"

"I was thinking it might be Capone's treasure," Oscar said. "Maybe the island was a temporary hiding place but it became permanent."

Anything was possible. "There's no place for Sandra and Daryl to be hidden there?"

"Not really," Coleman said. "Not that we could find, and we walked the island. The interior has some vegetation, but mostly sand. Walking in that deep sand takes awhile."

"Thanks for doing that. Both of you." I was appreciative and a little let down. Against my common sense, I'd hoped they'd turn up something.

"But we didn't come out exactly empty-handed," Coleman said.

"What?" Tinkie and I said together. She looked at me and I nodded. She turned and slugged Oscar's shoulder and I did the same to Coleman. They'd been toying with us.

"What did you find?" I asked.

"One of the dock workers on the island had a father who worked for Capone. He told us some stories, but also said he had a map of the docks and inlets where Capone unloaded booze for inland routes. I thought that might lead us to Sandra and Daryl."

"That would be great!" I felt relief creep around my heart. Maybe we would find them yet.

"Where's the map?" Tinkie asked.

"We'll pick it up tomorrow," Oscar said. "And he said he'd guide us if we needed his help."

"Thank you." I rubbed Coleman's shoulder and kissed his check. "Sorry I slugged you," I whispered.

"No, you aren't."

I grinned. "You're right. I'm not sorry at all. You deserved it."

We sipped our drinks and ordered creole delicacies for dinner. The seafood dishes were wonderful, and the worries of the day faded as I laughed with my friends and talked about the incredible Christmas trees.

"The people around here go all out," Tinkie said. "I wish we could keep the trees up all year round. I wish I had a storage warehouse to put them in and could just bring them out one after the other all year long."

Tinkie was a Christmas girl. She loved the lights and wrapping and decoration. I did enjoy the fresh cedar, holly, and magnolia leaves in the house. It reminded me of my childhood. But after the cut flora started to die, I was ready to clear out the decorations. Tinkie decorated Mardi Gras trees, Easter trees—you name it. She loved it all. And little Maylin was going to be a child raised in a world of glitter and fairy tales. As every child should be.

Tinkie and Oscar took the cars back to the inn, and Coleman and I strolled through the downtown where laughter and music came from several bars. The world spun on. I filled Coleman in on the threats to Sandra, and he wasn't surprised.

"Do you believe Sandra really got threats or do you think that was something she told Janet?" Coleman asked.

That was a take that I'd failed to consider, but Coleman was a smart man. "I'm going to assume the threats were real. I don't have a lot of leads on looking for Sandra, and at least this is a direction to pursue. That and the water route you and Oscar discovered."

He nodded and put his arm around my shoulders. We'd left most of the bars behind and the night was quiet as we walked along a stretch where the bay was clearly visible. A half-moon hung over the water, illuminating the bridge that connected Bay St. Louis to Pass Christian. During Katrina the bridge had been destroyed, and the new one, higher and longer, curved in the moonlight. A pedestrian and biking lane had been added and Coleman and I walked to the top where we could see the town spread out before us, the marina filled with boats and lights. It was a vision of peace on a crisp winter night.

From the bridge we walked back to the marina where so many of the boats were decorated with lights and trees and rocking chairs with Santas. One boat was slowly moving along the coast with a choral group on board singing the old Christmas songs I loved. There was a sense of real community. I wasn't in Zinnia, the center of my emotional safety, but tucked up under Coleman's protective arm, I was home. With the breeze from the bay blowing my hair about wildly and my nose a little block of ice, I burrowed against him. I had lost every anchor to my home except for Jitty. I'd come so close to losing Dahlia House and myself. I owed a lot to Tinkie and my friends, but it was Coleman who gave me back a connection to family. Living family. And Jitty was my golden thread that tied me to all the ones I loved on the other side.

"What are you thinking about?" Coleman asked. "You look very far away."

"My parents. At Christmas, they would sing songs to each other. My dad's favorite was 'Rudolph the Red-Nosed Reindeer.'"

"I'll bet that was his favorite to sing to you. Gene Autry would approve."

"The singing cowboy!"

"Yes." Coleman buried my cold nose in his cheek to warm it up. "You were the apple of your dad's eye."

"Is it better to be loved and lose that love or never to be loved at all?" I had wondered this more than once.

"If you've never been loved in that way, you don't know what it is, so you can't really miss it. But I think your soul never fully soars. That kind of love is a special gift, Sarah Booth. To be loved unconditionally is a foundation that cannot crumble or shake. One you'll know how to give your children. So many people go through their lives never knowing a minute of it. You had twelve years. Not enough, for sure. Riches that can never be counted."

Coleman turned me to face him. "And now you're going

to have the kind of love that two people can share in a bond that links them together for life."

His words were better than a warm blanket. Nothing could bring my parents back, but Coleman did love me. I could never doubt that. "We've known each other since grammar school. You know almost all of my faults."

"Almost? You mean there are more?"

I had to laugh. That was one of Coleman's most valued abilities—he could push me from sad to silly. "Yep. More, so prepare yourself. I know there were times I made you so mad you would have lit me on fire."

He laughed. "True. And vice versa. But I mostly get mad at you when I'm worried about you."

He was honest about that. I got mad when I thought he was trying to control me. Or withholding things from me "for my own good." "We'll do our best not to get mad anymore."

"Good plan." His grin told me he wasn't expecting a hundred percent compliance.

To stop the conversation before we got into all the ways I made him mad, I stood on tiptoe and embraced him. The moon was bright and the wind was cold, but all of that fell away as I put my arms around his neck and pressed into him, kissing him with a hunger that sprang to life from nowhere.

I took his hand and led him to the sandy beach beneath the bridge. We were only a short distance from the inn, but I couldn't wait to walk that far. I tugged at his coat, thinking only of removing all our clothes and doing what came naturally. It was Christmas, after all, and a little Santa in the sand was something we'd laugh about in our dotage. We were sheltered from any prying eyes on the bridge or along the coast road, and most of the town was sound asleep except for a few bars that catered to the young crowd and were half a mile down the road.

Coleman caught my eager hands. "Here?"

I laughed. "Why not? You're not a prude, are you?" It was so very rare for me to have Coleman on the run. I could remember only once when he'd been caught, butt naked, on the stairs in Dahlia House when Tinkie burst in the front door. He'd tried to hide behind me! To my disappointment, Tinkie had always refused to tease him about it. She was too much of a lady. But I sure wasn't!

"Right here. Right now." I unbuttoned his jeans. "A little less talk and a lot more action." I expected him to balk, but I was wrong.

Coleman never turned down a challenge. He pulled my jacket off and tugged my turtleneck up and off. We made a pallet with the pile of clothes and Coleman laid me back on it as he shucked out of his boots.

"Maybe it's a little too cold out here." It wasn't that cold and we were secluded, but I couldn't help seeing a splash of headlines in various newspapers. Worst of all was the *Zinnia Dispatch*. "PI and sheriff arrested for public indecency." There would be a photo of Coleman and me caught in flagrante delicto, eyes wide open and looking like a possum caught in the headlights of a car.

In one smooth move, he swept my jeans off.

"Coleman, maybe this isn't such a good idea."

"I think it's a great idea," he said. "You know I love to camp."

"The sand is freezing." I was about to capitulate and beg off, admitting that he'd won the challenge I'd issued.

"Now Sarah Booth, this is the pinnacle of romance." He pointed across the water.

The glow of the moon winked along the bay. The stars overhead were a million times brighter than I ever remembered. From one of the bars at least half a mile down the road, the Aretha Franklin version of "Hark! The Herald Angels Sing" rocked the night. Ready or not, Coleman was about to rock my world.

Coleman chuckled softly in my ear. "You know we could be arrested for this."

Oh, how well I knew it. I was already envisioning it, but I was too stubborn to call it off. "If I have to have a criminal record, I want it to be for this."

Coleman kissed me and I closed my eyes—until a horrified shriek cut the night. It came from about three feet away from us.

Coleman virtually levitated to his feet. "Hey! Who are you?"

I glanced behind me and saw a man standing there. His mouth was wide open and his jaw was moving but no sound came out. Until another wild shriek tore out of his throat.

"Stop!" Coleman reached out to him and he turned and ran like the devil was hanging to his coattails. "Hey, stop!" Coleman went after him. "Sarah Booth, get dressed!"

The man was screaming at the top of his voice as he ran across the sand. Coleman almost had him when he stepped on a seashell and went down in a tumbling heap.

"Coleman!" I was trying to find my pants and pull them on but my clothes were all tangled together. I saw lights coming from the road. Two flashlights were heading directly for us. Oh, this had so been a bad idea.

I finally got my pants and shoes on and at last I untangled my shirtsleeves and pulled the shirt over my head. I grabbed Coleman's jacket and ran toward where he was sitting on the beach. The first thing I saw in the moonlight was the blood. Not a lot of it, but he'd cut the bottom of his foot. I gave him his jacket. "Someone is coming." I tipped my head toward the fast approaching lights. Soon we'd be in their beam.

"Well, damn."

"I'll get your boots." By the time I got back to Coleman, the flashlight bearers were closer to us. The light blinded me as I shrugged deeper into my jacket.

"Well, well, well," Oscar said. "Boots off. Sarah Booth's shirt on inside out. Jeans twisted." He laughed. "Maybe you two should get a room."

"Dammit, Oscar." I was ready to clobber him. And Tinkie, too, as her light laughter sounded across the water.

"Honestly," Tinkie said, working hard to sound prim through her giggles. "You two have no decorum. No restraint. No sophistication."

"And no satisfaction, thanks to that drunk man we nearly scared to death."

"He scared you to death and raised a posse. It looks like the villagers coming after Frankenstein." Tinkie pointed west. A large group of people with tiki torches from a bar were coming toward us.

My underwear was forever lost to the beach and I wasn't going to complain—or admit it if anyone found them. Coleman stood up.

"How bad is the cut?" I asked.

"It won't kill me."

"No, a cut won't, but this video Oscar took is going to be hot stuff when you run your next campaign for sheriff," Tinkie said as she jumped back out of my reach.

"Don't give me a reason to kill you," I warned her.

"Ha-ha-ha." She didn't even pretend to be concerned. "Oh, I have you and Coleman now. What possessed you to get down and dirty in the sand when you have a perfectly wonderful bedroom right up the hill?"

"Adventure," Coleman answered her. He pulled me into his arms. "I'm a man of adventure and Sarah Booth is my match in every way."

"Well, Mr. and Mrs. Adventure Freaks, let's go back to the inn. In case you've forgotten, we have a case to solve and a lot of work to do."

14

I was up early the next morning and went down to the dining room to put together a tray of breakfast for Coleman and me from the bountiful offerings prepared by the owner of the inn. I didn't want to face Tinkie and Oscar at a breakfast table. That I deserved their teasing wasn't important. I could feel the heat in my cheeks just thinking about the drubbing Coleman and I were going to take. Whatever had possessed us to do the deed on a public beach? Sure, we'd had a few margaritas, but I wanted to claim it was the spirit of Christmas elves at work.

We ate our breakfast in bed, snuggled beneath the covers. Whenever I looked at Coleman, he grinned so wide I considered biting him—lightly. He wasn't in the least embarrassed by our late-night beach adventure, or getting caught. When Oscar and Tinkie realized they couldn't get a rise out of him, they would both turn on me. As Jitty would say, this was a lesson to be learned.

When my phone rang with Tinkie's number, I answered instantly. "Cece and Millie will arrive today. I can't wait to see them." I was trying to direct the conversation down a path that wouldn't embarrass me.

Tinkie paused and then laughed. "Oh, I can't wait either. I have fodder for their column, and photos to go with it."

Oh, she was a wicked, wicked woman. But I had committed to a strategy. "Do your worst. Depending on what you captured in your photos, it might get Coleman more votes next election."

Beside me Coleman laughed out loud. He approved of my handling of our paparazzi.

Tinkie dropped the subject and we made our plans for the day. Oscar and Coleman were staying on hand to welcome Cece, Millie, and Harold, who had finished at the bank. They would arrive for a late lunch. Jaytee and the blues band would travel down later in the evening. They were booked for several gigs.

"We need to find Sandra today," Tinkie said, "otherwise this case is going to bleed over into our weekend fun time with our friends."

She was right about that. "Why don't we check out the old O'Day and Malone homesteads. Maybe someone there can tell us something."

"I'm disappointed the police aren't taking this more seriously," Tinkie said, voicing one of my concerns. "It seems Sandra has annoyed so many people they're just glad she's not around causing trouble. No one is really worried that she could *be* in trouble."

"Do you think Janet is really worried?"

"I do. She's paying us a pretty penny to find Sandra." Tinkie was more pragmatic than I.

"Technically, she's paying us to prove she didn't have Sandra and Daryl abducted." It was a fine point, but one worth making. "She is the number one suspect if something has gone wrong with Sandra and Daryl."

"She has an alibi," I reminded Tinkie. "She was at the party. She was seen by a number of people. In fact, no one remembers when Daryl left the scene. Last we heard he was supposed to keep an eye on Janet."

"True. Chief Thibodeau doesn't have a conclusive time when Sandra disappeared. She was there and lots of folks saw her, and then when it was time for the book signing, she was gone. Along with Daryl. They could have been gone for an hour before that or five minutes. And other than that blood in the mudroom sink and the ransacked office, which may have been Janet's doing, there's no real indication of struggle or any problems. Chief Thibodeau thinks this is a stunt."

"It could be." I had to say it. "But we can't afford not to look as hard as we can. We took the case, and if Sandra and Daryl are in trouble, we're really the only people looking for them."

"Let's hit it," Tinkie said. "I'll meet you at the car, Gypsy Rose Lee."

Oh, I knew it had been too good to last. I wonder how many stripper names she and Oscar had looked up last night to hurl at me.

The wind was brisker this morning than the previous day when I met Tinkie at the car. Tucked under the windshield wiper was a sheet of white paper. I picked it up.

MIND YOUR OWN BUSINESS OR SUFFER THE CONSEQUENCES was typed in all caps, a big font. I held it up so Tinkie could read it. It sounded an awful lot like the notes Janet said Sandra had received.

"This is definitely not good," Tinkie said, getting into the car. "Not for my safety, but for Sandra's and Daryl's. She'd been receiving similar notes. I don't think this is a prank. This is an actual threat."

"And we'll take it to Chief Thibodeau. Now." I gave it to Tinkie, who held it by one corner.

The chief was not pleased to see us, but he sent the note to be fingerprinted. I was glad to notice he was at least more concerned for the two missing people.

"I had hoped it was all a stunt," he said. "But I can't dismiss this. Did you see anyone around your car?"

"No." Neither Coleman nor Oscar had seen anyone either. Tinkie had texted her husband. The men had offered to come back, but we urged them to stay on the quest for the dock worker who had a map. Tinkie and I were fine.

When my cell phone rang, I turned away from the chief and Tinkie, who were talking. Tinkie was giving him all the pertinent facts that we knew.

"Hello." I didn't recognize the number.

"Ms. Delaney, this is Mrs. Marcus. I got a call this morning from a woman who told me if you and your partner didn't back off hunting for Daryl, that he would be killed."

"When was the call?" I asked.

"About seven. I had to serve breakfast." She was sobbing as quietly as she could. "You have to stop whatever you're doing. Daryl has never harmed a living soul."

"I understand. Tinkie and I got a note, too, warning us we would be harmed."

"You did?" That seemed to make her feel a little better. "How do these people know what you're doing?" she asked.

"A very, very good question. Now I'm going to let you talk to the Bay St. Louis police chief. You have to tell him everything."

"No." The line went dead.

I relayed the conversation. "I know it isn't your jurisdiction out in the county, but she's scared. Really scared for her son."

"I'm very concerned myself," Thibodeau said. "I'm on this. If you hear or find anything, let me know."

"And you'll do the same?" Tinkie asked him.

"Yes," he said grudgingly. "The important thing is finding them."

Waveland was our destination when we left the chief's office. With any luck we could find Sandra O'Day's old homestead property, since the house was gone, and Janet Malone's family home, which if I understood her past, was still owned by the author though it was uninhabited. There might be people who could clue us in to any favorite haunts of either woman. Or it might be possible that we'd run across Sandra and Daryl. If it was a kidnapping based on a childhood grudge, we might be able to bring them home. And thus end a case that seemed to get stickier with each passing day.

"It's kind of wonderful both Sandra and Janet come from the same area," Tinkie said. "Maybe this competition thing started back in first grade." She grinned. "Wouldn't that be something? Two little six-year-olds who grew up so determined to outdo each other that they became best-selling authors."

"It would be silly. Honestly, if the two of them got together they could help each other. They write in completely
different fields. There's no reason for all this drama."

"You're right. But artists are often insecure and often fail
to act in their own best interests."

Tinkie was right about that. We'd seen it more than once.

We followed the beach to Waveland and found the lack
of traffic relaxing. Most travelers preferred I-10, a four-
lane that I considered the gateway to hell. The little town
of Waveland didn't hold the allure of the more artsy Bay St.
Louis, but it was a charming town and we started at the
logical place—the local diner.

Our waitress, Londell, knew everyone in the diner, and
when I asked her if she knew the O'Days or Malones, she
put two fingers in her mouth and cut loose with a whistle
that was like an ice pick in my eardrum. Everyone shut up
and turned to look at her.

"These ladies are looking for information on the Malones
and the O'Days. They're looking for Sandra and the man
who went missing over in Bay St. Louis. Jedediah, you knew
the families, right?"

A gentleman who looked too old and frail to still be alive
nodded slowly. "Knew 'em both. Good families."

"Would you mind talking to us?" Tinkie asked him.
"We're trying to help."

He assessed us slowly and finally nodded. Tinkie rose
and went over to his table. She turned on the charm for the
other gentlemen sitting around him but in a nick she had
him at our table, cut off from the herd. And she'd done it
with smiles and giggles.

When we had a plate of biscuits, bacon, ham, sausage,
and coffee in front of him, the interrogation began. I let

Tinkie take the lead. She had so much more ease at handling men than I did.

"Tell us about the O'Days," Tinkie said. "We heard about the terrible explosion. I'm sure it was a shock to everyone."

"Sandra took it hard. Heck, we all did." He looked out the window for a long moment. "Sandra wasn't such a spoiled brat when she was little. Her folks taught her manners and showed her how to act decent. She went off to New York and came back with all the trappings of a city hussy. Rude, loud, always goin' on about her possessions and her books and her prizes and all of that. She wasn't a braggin' girl when she was young. Neither was Janet Malone. I got a little more patience for Sandra. It likta killed her when her folks died. Janet, she's got no excuse."

"When did Mr. and Mrs. O'Day die?" I didn't have a clear time line on these events.

"Oh, around two, maybe three years ago. Right after Sandra bought that old mansion. She had big plans to move her parents in with her. They were in all the shops looking at décor and such. And then there was the explosion, and Sandra put her focus on Bay St. Louis. I don't know that she's been back here since, and I don't really blame her."

"You must have known both families," I said, hoping to encourage him to keep talking.

"I did. Like I said, both good families. Both good girls. Maybe too caught up in unimportant things. Neither one of them married or had babies." He shook his head.

This gentleman was old school and believed family should be a woman's first priority. A part of me wanted to argue with him, but Tinkie caught my eye and shook her head. It would do no good, and it would alienate him. I swallowed my objections to his worldview and asked, "I know the O'Day place was destroyed, but could you tell us where it was? And if the Malone house is empty?"

"Sure, sure." He signaled Londell. "Paper and pencil, please, when you get time."

She came right over and put a pad and pen beside him. "Anything for you. Want more coffee, Jedediah?" She gave him a smart-aleck grin.

"Go on with you," he said, but he smiled. He took the pen and began to draw a map. "This here is where the O'Day house was." He continued drawing. "And here's the Malone house. It's empty as far as I know. They could have sold the place a hundred times over, but Janet couldn't part with it. She told the local real estate agent that she wanted to keep the property so her folks could come home whenever they wanted. I guess we all cling to places where we were once happy. I doubt we'll ever see much of the Malones back here, living in luxury like they are."

"Do you think Janet is happy now?" Tinkie asked.

It was a surprise question. I hadn't seen it coming.

He thought about it. "Maybe a part of her, but that part where she was a child, living here, free to imagine anything she might be, I think she misses that. Folks don't understand it's the strivin' that makes a person happy. Not the gettin'."

Although Jedediah's views on women were dated, his wisdom was still keen in many other areas. "Did the girls have any special places they hung out?"

He picked up the pen and wrote a list of places on another page.

"Do you think Capone's treasure is still around this area?" Tinkie asked.

"I do," he said. "If Sandra and Janet don't have it, then it's still here. Most folks think Sandra found it and bought that old mansion in Bay St. Louis. They think that's why those two are at each other's throats all the time. Sandra took the treasure and wouldn't share."

That was an interesting twist. "Why would she share?" I asked.

He shrugged. "They were as close as sisters growing up. Whatever one did, the other one did, too. Janet didn't have any brothers or sisters, and Sandra was younger than her brothers. They were company for each other and always together. It just seemed natural they'd share, but greed can get the better of anyone."

"Thanks for talking with us, Mr. Jedediah," Tinkie said. She gave him a business card. "If you think of anything that might help us find Sandra, please call."

"Will do. Even though she misbehaves, I know she's a good girl. Please find her and that missing man."

"We intend to," I said.

15

The O'Day property was overgrown with weeds and sand-spurs, but we drove slowly until we came upon the charred timbers of what had once been a large home. We parked and got out to explore. Many of the big old houses built in the early 1900s were constructed from heart pine timber. It lasted for centuries, unless there was a fire.

"Do you think the explosion was accidental?" Tinkie asked. Sometimes she seemed to read my mind.

"The fire chief ruled it accidental."

"How much training do you think he had?"

It was a fair question. A lot of rural fire departments were all volunteer and didn't have the sophisticated equipment to determine the work of a smart arsonist. Especially one who blew up the evidence. A space heater flame going out, the gas building up in a closed room—it happened. But it could also be easily faked.

"You have a point there, Tinkie. Let's ask him. No point hanging around here. There's nothing to find."

We stopped by city hall and spoke with the fire chief, a young man who'd taken over only a few months before. The old chief had retired to Ohio, but the new chief knew a little about the O'Day explosion.

"That fire is still big news here. Close community and all. The O'Days were well liked. It's still a topic of conversation. Only happened a little more than two years ago," he said. "I remember because the writer had just bought the old mansion over in Bay St. Louis. Folks were talking about that and all her plans when her folks were killed. Awful."

"No one suspected foul play?"

He shook his head. "Not really. Folks from your generation have gotten away from those old space heaters in the newer houses, but this house was built back in the twenties when most houses were heated that way. Central heat wasn't a thing down here until the 1960s. My granny had those heaters and if you turned them too low, they could go out. The gas would accumulate in a room or the whole house, and if a light switch was flipped and sparked, that was it."

He seemed certain it was all straightforward and an accident. "You say the explosion happened just after Sandra bought the Buntman house across the bay?"

He nodded. "I remember. Folks thought she'd back out of buying the mansion and leave the Gulf Coast forever. She was that torn up. She didn't have anything to tie her here in the way of family. But she stayed. I never understood that, or why Janet came home and stayed. Both of them stayed in the area. That's all I know. You're welcome to look at the reports but I can tell you there's not much detail or photos or such. No one worried overly much about documentation."

We shook his hand and headed back to the car. So far, we'd accomplished little, and I could feel anxiety gnawing at my stomach. A lot of tragedy had surrounded Sandra O'Day, and now she and her assistant were missing. Was it just bad luck or had someone hung a target on Sandra?

The old Malone house was on our way home and we found the sandy driveway that disappeared in palmetto and ferns typical of the local plants. Pines, scrub oaks, and bayonet palms grew in clusters; quite a contrast to the rich alluvial soil of the Delta. Avoiding the deepest sand traps, I was careful not to get the car stuck as we drove toward the empty house.

We hit a grove of beautiful live oaks that had managed to survive the hurricanes and high winds. They cast a dense shadow over the sun-heated sand and I stopped the car to admire them. One joy of the convertible was the ability to be in the environment. "Amazing how they can withstand all the abuse those storms bring in," I said.

"Let me take a photo." Tinkie took out her phone but dropped it when a shot rang out. We both ducked, and a bullet struck the trunk of a tree right where my head would have been. I gunned the car and took off. There was no place to turn around so we headed to the empty house, which didn't seem like a very good idea at all. But if I tried to turn around in the sand, we'd probably become trapped and be sitting ducks.

Tinkie fished out her cell phone and sent a Mayday text to Oscar and Coleman. They were working on the Capone lead, but we knew they'd come as quickly as they could.

We bumped and spun sand for ten minutes before we

pulled up at the house, which showed neglect but was still solid. We jumped out of the car and I grabbed my gun out of the trunk while Tinkie tried the door to the house. It was locked. Before I could suggest anything she ran around the back, and in a moment, the front door cracked open. We hesitated in the doorway, but a rustling in the underbrush near the driveway made our decision for us. We hurried inside and locked the door.

"How did you get in?" I asked her.

She held up a credit card. "These locks are flimsy. The house was built at a time when folks didn't think about burglars."

I took a position by the big picture window in the front room and edged the draperies away so I could look out. Tinkie was scouting out the room, looking for a weapon of her own. I called her over and gave her the gun. "You're the better shot." She was. No doubt about it.

"You sure?" She took the gun gingerly.

"I'm sure. Maybe there's a shotgun or rifle here. I'll check the closets."

She took my place at the window and I checked to make sure all of the doors were locked before I went in search of a weapon. The Malones had left a lot of really lovely furniture when they moved, but I could understand. Life in Costa Rica would be a completely different style. The heavy, tapestried European furniture fit better here in the elegant old Southern home than it would in a Latin American paradise. The Malones had excellent taste, though. I'd love to have some of the furniture at Dahlia House.

I searched under the beds and in the closets for another firearm but turned up nothing until I opened a window seat in the master bedroom. A shotgun and a box of shells were tucked beneath a quilt. Perfect! I checked the gun, which seemed to be in working order, and went back to show Tinkie.

"Sarah Booth, they're coming." She nodded toward a bunch of ferns and brambles. Someone was moving through them.

I loaded the shotgun with birdshot and snapped it closed. "Cover me." I'd always wanted to say that. Tinkie only snorted and followed me to the door. When I threw it open, she fired a shot into the brambles and I cut loose with first one barrel and then the next.

A man screamed and cursed. "You little bitches. I'll get you for this!"

I reloaded and fired again, but he was gone. We stepped back inside and locked the door again. We were both sweating even though the day was dry and brisk. My cell phone buzzed and I read the text from Coleman.

"We're on the beach road about four miles from Waveland. Send address."

I did. They'd be with us in under ten minutes if I calculated right. "All we have to do is sit tight," I told Tinkie, who looked really worried.

"Do you think I hit anyone?" she asked.

I grabbed her arm and squeezed. "I hope we both did. Then they'll be picking birdshot out of their butt for days."

That made her laugh, and the worst of her worry had passed when Coleman and Oscar came down the drive in Tinkie's Cadillac. While Oscar ran inside to pull Tinkie into his arms, Coleman and I began to scout the thicket in front of the house where our stalker had been hiding. I started to ask some questions, but he waved me to be quiet and continued to search. We even went through two outbuildings, both containing more furniture, but found nothing. At last we went inside.

"Thank goodness you're both okay," Coleman said when the door was locked behind us.

"We are," I assured him. "Just a little spooked."

Tinkie and Oscar joined us in the big spacious kitchen around a farmhouse table. We needed a little time to let our nerves settle.

"I guess we should call the cops now," I said.

"No." Coleman shook his head. "I didn't find any blood. I'm not sure you hit anyone. It might be best not to bring this to the chief's attention."

"Why not?" I asked him quietly.

"If you shot someone, either of you, it's going to take a lot of time to untangle it. Y'all were trespassing. You didn't ask Janet for permission to be on the property."

"Because if she's involved with the disappearance of Sandra and Daryl, she'd hurry here to remove any evidence."

I had sound logic for my behavior, but that didn't cut it with Coleman. "I hear you, but the law is still the law. If the person you might have shot doesn't report it, you shouldn't either. There aren't neighbors near enough to have heard the shots. Just let it go. Deal with it if the stalker files a report."

"I agree," Oscar said. "This disappearance of Sandra and Daryl—something isn't right. And there's such a deep local connection with both of those women and this area that it's hard to decipher motives. I wouldn't kick a hornet's nest unless it was absolutely necessary to."

I was outvoted on calling the authorities, and truth be told, I was happy not to. But the person who'd tried to harm us still had to be found. *How* was the question.

"Have you searched the main house?" Coleman asked.

"Not yet."

"Then let's get after it. I'm going to try to get that slug that was shot at you out of the oak tree."

A great idea. Coleman knew more about ballistics than I did, and all evidence would be helpful. As we walked toward the stand of oaks, I had a moment to talk to him. "I really think Tinkie should take Maylin and go home." I felt like I was betraying my partner, but I would never forgive myself if Tinkie was injured on a case. "I have a little more compassion now for some of the things I've put you through."

"Yes, ma'am. You should, ma'am," he said, pretending to doff his cap.

"Coleman, do you think this is all a hoax? I mean a decent shot with a rifle could probably have hit me or Tinkie if they really wanted to." I blew out a breath in frustration. "This just doesn't feel right."

"I concur."

"So you think it's a publicity stunt?"

"The problem with that theory is that I haven't seen a lot of media picking up on it. I mean, Chief Thibodeau is very tight-lipped. Janet hasn't done any interviews. No one is talking about it, and I know for a fact the New Orleans television stations have been calling around looking for interviews. No one will talk to them."

"And you would think that someone from Sandra's publishing company would be here." This was an angle I hadn't pursued. "If it's a stunt, they'd be all over it and hyping it everywhere, knowing she was okay and would return to huge sales. Or they'd be disavowing these antics."

"Exactly," he said.

"So it isn't a stunt?"

"I didn't say that." A slow grin came into play.

I punched his arm, hard. "Stop trying to make me crazier than I am."

"That would be hard to do," he said under his breath, still smiling. "It could be a stunt that the publisher wouldn't get involved in. Or it could be real. There's honestly no way to tell so far, except that if this is a setup, someone went to a lot of trouble and the people involved are willing to go to jail for it. Someone shot at you. If you decided to press charges, they could do time."

He was right about that. "And that's another reason you didn't want me to call the police."

"Exactly right. If it is publicity they want, withholding that could flush them out. Calling the cops in is just going to blow this all up in the press."

"There's just no physical evidence to push us in either direction. Before this goes any further, I want Tinkie to go home."

Coleman put his arm around me. "I know this is frustrating. Oscar and I have tried to stay out of your way, but he's worried about Tinkie, too. I don't think she'll leave here. She's not the kind of person to pack up and run. And really think about what you're saying. Put yourself in her shoes."

"I was hoping you might talk to her."

Coleman's laughter was almost a bark. "Right. Not me. If I even suggested such a thing to Tinkie she'd hamstring me and roast me on a spit. Just like you would."

The image made me laugh, though I didn't want to. We'd made it to the oaks so I found the right tree and helped him search for the bullet. In a matter of minutes, he had it dug out of the tree. "It's a .22 caliber." He put it in a little plastic evidence bag. "The gun of an assassin who kills up close and personal, not a person shooting across distance. Like the note left in your car, it was meant to warn you off."

Which would indicate this encounter wasn't planned as a real attempt to harm us. The shooting had been intended to scare Tinkie and me off the scent. Coleman had led me to a conclusion. He'd allowed me to see the evidence as he saw it and come to a determination. And he'd helped me see that my concern for Tinkie was best kept to myself, as I should have known. Tinkie was as smart and tough as I'd ever be. Acting otherwise wasn't the conduct of a partner or friend.

"Hopefully, this will make finding Sandra and Daryl easier. Someone took them," I said. "It's the only thing that really makes sense."

"Now that you've settled on a theory of the case, let's find them."

16

Tinkie and Oscar were already searching when we entered the house. They'd started at the back so Coleman and I took the kitchen. The Malones had left their home with the shelves stocked with staples. The refrigerator worked, though it was empty. The beds were made with colorful sheets and towels hung in the bathrooms. It was as if the family had gone on vacation for a week and had never returned. Creepiness oozed in every shadow.

"I wonder why Janet doesn't sell this place," I said to Coleman as I pulled a cookie jar collection down from the top of some shelves. I checked each one to make sure there was nothing hidden inside. This search required patience and diligence to do properly, even with four of us working.

By the time we'd taken everything off the shelves and returned it all, Tinkie and Oscar had finished the bedrooms. The living room and den were left, along with the attached garage and laundry room and a couple of tool sheds in the back.

"I'm hungry," Tinkie said. "Since I've given birth, I'm used to eating every three hours. I have to make milk for Maylin."

"I could make a food run," Oscar suggested.

"We'll be done soon enough," I grumbled. I was hungry, too, but I didn't want to slow down. I was ready to do something else. Hunting for treasure that never appeared had made me weary and frustrated. Tinkie, too. I could read it in her posture. We were both tired from the adrenaline high that had plummeted us to the depths of drudgery.

"Let's finish." Coleman looked around. "Another half hour ought to do it. Oscar, let's take the outbuildings and let the girls stay inside where it's warmer."

"Good plan." Oscar, too, was ready to finish. "If we knew what we were looking for it would help. It could be a key or a steel safe. So that means we have to look everywhere, even the smallest hiding places."

He was right about that. They banged out the back door and I put a hand on Tinkie's shoulder. "We're almost done."

"I'd really hoped to find something but I'm feeling hopeless."

"Me, too. But if we find nothing, we'll never have to see this place again."

"We could just call Janet and ask where the best hiding places are." Tinkie's blue eyes sparked with mischief.

"What Janet doesn't know won't hurt her." I said it boldly, but I felt a bit like a heel that we hadn't told our client we were searching her parents' home. But she was the prime suspect in the disappearance, or at least Chief Thibodeau thought so. "Technically, we're clearing her name. If we'd told her beforehand and we found something that cleared her, it wouldn't have had any meaning."

"You're right." Tinkie pointed to the fireplace. "I'm going to check around that. If I get all sooty, we have to go back to the inn to change clothes. I can't go around town looking like a chimney sweep."

"Chim chim cher-ee!" I jumped up and clicked my heels in the air, proud that I could still perform that maneuver. Moping was over; it was time for action.

"I never took you for a *Mary Poppins* fan," Tinkie teased.

"I have many secrets. Many dark secrets. Now I'm going to check the attic." I hated attics more than anything except basements. In the South, there were no basements, thank goodness. Attics were bad enough.

The pull-down ladder was in a back room obviously used as an office. If I remembered correctly, Mr. Malone had run a business. We went through two filing cabinets and found nothing that might indicate treasure or anything else. I dropped the ladder and climbed up, unzipping the foil cover that helped insulate the house. When I pushed through into the dark attic, I took a moment to catch my breath. A form in the darkened attic looked too human for comfort, but as my eyes adjusted, I could see that it was a mannequin in a coat.

Who put a mannequin in their attic? And why? Damn. Maybe to give burglars a heart attack. I clicked on the heavy-duty flashlight I'd found in the cedar chest where I'd found the shotgun and scanned the room, which was big. Boxes, dog cages, and all kinds of things filled the space chockful. Strangely, there was no furniture. The attic stairs weren't sturdy enough to support moving furniture up there. But the stacks of boxes and smaller things could easily have hidden someone.

I shone the light on the mannequin and had to laugh. Under the trench coat she wore a beautiful 1940s pale blue negligee. I wondered if Sandra and Janet had played together as young girls, dressing the mannequin and making up stories about her life.

When I assessed all the work ahead of me, I sighed again. It was going to be rough going opening boxes while holding a flashlight. To my immense relief, I found a light with a string to turn it on. In a moment the attic was flooded with illumination.

The shadows took on more definitive shapes. I knew I was being silly but I couldn't shake the sense that someone was watching me. Heebie-jeebies. Good thing I'd left the gun with Tinkie or I might have shot a box.

The attic was floored, and I walked around, using the flashlight on the denser shadows, finding nothing. The only thing that really interested me was an old humpback trunk that looked as if it might have led an interesting life. I opened it up and gasped at the wedding gown inside that had yellowed with age, but was nonetheless a work of art. I carefully removed the dress and found, tucked beneath it, exquisite shoes, beautiful lingerie, and a box with a pearl necklace in it. I couldn't believe Janet knew about this dress and had left it to decay in the attic.

I put everything back and moved on to some boxes of old clothes and toys. I wanted to be sloppy and fast, but I forced myself to be thorough. When I came to some cartons that looked like they held legal papers, my curiosity was piqued. I opened the first one and stopped. These were very, very old records, dating back to the 1920s. And they detailed the location of funds under the name Helene Buntman.

I took a stack of documents to the overhead light and began to study them. It became clear they were payments to Helene from various people along the bay. This was likely the record of Al Capone's delivery service of booze. It probably held little value, except to Sandra O'Day for her research and book on Capone, Buntman, and the distribution of booze.

"Tinkie!" I called to her. "Help me get these boxes down. We need to take them with us."

It was awkward and tiring, but we ended up with six boxes filled with financial records and some odds and ends. We needed a place to work where we could spread them out and really study them. Actually, I needed Tinkie to study them. She was the financial genius of Delaney Detective Agency.

It was time to get back to town and some food. Tinkie's stomach was growling and I had a headache from hunger. Coleman and Oscar came in from the shed, empty-handed and also hungry.

Tinkie and Oscar agreed to go over the financial records, so we started loading them into her car. My partner knew how to make herself useful, but I found myself at sixes and sevens.

"We should search the Buntman mansion again." I threw it out there to see who might bite.

Coleman nodded. "We could, if we had a warrant."

"I don't know what to do next." I was frustrated and impatient. "Maybe I can find something at the mansion that tells me where Sandra and Daryl might be."

"You're grasping at straws, and we don't have a warrant."

He was right, but that didn't make me feel any better. "I

don't have any other leads, unless Tinkie turns something up in those dusty records."

"We have the liquor distribution map. Those locations where Capone had someone meet the boats to haul the liquor inland. We met up with the guy whose family worked with Capone and he had a copy for us. It's in the car. I don't know how helpful it will be. We had time to check a few of the locations and no one even remembers anything about the Capone era. It was a hundred years ago. Folks have short memories, especially if they made money off illegal activities."

"Thanks for trying." I got up and walked behind Coleman so I could wrap my arms around him. Whatever else, he was one constant I could count on.

"I've been thinking about the person that shot at you." Coleman pulled me into his arms so I could face him. "Maybe we should have reported it."

"Why?"

"You had that note on your car windshield, threatening you. I worry that someone is following you with the intention of harming you."

"But I was trespassing."

"It would be awkward explaining breaking into the Malone house, but you are working for Janet. You should call her and tell her what we found. She may be able to shed some light on all of this."

"Do you think her ancestors worked for Capone? Keeping his records and all?"

"It's very possible."

"I wonder if Sandra knew about these records." I was musing out loud, but Coleman nodded.

"It's a motive, Sarah Booth. If someone thought the records . . . No telling what people would do to obtain information that might lead to a treasure. Who would have thought the records would be out here."

"Why *does* Janet have these records?"

"Well, it appears her grandfather"—he pointed to the name of Samuel Malone—"was Capone's accountant or bookkeeper back in the day. It makes sense the records would be his, unless Capone or Helene's family asked for them. Truth is, I doubt Janet even knows they exist."

"I don't think anyone has been in that attic for years." The thick layer of dust hadn't been disturbed. "There's a wedding dress there that's incredible. And there are other boxes. I looked in them but I didn't dig through them. Some more old papers that look like family correspondence and old photographs. I should probably bring those down, too."

"Yes, I'll get them and we'll take those boxes with us since Tinkie has the financials. Or why don't we bring Janet over and go through the rest of them with her?" Coleman suggested. "That's something to think about tomorrow, but right now, we should prepare for the arrival of Cece, Millie, and Harold." He tapped his watch. "They'll be here soon."

We hauled the last of the boxes out and locked the door. I couldn't wait to see my friends, but I also had the case hanging over my head. I wasn't in the mood for holidays or anything else. I wanted to find Sandra and Daryl and be done with this. One day I'd learn not to take cases at Christmas.

We loaded the last carton and watched Tinkie and Oscar head out. I stood at the car door, one foot on the running board, to look back at the house. It had once been the home of a family. Now it was a shell. I felt a sense of sadness. This house held memories and secrets. Would anyone come take an interest in them once we were gone? I didn't have an answer.

"Load up, Sarah Booth." Coleman was behind the wheel and ready to go. I slipped in and closed the door. Feeling melancholy wouldn't help a thing. We headed east toward Bay St. Louis. While Coleman drove, I checked my phone for the news of the day.

One breaking news story stopped me. The Beer and Bait, the restaurant run by the Marcuses, had been set on fire. The blaze was extinguished before any real damage was done, but the fire marshal had declared it a case of arson.

I read the story aloud to Coleman.

"This isn't good," he said.

"Understatement."

"It may not be related to Daryl."

"The only way to tell is to talk to the Marcuses. Let's head there. I'll text Tinkie and—"

"Sarah Booth, it would be best if I go alone and talk to them. They already know you're working for Janet and if they suspect she has anything to do with this, they won't talk."

"But . . ." I stopped. He was right. Donnie Marcus was a man's man. He'd relate to Coleman a lot better than me, and I believed Tinkie had gotten everything she could from Mrs. Marcus. "Okay. I talked to Mrs. Marcus earlier this morning and she asked us to drop the search for Daryl and Sandra. She was afraid someone would get hurt. So it probably is best you talk to her."

Coleman reached across the seat and put his hand on my forehead. "Are you running a fever?"

"Smart aleck."

"Yeah." He grinned. "It's one of the many reasons you love me."

When we pulled into the inn parking lot, we helped move the boxes of photos and old letters to our room. Once Tinkie agreed to our strategy, I gave Coleman directions to the little marina where the Marcuses' restaurant was located. Tinkie and Oscar went to work and I slipped over to my room and mixed up a pitcher of Lynchburg Lemonade—and just in time. Cece, Harold, and Millie had arrived.

We took our drinks out to the patio by the pool and I filled them in on everything that had happened so far.

"What's on the agenda for this evening?" Cece asked.

"My plans were to go clubbing and hear some great music." Normally Tinkie mapped out our social agenda, but there were several places I wanted to check out.

"Why are you talking about that in the past tense?" Harold asked. "Remember, I left Roscoe with a new warden so I could come and play."

Harold's dog Roscoe was so smart and so bad he needed a full-time human attendant to keep him from ending up in the county shelter.

"You guys need to go. Oscar and Tinkie will take you. Coleman and I need to work on the case."

"Tinkie has agreed to that?" Millie asked. She knew my partner well.

"Not exactly."

Cece only arched her eyebrows. "That isn't going to happen and you know it. So we might as well all work on your case with you. Besides, I owe you. Those videos of the catfights between those crazy writer chicks you sent have increased our subscription rate again. I'm hoping to see some of that action myself as soon as we find Sandra." Cece held up her new cell phone with the super-duper camera that shot videos she could edit. "We're moving into the big league here."

I was pleased for her. Cece, who had turned down plenty of chances to work for bigger papers or television stations, had chosen to stay in Zinnia. She'd gone from society editor to news editor to international columnist. The column she and Millie wrote together, "The Truth Is Out There," was fast becoming a part of popular culture.

"When we locate Sandra, I'm sure you'll see a lot of hair-pulling and name-calling. I don't think Janet and Sandra can stop themselves. But we have to find her first. And Daryl."

"How can we help?" Millie asked.

"I have an idea." I turned to Harold. "How would you feel about turning on the charm for a wealthy writer?"

"Janet Malone?" Harold asked, looking puzzled. "Why? She's hired you to find Sandra. Surely she's told you everything she knows."

"Maybe and maybe not," I said. "But it couldn't hurt to have you find out if she knows more. If this is a publicity stunt, which I don't think it is, I am personally going to punch her and Sandra in the nose."

"Music to my ears," Cece said. "Just be sure I'm able to get it on video."

17

Cece, Millie, and Harold were booked into rooms at the inn, and once they were settled, we held a meeting. We had a free night—one where we'd planned to listen to music—but Cece and Millie decided to attend a holiday gathering of news media at the Beau Rivage in Biloxi. With Cece's journalism connections, she was the best person to investigate the fire at the Marcuses' marina, and Millie had the uncanny ability to make anyone talk. She was so friendly and knew so many frazzling details about celebrities that she could find common ground with almost anyone.

Harold would be deployed to woo Janet Malone into revealing any secrets she might be hiding from us about her relationship with Sandra or the Capone history. I'd join the two of them later in the evening to grill Janet about the Malone relationship with Al Capone and his hooch distribution business. I also wondered about the wedding dress in the attic, but it would be hard to ask about it until I was ready to confess to searching her parents' home. I wasn't quite there yet.

I took a long, hot shower, put on some jeans and a hooded sweatshirt, and mixed another drink for myself. Night had fallen, and I called Janet and found out she was going to the Blues Muse to hear a singer. I told her a friend of mine would be there to say hello. With the address in hand, I dispatched Harold to open her up like a box of candy.

When he was on his way, I put my phone on the charger and sat down beside it with a box of photos from the attic. In a matter of moments, my jittery anxiety dissipated and I found myself reliving a fascinating history through the old pictures.

I found a photo of Capone sitting across a desk from a handsome man who bore a remarkable resemblance to his descendant, Janet Malone. They both had the gray-blue eyes and auburn hair, the same smile. This had to be Samuel Malone, accountant. There were dozens of photos of the men eating at restaurants, drinking, fishing, laughing. They had been not only business associates, but friends.

The photos weren't arranged by date, so I tried to order them into a few piles to make it easier to show my friends. They would be fascinated, as would Janet. Color and technology improved as I dug deeper into the box, and I came to pictures of people I didn't know that had been taken during the eighties and nineties. The pictures of two young girls on the sandy beach, digging for shells, playing with toys, laughing and running, carefree and sparkling with good times, reminded me that Janet and Sandra had actually once been very good friends.

What had come between them to make them hate each other so? Money? A man? Secret family stuff? I thought about Tinkie, Cece, and Millie, and I couldn't imagine anything more valuable to me than their friendship. It had to be something spectacular.

I'd finished one box of photos and was picking up another when something hard and heavy chinked into the window in my room. I was on the second floor so someone had to have tossed whatever it was at the window. I got up and slowly moved the drapes and looked out.

The parking lot was empty.

Through the branches of the oak trees the moon glinted on the moving water of the bay. If I stepped outside I could probably hear some of the boats moaning slightly at their moorings. There was just enough wind to lift and settle them at the dock.

The moon was waxing but it was plenty bright. I thought about the dancing couple on the yacht. Such a night for romance.

I closed the draperies and sighed. Coleman and my friends would be back soon, all with reports to give. We'd resolve this case and get on with our Christmas celebrations.

I was about to take my seat again when something else plinked against the window. Some jerk was going to break it if they kept throwing things at it. I picked up the phone and called the front desk to alert the owner, but no one answered. The faintest chill tingled my spine. There was always someone at the desk.

I put my phone in my pocket, got my gun, which Coleman

had put in a drawer in the kitchen, turned off the lights in my room, and eased out the door. For a moment I stood on the porch and let my eyes adjust to the night. The two rocks that had hit the window weren't hard to find. They were the size of eggs, and I was surprised they hadn't cracked the window. If it had been ordinary glass, they would have, but I supposed the inn had installed more durable windows to combat the high winds of hurricanes.

Someone had tried to break my window. Why?

I remembered the note on my windshield. I'd been warned. It was obvious the person who'd left the note knew I was staying at the inn. I walked to the end of the porch but there was no trace of anyone on the second-floor porch or in the parking lot. I walked to the opposite end and took the stairs down to the pool area. When I got to the gate that was normally closed with a childproof lock, I found it wide open.

The chill touched me again and I walked quickly to the office. The door there was open. I didn't knock, but I drew my gun as I entered.

"Martha!" I called softly. "Ellie!"

I heard something clatter in the room next to the office. I rushed in, kicking the door open just in time to see a form fleeing out the front door. I gave chase but he was fast. Truly a sprinter. He cleared the steps in one leap, vaulted the wrought iron fence in the front yard, and was gone down the road. By the time I got to the gate, he was two blocks ahead of me and disappeared down a dark alley. Better to call the police and check on Martha than chase someone I didn't have a prayer of catching.

I hurried back to the office at the inn. "Martha, are you okay?"

The place was eerily quiet. Martha or Ellie were always

there. The main house was their home, and the office was located on the west side and with a separate entrance.

"Martha? Ellie?" I began a search of the property. My impulse was to call the police, but I didn't want to panic. I would look for the ladies first.

I felt like a trespasser as I pushed through the dining room and living room into the kitchen. I stopped. Broken dishes were on the floor and knives from a butcher block were scattered across the kitchen island.

A soft moan caught my attention and I went into the big laundry room that contained several commercial washers and dryers. Martha was lying on the floor, blood around her head from a gash in her scalp.

"Martha!" I ran to her and ascertained she was alive and breathing with a steady pulse. Something had struck her on the head. "Martha, can you hear me?"

"Where's Ellie?" she asked.

"I'll hunt for her if you're okay. Shall I call an ambulance?"

"No. No ambulance. Find Ellie." She pushed herself up to a sitting position, leaning against a washing machine. The wound on her head wasn't serious. The bleeding had stopped. She needed to be checked by a doctor, but she was good enough for me to hunt for her sister.

I left her there as I went into one of the bedrooms. Ellie was sitting on the floor by the heavy bedstead, her hands tied behind her to the bed and a gag in her mouth. I removed the gag and freed her. "Are you okay?"

"Mad as a wet hen. Where is Martha?"

"You should call an ambulance and take Martha in to be checked. She was hit on the head. Who did this?"

She shook her head. "I didn't get a look at him, but when I find out who it is, he is going to be very, very sorry."

"Martha's in the laundry room. Call an ambulance and then come be with her. She's worried about you."

Once Ellie was comforting Martha, I called the police chief. Lester Thibodeau wasn't happy to hear from me, but he came personally. When he saw the damage, he was less annoyed and a lot more furious.

"Thank goodness you found them," he said. "Why were you here at the office?"

I didn't really have time for an interrogation, but I could give the highlights and the superficial glimpse I got of the attacker. I told him everything and he sent officers to collect any evidence on the porch in the hopes of getting a fingerprint.

"Did you see anything about the attacker? Any identifying details?"

"He was tall and slender and really fast. Like a professional athlete fast."

"Some of the high schools have track teams. It won't hurt to ask there. Thanks. You sure you're okay?"

His mustache worked up and down and I couldn't tell if he was mustering up sympathy or trying not to laugh. I wasn't hurt and he knew it.

"I'm all good. Now I have to go."

"I met one of your Zinnia cohorts over in the blues bar on Nineteenth Street. Handsome man. Took a shine to Janet Malone. You wouldn't know anything about that, would you?"

Thibodeau acted like a sleepy, small-town cop, but he didn't miss much at all. "Harold Erkwell, a banker from

Zinnia. I asked him to make friends with Janet. To be sure this isn't some prank she's playing. I don't think it is, but just to be on the safe side."

He put a hand on my shoulder. "Thank you. We had another break-in at the O'Day mansion. Luckily a couple walking on the beach saw flashlights in the house and called us. We rousted the burglars before anything could be taken."

That was interesting to know. "You sure it was just burglars?"

"I'm not sure of anything about this case," he said.

"Any word on the fire out at the Marcuses' marina?"

"Not my jurisdiction, but I did talk to the fire marshal. Obvious arson and they found some heavy-duty locks and chains under the restaurant." He let that sink in.

"You think someone was going to lock the people in the restaurant and burn them to death?" This had taken a much darker turn.

"I didn't say that."

"But you don't disagree?"

He didn't answer for a long moment. Then he said, "You take care. And ask that sheriff fellow of yours to stop by my office in the morning if you would. I'll be damn glad when all of this is over."

"Me, too, Chief. The sooner this is over, the better. I'll be glad to get back to my sleepy little Delta town."

I saw the police chief off and went back to my room. I'd barely had time to settle on the bed when Tinkie and Oscar knocked at the door. "Maylin is asleep," Tinkie said. She looked ready to drop but she was wearing her game face. "Let's go find Harold. I have some questions for Janet."

"Did you find anything helpful?"

"Plenty," Tinkie said. "But let's have the conversation

with Janet at the blues club. We're going to get changed and we'll see you on the porch in thirty. You can ride with us. I'll text Millie and Cece and tell them where to meet."

"I'll be there." I sent Coleman a text with the location and the gist of what was going on. Then I showered, threw on some jeans with a red-sequined top—after all, it was Christmas—and went down to catch a ride with Tinkie and Oscar.

They were just coming out of their room and we stood on the balcony for a moment, drinking in the night.

"Ladies, I'm going to have to insist that we don't get involved with Christmas crimes next year," Oscar said. "I love helping you, but we all need a break from work."

I wasn't going to argue with him. I wanted nothing more than some Jack, a good belly-rubbing song, and Coleman to dance with.

"We can worry about next year in eleven months," Tinkie said. "Let's finish this case and get back to celebrating the holidays."

We loaded up in the Cadillac and headed into the night.

18

The club was everything I'd hoped it would be. Neon sizzled in the crisp night as we arrived and the music that came from inside was pure Delta blues. The best music on the planet. I didn't know the band, but whoever was on lead guitar could make that instrument sing and moan.

Tinkie and Oscar took the lead, pushing into the club, which looked surprisingly like a 1950s ballroom with linen-covered tables, waiters in tuxedoes, people in fancy clothes, and some in jeans moving with the music on the dance floor. Throw in a 1980s disco ball and you had it. We stood at the entrance, getting a feel for the atmosphere.

"This is incredible," Tinkie said. "Cece is going to love it!"

"There's Harold." I spied our friend at a corner table

where a waiter filled champagne flutes for him and Janet. He toasted her and they clinked glasses. Janet looked happier than I'd ever seen her.

"Is that the author?" Oscar asked. "She's lovely. Watching that video of her and the other writer fighting, I had no idea she was such a beauty."

"That's Janet Malone," Tinkie confirmed. "She's beautiful and she's the one who writes the steamy novels."

"Got it." Oscar caught Harold's eye and gave him a thumbs-up.

The lead singer for the band tapped the microphone. "Now for a little change of pace, we have a very special treat for you tonight. Ms. Janet Malone is going to sing a few numbers for us. Janet? Would you mind?"

"Tony, that isn't necessary." Janet actually seemed to blush. She cast a shy glance at Harold.

"Not necessary," Tony said, "but certainly a pleasure."

Harold assisted her to the stage. As she took a stand in front of the microphone, we all quickly found our seats with Harold. Coleman slipped in beside me, whispering, "The Marcuses are fine. Mr. Marcus wasn't there, but Mrs. Marcus was happy to talk. She was alarmed, but she didn't know anything helpful. She didn't see anything, but she did say the chains and locks found at the diner belonged to Donnie Marcus. He used them to lock up the boats when necessary. Ultimately, I got nothing except they're decent people. Mrs. Marcus loves her son."

I squeezed his hand and kissed his cheek. "Thank you."

Our attention turned to the stage. A single light illuminated Janet, and she began to sing an Etta James rendition of "Stormy Weather." We all simply sat at the table, mouths open. Janet Malone could sing. Really sing. Before the song was halfway over, the audience was on its feet clapping and whistling. I was stunned.

"Did you know she could do that?" Coleman asked me.

"Not a clue. She could have made a living with her pipes instead of writing."

Janet tried to leave the stage but the audience kept clapping and stamping their feet until she sang another number. She surprised us all by singing "The House of the Rising Sun," a song that never failed to make me think of so many good memories in New Orleans.

Amid applause and whistles, Harold escorted her down from the stage and back to our table while the band took a break. Harold lightly stepped on my toes under the table, letting me know he had something to tell me out of Janet's earshot. It would have to wait until an opportunity to slip outside came up or we got back to the inn.

Everyone was all ears when I told them about the attack on Martha and Ellie at the inn and the rocks hurled at my window.

"You saw the man who did this?" Tinkie asked.

"I did, but not clearly enough to identify him. I'll give all the details when Cece and Millie get here." I heard my name and when I looked up, Cece and Millie were dodging through the tables to get to us. They were beaming with excitement as they took seats.

"You found out something!" It wasn't much of a guess since it was obvious by their faces.

"We did."

"Did you find Sandra and Daryl?" Janet asked.

I kicked Cece lightly on the shin under the table.

"No, we only found out that Daryl owns a home in Pass Christian. I'm sure you knew that." Cece didn't lie, but she sure skirted the truth, and luckily Millie picked up on the situation and didn't reveal anything.

"But I didn't," Janet said, confusion on her face. "Not that it matters, but . . ." She looked up at the stage where the band was setting up again. "It's just odd they wouldn't have told me. Sandra hates me, but she likes to keep me abreast of all their purchases. Especially a house. You know, to rub my nose in it. And I'm sure she bought it for Daryl. Where is it located?"

"I forget the name of the street, but it's just off the beach and isolated. I gather it's a newer home, meeting the standards for elevation above sea level and all of that. I'll look at my notes and tell you when I see it."

"That would be lovely," Janet said. There was a hint of hurt feelings in her expression, as if Sandra and Daryl had betrayed her by not keeping her informed. It was interesting. I guess the term *frenemies* fit them perfectly. They loved bickering and fighting with each other—it was the basis of their friendship.

The band kicked into high gear, and since we couldn't really talk with Janet there, we gave ourselves over to having fun. It was, after all, the holiday season. After two hours of drinking and dancing, I realized I was exhausted. We'd all had a day, but I'd been shot at *and* stalked. All I really wanted was to snuggle up in bed with Coleman and sleep. As I looked around the table, it was clear Tinkie and Oscar, too, were winding down. Harold, though, was hanging on Janet's every word. I'd sent him to meet her as a means of gathering information, but it seemed there was a real spark of attraction.

"I think I'm about ready to turn in. Janet, I'll have a report for you tomorrow," I said.

"I'm worn out, too," Tinkie agreed.

"I'm having a great—" Cece frowned when she saw my face. "Yeah, me, too. I'm totally exhausted. Come on, Millie, let's turn in. Tomorrow we have a heavy-duty day of shopping."

"Right," Millie said, grabbing her coat and purse. "Let's go before I turn into a pumpkin."

If we were less than subtle leaving Harold and Janet alone, the couple didn't notice. They were too wrapped up in each other. I put a hand on Harold's shoulder. "See you later," I said, pointedly looking at my watch. "Remember, that report is expected."

"Duly noted," he said, but his eyes said he was hungry for something other than reporting to me. I had a disturbing thought that perhaps I'd fed Harold to a shark.

The ride to the inn was silent as I pondered the danger to Harold if Janet was a kidnapper and killer. Not likely, but my guilt was in high gear as we pulled into the parking lot. We went up to the room, where we were joined immediately by the gang.

Coleman shook his head at me and finally spoke. "Harold's a big boy. He can take care of himself."

It was exactly what I needed to hear. Tinkie laughed out loud. "He was smitten. Harold normally has the ladies eating out of his hand, but he was hit hard by Janet."

"Wait until he sees her dark side," Oscar said.

"Maybe her dark side is only for Sandra, though I got a

distinct feeling Janet was hurt that she didn't know about Daryl's home," Cece said. "But why should she know?"

"They have a symbiotic love-hate relationship," Tinkie said.

"And that is an understatement," I agreed.

"Do you think Harold is coming?" Tinkie asked, looking at her watch.

Cece rolled her eyes. "I won't reply with the wiseass remark that question deserves."

"He'll be here," Millie said. "Harold may be intrigued by Janet, but he wouldn't desert his mission. He'll be here to report any minute now."

"If he can shake loose of Janet," Oscar said with a wicked grin.

"Let's focus on the new information." I was eager to add pieces to the puzzle. "Cece and Millie, what else did you find, other than Daryl's house?"

"Daryl Marcus grew up in the Bay St. Louis library," Cece said. "He was the walking epitome of a bookworm."

"That made a lot of people think he was strange," Millie added. "Most of the locals hunt and fish. Daryl refused to harm anything. That put him at odds with his surroundings."

This was information I'd learned, but confirmation was a good thing. "He was different from most of his peers, true. I can't see him being a threat to any of the good old boys."

"Right. He was more of a tender guy," Millie said. "Someone we'd probably like a lot." Her eyebrows rose. "But there was an incident recently at his parents' diner."

"What kind of incident?" I had a tingly feeling along my spine.

"Daryl had gone to see his parents a few weeks ago. He

was standing on the dock at the marina when a motorboat sped past and someone threw a container of fuel on him. The boat kept going and Daryl wasn't injured."

"This was reported?" I asked, wondering why his parents had totally failed to mention this to me or Coleman.

"Yes, but Daryl said he couldn't identify the boat or the person driving it or the passenger who threw the balloon full of gasoline. The reporter thought that Daryl probably knew who it was and decided not to tell."

"Why would he do that?" Coleman asked.

"Maybe to keep conflict from his folks," Millie said. "Daryl was teased a good bit growing up. The reporter I was talking with, a local, said Daryl never liked confrontation or conflict. And he wouldn't want to bring trouble to his parents. But it was just curious that he was doused with fuel, like gasoline, and then a few weeks later, the diner was set on fire."

She had a good point.

"Was there any speculation from the area journalists about where Daryl and Sandra might be?" I asked. Cece and Millie had gone to the association of journalists gathering to meet their local counterparts and to gather information.

"Typical stuff," Cece said. "It's about fifty-fifty. A lot of the journalists don't care for Sandra. They think she's high-handed and thinks only she knows how to research properly."

That would stick in any journalist's craw, especially one who prided themselves on digging for the truth.

Cece continued, "So a few that had covered her feel that this is a stunt. You know, keep the spotlight focused on her."

"Especially since her book came out only a couple of weeks

ago," Tinkie said. "This kind of sensational story—an abduction and certainly a rescue—is just the boost her book needs to stay at the top of the charts."

"Except there hasn't been any coverage," Oscar pointed out.

"Not yet," Millie said. "But the local paper is about to do a big exposé about the disappearance on Sunday."

The Sunday paper had the largest circulation, so it made sense. It would be the beginning of a landslide of publicity once the local law enforcement officials and those close to Sandra or Daryl agreed to interviews. It was going to be mayhem for anyone even loosely associated with Sandra. If it played out the way I saw it, by Sunday we would be finished with the judging and if the case was solved, we'd be on our way home. That was a life raft thought I could cling to.

"What else have we learned?" Coleman asked.

Tinkie and Oscar filled everyone in on the physical search of the Malone house.

"And Tinkie and Oscar have been going over the financial records of Al Capone," Coleman said, generating a buzz from Millie and Cece. "Tell us what you found, please."

Oscar deferred to Tinkie with a wink and a nod. She cleared her throat and raised her eyebrows at me. She knew this was what I'd been waiting to hear. "Capone had a lot of business savvy. He was raking in funds from the smuggled liquor, mostly rum made from sugarcane in the Caribbean islands and brought into the bay by the smaller fishing vessels of the Buntman family. The locals around here were also making whiskey that Capone was moving inland. It was very lucrative for Capone and the local people involved."

"Any evidence of a treasure?" Coleman asked eagerly. He'd fallen victim to the lure of a buried treasure hunt, as had I. And from the looks of it, Tinkie, Oscar, Cece, and Millie were in the same boat.

"Some of the financial information is written in code," Oscar said. "Tinkie and I tried to come up with a key, but we didn't have success. There has to be a way to break the code. We aren't giving up. Now that Harold is here"—he checked his watch—"if indeed he ever comes, we'll get him to help. He's clever with that kind of thing."

"He'll be here soon," I assured them.

I could count on Harold. Always.

A soft knock at the door made me jump to my feet with a smile. I opened the door and Harold strolled in. There was lipstick on his collar and a knowing expression in his eyes. He looked very pleased with himself.

"What did you find out?" I asked.

"I don't kiss and tell," he said loftily.

I picked up a pillow and went after him. Chuckling, Harold pointed to a seat at the table. "Sit down and I'll tell you everything."

Since I was dying to hear what he'd learned, I plopped down and waited.

"Janet is sincerely worried about Sandra and Daryl. She said at first she thought it was a prank or some kind of stunt, but now she's really worried. She told me that someone had doused Daryl with gasoline a couple of weeks ago at the marina. And just this morning, someone set the place on fire—while people were inside."

"Does she have any idea where they might be?" Coleman asked.

Harold shook his head. He reached in his pocket and came out with a key on a chain. "She wants me to search the mansion. She gave me a key."

"Why does she have a key to Sandra's place?" Tinkie asked.

"As much as they hate each other, they are each other's literary heirs. Janet is charged with making sure Sandra's papers are kept safe and all of that copyright business. While I'm there, I'm supposed to open the safe and make sure all of the paperwork is still there."

Now that was a revelation. And another motive for murder!

19

By the time we'd all shared our discoveries, it was into the wee hours of the morning. We called it quits and Coleman and I snuggled in bed.

"Do you think Janet realizes how much of a motive being Sandra's literary heir is?" Coleman asked.

"It makes me think she really isn't involved. She has to know how significant that is."

Coleman kissed my ear. "Tomorrow I'm going to set a trap for the person who keeps trying to intimidate you."

"Okay. I know Martha and Ellie will be glad to hear that. I'm sure they're ready for me to pack up and go home."

"The Christmas tree judging is almost upon us," Coleman reminded me. He gave a big yawn. "I'll be glad when this is done."

"Me, too." The beautiful December days had made me long to ride my horses through the fallow cotton fields. I missed the animals and my routine at home. And I was frustrated by a case that should have been simple and straight-forward but wasn't.

We drifted off into sleep and I had the strangest dream about Janet and Harold—that she was moving to Zinnia. I wondered how she'd take to Roscoe, Harold's demonic dog. I woke myself up laughing.

Then I heard a car alarm in the parking lot. Coleman woke, too, and we swung our feet out of bed, grabbed pants and jackets, and headed out the door with a flashlight and my gun.

The parking lot was eerily empty, but Tinkie's car horn was blaring. In a moment Oscar appeared on the balcony with the key fob and stopped it. "Anything amiss?" he asked.

"Not that I see," Coleman said. We walked all around the car and found nothing. "We'll search first thing in the morning," he said to me. "Let's get back inside."

We were both shivering, and in the dark night, if there was anything to see, we'd likely miss it. I sent him back to the room, but I checked on Martha and Ellie's office. It was locked up tight and I didn't disturb them. They'd had an upsetting day already.

I'd taken the path by the wrought iron fence and the pool. Coleman had disappeared, and I assumed he was in the room waiting for me. The night was beautiful and only a little cold. I stopped to take in the lighted pool area, the moon through the branches of an oak tree, and the lights on docked boats in the marina. The night was still and calm. I felt the air tinged with magic.

On the way back to the room, I had some difficulty with the gate to the pool area. As I tussled with the latch, I saw something in a nearby holly shrub. I had the flashlight so I was able to examine the fabric caught in the prickly shrub.

I didn't touch it because I didn't have any gloves or evidence bags, and if there was something there, I didn't want to contaminate it. But I knew the fabric, blue flannel. And I knew where I'd seen it. Donnie Marcus had worn a shirt with that exact pattern the day I'd been to his diner and marina.

The strange sound of an orchestra tuning stopped me in my tracks at the pool apron. I looked all around and faintly heard the strains of a tinny 1920s tune, "Dear Heart."

I spun around looking for the orchestra and singer, but no one was in sight. Pink feathers from a boa drifted down from the oaks and fell into my hair. What the heck?

Movement beneath the oaks caught my eye, and I started to punch on the flashlight, but something stopped me. A bevy of beautiful women, in long gowns dripping with sequins and feathers, danced among the trees.

"Damn." Of all the things I'd expected, it wasn't a Ziegfeld Follies revue in Bay St. Louis. The beauty of the dancers, the costumes, the song, the night all lulled me into a mesmerized state. It was as if I'd truly stepped into a Hollywood fantasy from a time long past.

A slender woman with short, wavy hair came toward me and the other dancers vanished. Little curls of perfectly placed hair adorned her forehead. I didn't recognize her, but I knew who was at work here. Jitty.

"Magnificent Christmas vision," I told her.

"Billie Dove, a pleasure to meet you."

"Dancer?"

"Yes. And actress for a number of years. Most of my earlier films were destroyed in a fire, but I'm probably best known for the rumors of my four-year affair with Howard Hughes."

"Really? I thought he was too germophobic to have affairs."

Her laughter was warm and soft. "We all change over time, Sarah Booth. It will happen to even you."

"That almost sounds like a threat." Jitty had definitely gone a little dark.

"Not a threat. A promise of the inevitable."

"Were you really Howard Hughes's lover?"

Her smile was fleeting. "Time has taught me that discretion is the better part of valor."

Once Jitty's lips were sealed, nothing could pry them open. I was tired and ready for bed. "You're beautiful tonight, Billie."

"I had a good life. Better than so many women who went to Hollywood. I got out when the getting was good and lived on a ranch. My family and I were happy."

She had been lucky. Getting old while vying for movie roles was a brutal way of life. "So why are you visiting me?"

"It's Christmas. Perhaps I should have come in on a Christmas number instead of 'Dear Heart.' I've always been a sentimental fool."

Her costume changed and she was wearing a diaphanous gown that clung to her slender body. She struck a profile pose and I was in awe of her grace and beauty. Billie Dove embodied femininity. Not even the passage of time could dim those qualities.

"Why are you here, Billie?" I asked again.

"Balance, Sarah Booth. Always seek balance. Remember that the past and future meet in the moment. Libby wanted me to tell you that."

A wind blew out of the oaks and set her dress to flying behind her, and then she was gone.

"Jitty! Jitty!" She'd brought me a message from my mother, but what did it mean?

I waited a few moments longer, admiring the glow of the moon through the oaks. When it was clear Jitty was gone for the evening, I went up the stairs to the inn porch. Coleman was inside our room. He was all ears about the tag of fabric and agreed it was best to wait until light to collect it.

"Why would Donnie Marcus want to spy on us?" Coleman asked me.

"Maybe he thinks we really know where Daryl is." It was the only explanation I could come up with that didn't involve kidnapping on his part.

"I hope that's true. If he's behind this, it's going to be bad for his family."

Coleman said out loud what I didn't even want to think. We settled into bed and before long, he was asleep. After some time, I slipped into a peaceful slumber, too.

Coleman and I were up at the break of day. Ready to collect evidence, I took the shortcut to the office where I intended to borrow a plastic baggie and some cleaning gloves from Martha. Coffee was brewing, but she was still in her pajamas and slippers. She assured me she was totally over the events of the day before. She was her normal, upbeat self, brushing off the intruder as someone who'd thought to grab a few valuables, thinking she and Ellie were defenseless.

"I think we scared him as much as he scared us," she said. "It's over and done. Ellie and I are fine. I need to get to work on breakfast. Would you grab the paper from the front lawn? I haven't had a chance to go outside."

I picked up the paper from the front sidewalk and opened it up as I walked back to her kitchen. There were photos from the journalism convention, including of Cece and Millie—who'd obviously been given an award they'd never said a word about. The cutline said they were honored for the Most Entertaining and Innovative weekly column.

Those scoundrels had kept the honor all to themselves. They definitely had some explaining to do.

I chatted with Martha in the kitchen for a few minutes, waiting for the rising sun to take the chill off. When I was ready to get to work—after a cup of coffee—she gave me the gloves and baggie without asking why, and I didn't mention the flannel. I didn't want to get her hopes up that I had a real clue. And a good thing, too. By the time Coleman and I got to the hedge, the piece of material was gone.

"Someone had to have taken it," I said.

"It couldn't have blown away?" Coleman asked.

I shook my head. The fabric had been snared into the shrub strongly enough to tear out of a shirt—and yet it was gone. Someone had removed it. And it wasn't Martha or Ellie. Neither had been outside even for the paper.

I'd snared two cups of coffee when I was in the kitchen, and Coleman and I drank them on the balcony porch, waiting for the others to wake up. "Tinkie and I have to be at the library today," I told him. "We finish the judging, and then tomorrow is the announcement of the winners and the big gala fundraiser."

"Oscar is donating a hefty amount," Coleman said. "And he's arranging for the same kind of tree decorating competition in Sunflower County next Christmas."

"He's a good citizen and a generous friend." I meant every word.

Tinkie and Oscar joined us, and by the time Martha had brought fresh coffee up to the porch, Cece and Millie arrived. Harold was absent and Cece was dying to knock on his door to see if he'd stayed at the inn or returned to Janet's house. I did my best to dissuade her, but her mind was made up.

"I'm going," Cece said, and before I could stop her she was down the porch and pounding on Harold's door. "Up and at 'em," she sang out. "Sarah Booth is looking for you."

If Harold was asleep, she would be lucky if he didn't pinch her head off. And somehow I'd get the blame. Still, I watched the door with my own eagerness. Had Harold taken the plunge and spent the night with Janet?

"Hey, Harold," Cece said, knocking really loudly.

When there was still no answer, Coleman stood up and walked over. He banged on the door. "Harold, open up and let us know you're okay, please."

No response.

"Let me check the parking lot for his car," Oscar said.

It wasn't like him not to keep us informed. I called his cell phone. No answer there either. Oscar came back. "No car."

"Where is he?" Millie asked. She was the mother hen, even for Harold. "Call Janet, just to be sure he's okay."

I hesitated. If they were engaged in a fling, I didn't want to hover. Both of them would likely resent it.

Tinkie rolled her eyes at me and pulled out her phone. She dialed Janet with a determined set to her jaw. When the writer answered, Tinkie got right to it.

"Tinkie here. Is Harold with you? His car isn't here so we thought he might be."

I couldn't hear Janet's answer, but a heavy line appeared between Tinkie's eyebrows before she said. "He didn't?"

In a moment she put her phone away. "Harold left the blues club shortly after we did. He told her he was coming here to the inn, which he did, and that he'd see her at the library. She doesn't have a clue where he might be."

True worry touched my heart. "Maybe he went into town or down to the marina. He likes boats."

"Could be," Oscar said, obviously trying not to upset Tinkie. "I tell you what. Let's get some breakfast and give him a minute to wander back. Then you girls go on to the library and Coleman and I will look around for our missing friend."

He said it with such casualness that I had to admire his theatrical abilities. He was just as worried as I was. His right hand gripped the arm of his chair with white knuckles.

"Oscar and I are becoming quite the team," Coleman said, also jovial. "I may have to hire him as a deputy."

"You'll need to up that pay scale a bit," Oscar said.

The boys' banter served to break the tension and we all got up to shower and get dressed for the day. I was glad to get Coleman alone.

"Are you worried?" I asked him.

"I am." He didn't sugarcoat it. "This isn't like Harold. Where is he if he left the inn and didn't go to Janet's? I'm going to talk to Thibodeau and get an APB out on Harold's car. Who would know to pick on Harold, though?" he asked.

We both arrived at the same answer, and we said it together.

"Janet."

"Could she be that devious and awful?" Coleman asked.

"I sure didn't think so." I was shocked at the possibility. "But the flannel piece. I'm certain it was from Donnie Marcus's shirt. It seems far more likely that Marcus would be involved in an abduction."

"True, but why? What would Donnie Marcus gain from kidnapping Harold?"

"I don't know exactly. But he could have lain in wait in those shrubs and grabbed Harold as he was heading up the stairs to his room, forced him back down to his car, and made him drive away."

Coleman nodded. "It could have happened just like that, but I hope not. And I still don't see the benefit. Harold has nothing to do with your investigation."

I knew what he wasn't saying. Someone willing to abduct a man in the middle of a business parking lot was someone with a lot of brass. Which led me to the possibility that we were working with professionals. Not local treasure hunters or some feud with Janet Malone, but someone skilled in abductions and hostage taking. Someone who might be a lot more interested in the research on the Dixie Mafia that Sandra had been doing. After all, Janet and Daryl had been taken from the middle of a Christmas party with at least a hundred people on the property. And no one had noticed a thing. Janet had been nicely framed for it. Now she could also be framed for Harold's disappearance. And it was on

Janet's property that we'd found Capone's business records. There might be something significant there.

"The stakes have just been upped," I said. "What if Donnie Marcus is involved with the Dixie Mafia? His marina gives him access to a lot of places. I know folks believe the mafia is gone, but what if they aren't?"

"Don't poke that snake, Sarah Booth. Let's shower and get dressed. We need to get busy," Coleman said, holding the bathroom door open for me.

20

Cece, Millie, Tinkie, and I arrived at the library just on time. My two journalist friends had opted to come look at the trees rather than shop. They were worried about Harold and wanted to be at the ready if any news came to us.

Millie was in bliss when she found a very strange tree pruned in the shape of Elvis dancing. He wore white and silver ornaments and a real bejeweled cape was draped on his shoulders. The ornaments were shaped like little guitars and microphones, and a recorder had been hidden in the tree that kept saying, "Thank you. Thank you very much."

"Winner, winner, chicken dinner!" Millie sang out.

"It's certainly original," Cece conceded. She looked all around the library. "Where's Janet?"

That was a good question. She was nowhere in evidence. I hated to do it but I stepped outside and called her.

"We're getting started," I told her.

"I can't come. What if Harold comes here looking for me?"

"It's a small town. Leave a note and tell him you're at the library."

"I can't." Janet wasn't budging. "Sandra, Daryl, and Harold are missing. The only thing they have in common is me. This is somehow something I've done, and I can't judge Christmas trees. Can't you find someone to step in for me?"

I was looking directly at Millie. "I can suggest something to Mary Perkins, but you need to make it right with the librarian."

"I'll do that if you can find judges."

I didn't have a lot of choice except to dump it all on Mary and let her have the final say. "I'll speak with Mary."

"Thank you, Sarah Booth. Thank you. I'm just a nervous wreck."

"After we're done at the library, you, Tinkie, and I need to talk. About what we found in the attic in your parents' home."

"What do you mean?"

"Long story, we'll talk this afternoon when we have time to get into it. I'll tell you all about it. If you see Harold, please have him call me."

"Will do."

Three hours later, after much oohing and aahing from Millie and Cece, we had winners picked. Mary had shown masterfully stoic acceptance of Janet's failure to show up. She couldn't blame Sandra—yet. And she was worried sick about Daryl. A sensation I shared.

She took the list of winners and thanked us all. She had

tickets for the evening soiree and gave us each one, which included a guest. If Harold showed up, he'd be at the party. If Harold didn't show up, I didn't know that any of us would be there, as unfair as that was to the library committee.

But as it stood, we had the rest of the day to find our missing friend, Sandra, and Daryl. The problem was that we didn't have any real clues as to where any of them might be.

It was time for a meeting with Janet. A come-to-Jesus meeting, as my third-grade teacher would have called it. I knew that for a fact because I'd had more than one of those with her about my "rough" behavior. She didn't approve of tomboys. Mrs. Opal, who said she had a direct line to Jesus, said that neither he nor she liked girls who beat boys at sports. So then my mama had a come-to-Jesus meeting with her.

Tink and I left Cece and Millie downtown to finish a little Christmas shopping while we drove to Janet's house. We were greeted by two very handsome yellow tabby cats. Sphinxlike, they watched us. Then a parade of black cats came from the front patio area and led us to the back where there was a beautiful pool. Cats were everywhere. In shrubs, in trees, in planters, in chairs, on tables, lolling on the diving board. Janet Malone loved her cats.

She was seated in the shade, toiling over a notebook.

"Janet?" I didn't want to startle her but I did anyway. She leaped to her feet.

"Sarah Booth! You scared the hell out of me."

She was mighty jumpy. "Sorry, the cats led us out here. Has something happened?" I tried to get a look at the notebook but she closed it.

She frowned. "Have you talked to Coleman?"

"No, why?" Before my heart could begin to race with

dread, my phone rang and it was him. I answered. "What's going on?"

"Don't get upset, but we found Harold's car at the dock for the ferry to Ship Island," Coleman said. "No sign of him at all, but there was blood in the driver's seat. Not a lot, but enough to indicate someone was injured. Chief Thibodeau is running it now to see if it matches Harold's."

That news was like a kick in the solar plexus. "Does anyone know what happened?"

"Thibodeau will find out. It's a jurisdictional complication right now. The ferry runs out of Harrison County and Harold disappeared from Hancock, but the authorities are working together, and the Mississippi Bureau of Investigation will take over the case as soon as they arrive." Coleman kept his tone matter-of-fact.

"Who called the MBI?" I asked.

"Thibodeau." Coleman was masterful at keeping his voice level. Sometimes the MBI was an asset and sometimes a pain in the butt. "It's the best solution because of Ship Island, which is a national park. We don't want the feds mucking around in this. They'll slow the process."

I wasn't about to ask who had jurisdiction over the ferry. Oftentimes Coleman, with the legal authority of the badge, had so much more power than Tinkie or I would ever have. But there were other times when our status as private investigators cut through jurisdictional red tape and the finer points of the law. If the car was still at the parking lot in Gulfport, Tinkie would charm our way into taking a look at it. After we finished with Janet.

I relayed the information to my partner and Janet. Tinkie sent a text to Millie and Cece while I set up to interview Janet.

"Aren't you going to chase down where Harold is?" Janet asked. She did seem a little sweet on Zinnia's most eligible banker. "You can't just let him be taken without trying to find him."

"We're looking for all three missing people," Tinkie assured her. "The law is on it and so are we."

"Well, get out of here and go look!" Janet was a bit cranky.

"First, we have some questions for you," I said quietly. "Was your grandfather Al Capone's accountant?" Sometimes bluntness was the only ticket.

"He was, or that's what I was told. And it was my great-grandfather, Samuel Malone. A brilliant accountant and money manager. He was also a fine architect." She narrowed her eyes. "How did you hear about this?"

Confession time was upon me. "I searched your family home. I was thinking Sandra was possibly hiding out there. She'd know about the house and so would Daryl. They'd know it was empty. So we searched the house and I found some things in the attic."

"This is not something I want publicized," Janet said, rather tersely. "Why didn't you call and ask permission?"

"No cell service," I told her, which wasn't the truth but there was a lot I didn't want her to know.

"Right." She didn't believe me. "You still think I'm involved in this, don't you?"

"I think it's a possibility." Tinkie put a hand on her arm. "Don't take it personally. Doing the work we do often makes us suspicious. But honestly, right now we're a lot more interested in Capone and his relationship with your family. It's kind of . . . intriguing that your family worked with him, as did Sandra's. And you two were close in childhood."

Janet closed her eyes and licked her lips. "Yes. Sandra

and I were inseparable. We played together every day. My family dropped me at her place or vice versa. Every summer day. And we were always in trouble in school for talking and scheming. We both had big imaginations." Melancholy touched her features. "The adventures we had. We were in the same grade in school, and we were our own clique."

"What happened?" I asked.

She shrugged. "Competition. Jealousy. Both going into the writing field. The sense that there wasn't enough pie for everyone, which isn't true."

"But your work could complement each other's," Tinkie said. "You don't have to be adversaries."

"We were close and helpful for the first few years. Then I made a bad mistake." She hesitated and I thought she wouldn't finish, but she did. "I stole an editor that Sandra had a crush on. That was the beginning of the end."

Yowza! I could see where that might not go down smooth in the Sandra O'Day world. But I was confused. "How did you steal an editor?"

Tinkie followed quickly with, "When was this?"

"Twenty years ago. He was her first editor at the big publishing house that bought her book for a lot of money and told her she'd be a star. He didn't edit nonfiction, but he loved her book and after she met him in person, she was smitten."

"And you were in New York together and you met him." I could fill in some of the blanks.

"Yes, he wasn't my editor, but I saw him all the time at parties and writers' conventions. Sandra was too shy to make a move on him, so he thought she wasn't interested. I stepped into the shadow of her timidity." She heaved a sigh. "She never forgave me and, believe me, if I could do it over

I wouldn't. He was a swell guy and great in bed, but not worth the damage it did to our friendship."

She had more depth and maturity than I'd expected. "Have you ever told her that?"

Janet shook her head. "She'd put a stiletto through my eye before I could get the words out."

That was a possibility. "Promise me that when we find her you'll make this right." It was clear to me Janet still longed for her childhood friend. The fights and slugfests were ridiculous. Understandable, but also ridiculous.

"Just find her. And Daryl. With each passing hour I get more and more frightened for them. And the media have been calling me, demanding an interview. Chief Thibodeau has asked me to speak at a press conference today."

"When?" Tinkie asked.

"He's going to call with details, but I can't do it. Not with Harold missing. I mean Harold is what made me see the light about what I've done to Sandra in the past. I really like him. And now he's just suddenly gone. It's awful."

"Did Harold mention last night anywhere he might go looking for Sandra or Daryl?" I didn't trust her completely to tell us the truth. What if she had sent Harold on some wild-goose chase to Ship Island? What if she had set him up to be injured or killed, thrown off the ferry? Or maybe he'd uncovered something she was hiding from us.

"Harold was very interested in the mansion that Sandra bought. He was captivated by the idea of Capone's treasure. I mean every little boy that has ever read *Treasure Island* dreams of finding a pirate treasure. Capone is the closest thing most of them will ever come to an American pirate. A land pirate."

She was right about that. And such an adventure would

appeal to Harold. Not for the money, but the excitement of hunting and finding something sought by so many for such a long time.

"I gave Harold a key to Sandra's house," she said, gaining a little more of my trust with her revelation. "Could he have gone there?"

"Why do you have a key to her house?" Harold had told us about the key, but I was curious what reason Janet would give.

"Sandra and I are bound together in ways few would understand."

They had been close friends, almost sisters. I felt like that about Tinkie, Cece, and Millie, too. I would trust them with anything I cared about. But we treated one another with respect and caring. We weren't trying to slug one another into the next week. "You have to give me a better reason than some old bond of friendship."

She shrugged. "I don't have anyone else I can turn to. And she's in the same boat, except for Daryl. When her parents were killed, we made this agreement. To make sure each other's final wishes were carried out. I felt sorry for her. She isn't close with her brothers and when her parents were gone, she had no one else. I agreed." She sighed loudly. "We're both smart and good with business. It was a wise thing to do. Now how about you start looking for Harold? I want him to be my date for the soiree. I think I'm falling for him."

21

After the shock of that pronouncement faded, I pressed Janet harder. The two women were each other's literary heirs and would control the books and whatever came. I still found it hard to believe. "You can't even talk to each other without getting into a hair-pulling fight but you entrusted her with what happens to your work?"

"I know it sounds crazy, but no one loves her books more than I do. And she loves mine. It's part of the competition. We both recognize the other's talent. I would honor Sandra's literary heritage, as she would mine. And we both left very clear instructions on what is to happen. I have her key, and she has a key to my house. The only thing I worry about, should I die unexpectedly, is the cats. Sandra isn't a great lover of felines, but Daryl adores them. That's why I was so startled to learn he bought a house in Pass Christian. Daryl was supposed to inherit my house and my cats. He knew I'd be joining my parents in Costa Rica in the next few years and the house would be his. That was part of our deal."

The relationship between the two women and Daryl was very complicated. A team of psychologists could work on sorting it out for the next fifty years.

"Do you have another key to Sandra's we can use, in case we can't find Harold this morning? We probably will, but just in case." I tried not to worry her about Harold, but I wanted to see her reaction.

"You don't have a clue where he could be?"

"He was at the inn, but I thought he might come back to visit more with you." I put it out there.

"No, he saw me home like such a gentleman, but then he drove on to the inn." She bit a corner of her bottom lip. "It was late. Where would he go?"

She seemed worried, but I didn't trust her as far as I could throw her, an image that gave me a tad of satisfaction. "Maybe he's at the mansion." His car in the parking lot of the Gulfport marina told another story, but she didn't have to know that. "If you have that key . . ."

"I do." She got up and went to a small secretary in the room and found another set of keys. "Front door, back door, garage, and two others for who knows what. Also, keys to Sandra's car and Daryl's. Although Sandra usually left a key in her ignition."

"Daryl had a car?" This was news.

"Yes, a black BMW something or other. Men and their cars. Sandra has a car fetish, too, now that I think about it, but at least her car has some style."

"And it is?"

"T-Bird. Red, white interior, convertible." She frowned. "I haven't seen it at her house, now that I think about it."

"Garage?" I asked.

"Check when you go."

She could bet that I would. "Surely Thibodeau knows about this?" I asked.

"Everyone in town knows about it. Sandra would take up two parking spaces to keep her car from getting dinged."

Neither car sounded like a nondescript getaway vehicle, but I would tell Coleman and he could get the chief to run the plates. If the cars were seen anywhere . . . it would only be good for us.

But none of this was helping us find Harold. "Janet, who would want the old accounting records in your attic?"

She shook her head. "No one . . ." Her eyes widened.

She was definitely hiding something now. "Why haven't you put that empty house on the market?" I asked. There had to be some reason the house was empty but hadn't been sold. Empty houses tended to fall apart quickly in the salty humidity of the Gulf Coast. "Do you have relatives who want to live there or keep the property?"

"No. There's just my parents and they're happy in Costa Rica. I'll bet they never come back here." But she wasn't looking at me.

"They don't come home to visit?"

She frowned. "No."

"Then why?"

"I'm too lazy to clean it out, if you must know. I knew there were boxes and boxes of records in the attic. Things my parents wanted me to donate to museums or worthy causes. I just haven't gotten around to it."

I wasn't buying that for a minute and neither was Tinkie.

She came at Janet from another angle. "Tell us about Sandra's brothers. Where are they?"

"Ben is in Houston and Ray is in Knoxville."

Both close enough to easily drive here. "Could you give us their numbers? Maybe Sandra has checked in with them."

"I don't think they'll know anything about this. They aren't close with Sandra. In fact, I'd say 'estrangement' isn't an adequate word. There's animosity among the three of them. The boys haven't been back to the Gulf Coast in years."

"I want to at least call them and alert them to the fact their sister is missing."

She gave me the numbers, which forced me to ask her why she had contact info on two men she claimed not to like.

"Sandra keeps the contact info up-to-date with me in case of emergencies."

I didn't waste a minute calling Ben's office. "May I speak with Ben O'Day?"

I listened to the woman in the corporate office explain that Ben was on vacation and wouldn't be back until next week. I did learn he'd been on vacation for five days, plenty of time to get down here and abduct his sister. "Thank you."

I hung up and looked first to Tinkie, then Janet. "Ben isn't at work. On vacation. Is he here, Janet? Is Sandra's brother here on the coast?" My temper was hot. If Sandra's brother had been here all along and Janet had failed to tell any of us . . .

"I don't know!" She jumped up from the table. "I haven't heard from those two in a long time. They were mean to Sandra when we were younger. Mean to both of us. I don't care where they are."

Once bitten, twice shy, as Aunt Loulane would say. The

fact was I didn't one hundred percent believe my client. She'd failed to tell us several crucial things.

I called the work number for the second brother and learned that Ray O'Day had been working remotely for the company for the past fifteen years as an expert on evaluating geological sites for oil and minerals. His office wasn't certain where he was and didn't care as long as he turned in his work.

"Ray works remotely. He could be anywhere. Do you know where he is?" I asked Janet.

"I don't. Ray was even meaner than Ben. I think it was his name. Everyone teased him. Ray O'Day. The way it rhymed made him a target."

"I can try to track him down," Tinkie said. "I have some of those programs on my computer. You got the name of his company. It shouldn't be that difficult."

I had a sneaking suspicion both brothers were on the Gulf Coast. The issue was whether they were up to legal or illegal activities. Had they taken Sandra and Daryl? Were they after the Capone treasure? Was it one of the brothers who'd taken a potshot at me?

Tinkie, who'd gotten up to walk to the porch window that gave a lovely view of the isolated beach and the bay, came over to me. "Let's get out of here," she whispered in my ear. "There's someone on the beach watching the house with binoculars."

"Janet, if you hear from Sandra, Daryl, or Harold, call me instantly. Tinkie and I have to go."

We beat it out of her house, stopping only once to pet a clowder of cats that swarmed my legs. Pluto would be at Dahlia House, waiting for his cuddles once I closed this case.

Tinkie got the gun out of the trunk, just in case, and we

split up and flanked what appeared to be a man on the beach. He was facing the land, not the water, his binoculars trained on a patch of sea oats growing on a small hillock of sand in front of Janet's house. He was oblivious to our approach.

When Tinkie pressed her finger into his ribs, he almost jumped out of his skin.

"What are you doing spying on Janet Malone?" Tinkie asked him, still using her finger to make him think a gun was poking him.

"It's those damn cats! I'm protecting the seabirds. Those cats are predators." The man wore an army vest with net pockets and several bird guides were tucked in them. Which could indicate he was telling the truth, or just that he was detail oriented with his disguise.

"You think Janet Malone's cats are over here on the beach chasing seabirds?" The cats I'd seen at Janet's were hefty girls and boys and mostly happy to lounge around in the sun. They were not hunters by any stretch of the imagination. Well-fed cats seldom hunted anything except a soft pillow or a fireplace to lounge in front of.

"They're brutal murderers of birds." He pressed his lips into a thin line.

"I presume you have evidence that Janet's cats are killing things?" Tinkie asked.

"What, you want to see feathers or a carcass?"

"I want to see video or photographs of a cat doing this. Maybe it was a kid with a BB gun."

"I don't have to show you anything. I intend to make sure those cats are removed."

This guy was pushing my hot button. "You are aware that the cats are within a twelve-foot chain link fence that can't be climbed?" I pointed out.

"She can't contain those cats. No one can. Cats are evil."

"Listen, buddy." Tinkie was in his face. "Those cats never leave her yard. You are stalking her. I think Chief Thibodeau will want to know about this."

"I'm on the city council. You can call him, but he won't arrest me."

Oh, Thibodeau would love hearing this. He didn't strike me as the kind of lawman that let a silver-spoon official determine how to enforce the law.

As much as I wanted to plant his privilege right up his . . . I realized he might be valuable. If he was watching the Malone home this closely, he might know something. "Did you see a gentleman leaving Ms. Malone's last night about midnight? Silver Lexus."

"What if I did? Are you still going to report me?" The bird watcher was ready to bargain.

"Give us something we can use and we won't call the chief, if you promise never to spy on Janet again."

"Yeah, I saw him leave. I figured some of those cats would get out when the automatic gate opened so I was paying close attention."

"Did you see anything else?"

"You gonna call the chief on me?"

"No. Tell us," Tinkie said.

"There was a dark-colored pickup truck that had parked down that side street. It followed the Lexus man when he left in his car."

"Did you know the person who drove the truck?"

"Didn't get a good look at the driver or the truck. I ducked behind the sand dune over there. I mean no one bird-watches in the dead of night. I didn't want to get caught and end up in trouble."

Well, the busybody neighbor did actually have a brain for crime. "Okay." I took down the man's name and address and warned him to leave Janet's cats alone. It was time to fly. Tinkie and I had two destinations. First, Sandra O'Day's mansion, and then the parking lot at the Gulfport docks. If Harold was at the mansion—though it was unlikely—I would beat him up and then kiss him. If he wasn't, the search of his car would be even more important.

22

We pulled up the driveway to the mansion and I parked in the shade of some oak trees beside a portico. The slight slant of the sun told me it was late morning. I had to move faster. Precious hours were slipping away from us.

There was no sign of Harold or anyone else in the house, but I clung to my hope that maybe he was inside, maybe restrained and fighting mad. I could only wish Harold's devil dog Roscoe was with us. He would find his owner and punish anyone who looked cross-eyed at Harold.

"Are we going in?" Tinkie asked.

"Gun and tire iron blazing," I replied. "In just a moment."

Stillness enfolded the house, and I turned three hundred and sixty degrees to see an incredible view of the bay. The mansion was on high ground and the site had survived numerous floods and hurricanes. The worst hurricane in modern history for this region was Katrina. In 2005 it had wiped a lot of Bay St. Louis off the map. Winds, flooding, and tornadoes had destroyed property from New Orleans to Point Clear, Alabama. The Capone mansion, empty at the time, had survived with the loss of some clay shingles and shutters, according to what I'd read at the library. It was on the highest ground in the area. Even though climate change hadn't been an issue when Capone built it, he'd chosen the primo real estate in the whole region. The house would likely endure long after Sandra was dead and gone. Assuming she wasn't dead and gone already.

I pushed that depressing thought away and unlocked the front door.

The house was big, so Tinkie and I split up to cover more ground quickly. I'd given her the gun; I had a tire iron from the car, but I didn't think I'd need it. I honestly felt the house was empty. There was just a sense of stepping into a void. The essence of the humans who brought a house to life was gone.

The detritus from the party was still everywhere— champagne flutes and wineglasses sitting on tables and counters, plates and cutlery stacked on serving trays. Someone had cleaned up the food, thank goodness.

Boxes of Sandra's books were piled in a corner of the front parlor where she should have held her book signing.

I went to the mudroom to check out the blood. The rusty stain splashed in the sink looked to have come from a cut— nothing really serious. If Daryl had been injured, this wasn't enough to cause severe damage. I took photos of everything, moving from the mudroom to the laundry, the pantry, and into the kitchen. I didn't see anything out of the ordinary,

and when I accessed the back door to the garage, I saw that
Sandra's car was there as well as Daryl's BMW. So, where
were they? Had they just walked out of the party and into
thin air? It was beginning to look that way.

A set of house plans would have been helpful to look for
hidden rooms, but we didn't have access to those. I'd read
too much Poe in my youth and I imagined Sandra and Daryl
locked up in the house somewhere, slowly starving to death
or dying of thirst, so that their desiccated carcasses would
one day be found to whispers of, "Oh, so this is what happened to them."

Without the architectural plans, though, we were flying
blind. In every room I checked cabinets, pressed crown
molding and mantels, jiggled built-in light fixtures and
sconces. It was a huge house, but luckily Sandra was a neat-
nik and many of the drawers and closets were empty.

I found two hidden areas where several people could
hide for a period of time. There was no evidence Sandra or
Daryl had ever been there. I could see how handy the rooms
might be if the mansion was raided by the feds, though. I
had no doubt the hidden spaces were designed by Capone
for those emergency situations so he could escape capture
by the law or competing gangsters.

Sandra, Daryl, Harold, and the treasure remained elusive.

I met up with Tinkie on the third floor and told her about
the two hidden rooms. She told me about a passage from
a first-floor bedroom to the garage. That explained how
our missing author and assistant could have left the house
without anyone seeing them leave, but she saw no signs that
they'd gone that way.

Looking at the office, which was jam-packed with floor-
to-ceiling bookshelves, cabinets, stacks of research books

on the floor, and filing cabinets brimming with papers, I sighed aloud. It would take forever to check each book, each journal, each photograph or framed painting to see if something was hidden there.

"We'll be here the next two weeks," I told Tinkie.

"We don't have that kind of time." She checked her watch. "I feel like the sand is slipping through the hourglass for us and Dorothy."

I knew exactly what she meant. "Let's try looking for other rooms or passages."

For an hour we moved books, pressed wood panels, shifted items on the desk and tables, hunting for any indication of what could have happened.

I hated to do it, but I dumped the contents of her desk drawers on the floor—as neatly as possible. We got garbage bags from the kitchen and loaded the stuff in them so we could get help going through them. There just wasn't time to do it on site.

"We need to get to the dock and check Harold's car. As much as I want to find Sandra and Daryl, I want to find our friend more."

"Me, too." A bubble of frustration spun through my brain. "What in the hell was Harold doing out of his room?"

Tinkie gave me a look.

"But he didn't go to Janet's. If he'd gone to Janet's he would be . . . there." I'd almost said "safe" but Janet looked like she could put a kink in a man if she chose to do so.

"Janet *said* he hadn't gone there. That doesn't mean it's true."

Tinkie was right. We had no reason to believe Janet would tell us the truth about anything.

Even though the house was chilly, I was sweating from

exertion. We took a seat on the stairs outside the office. I called Coleman and told him about Sandra's brothers, who were both basically MIA. He'd have the best chance of working with the local authorities to verify their locations. He agreed to visit Thibodeau and get the local coppers on the job.

"Tinkie and I haven't found anything." I couldn't help the note of defeat in my voice. I'd hoped so hard that Harold would be in the mansion, detained but okay.

"Don't forget to check the burial vault," Coleman suggested. "If you need help, Oscar and I can come."

It was a tempting offer, but Coleman was more useful liaising with the local law. "Where are Millie and Cece?" I asked.

"They went to look over Harold's car. The Gulfport police are going to fingerprint the car and see if the GPS can tell them anything."

"Thank you." It was a relief Coleman had covered that base. "I'm worried sick about Harold. Do you have any theories of where he might be?"

Coleman hesitated for a moment, but then said, "I had hoped he was in the mansion. That he was tied up or locked in a room. Are you sure you've searched the place thoroughly?"

"No. To be honest, we found some hidden rooms and a passageway from the first floor to the garage, but there could be more here. We need floor plans."

"I can ask Thibodeau about that. He can get a warrant if we produce enough evidence."

Coleman knew how to make the legal system work for him, a fact I never took for granted.

"How'd you get into Sandra's place?" Coleman asked.

"Janet had another key. And, by the way, Janet's and Daryl's cars are here. I'm sure Thibodeau knows that."

"I'm sure he does. Which begs the question, how did they leave the premises?" He let a beat go by. "*If* they left. Something tells me they're still there."

I didn't doubt Coleman's gut. But Tinkie and I had looked everywhere in the house. If Sandra and Daryl were secreted there, we'd missed it entirely. "Did you have time to check out the flannel shirt?"

"When I see Thibodeau, I'll tell him. He might be able to get a search warrant for the Beer and Bait. We can hope. But even if Donnie Marcus was hiding in the shrubs, it doesn't prove he had anything to do with the disappearance of Harold, Daryl, or Sandra."

"How do we find hard evidence?" I was frustrated with my inability to bring this case home. It should have been so simple. Three people didn't simply disappear from a small town with a population of less than 14,000 people. "I really thought I'd find something here that would point us in the right direction."

"I had hoped so, too."

"Coleman, do you think Harold is okay?" I tried not to ask him questions like this, but my lack of success in the mansion had left me feeling vulnerable.

"If he was taken because of Sandra and Daryl, the kidnapper has no reason to harm him. If he was taken for money, we'll get a ransom demand. Let's try not to jump to the worse conclusion first. Most people in town have no reason to associate Harold with you and your investigation."

"Thank you." Coleman and his facts made me feel better.

"But if someone is directing this at Janet . . ." He left the sentence blowing in the wind.

"If they saw Harold with Janet last night, maybe it is about her." Janet, with her fabulous singing and performance, had called a lot of attention to herself.

"That's a direction I'd follow—after you check out the mausoleum."

"Headed there now."

23

Tinkie and I found the mausoleum on the western slope of the lawn in a stand of beautiful oak trees. Spanish moss waved in the gentle breeze, and in the distance I could hear a large boat on the bay. We used caution as we approached the stone building that looked like a miniature temple to the Greek gods, including a statue of what I took to be Diana with her hounds in front of the entrance.

"There's a padlock," Tinkie pointed out.

"And so there is." The set of keys Janet had given me for the house included five. One to the front, one to the back, one to the garage, and two of unknown use. I pulled them from my pocket and the first one I tried opened the padlock.

"Why would you padlock a grave?" Tinkie asked.

"Vandals." As hard as it was to believe, it was not uncommon for lawbreakers to go into cemeteries and destroy graves and statuary. "The mansion was abandoned for a long time before Sandra bought it. Maybe the padlock dates from that time."

The sun was warm on my shoulders, and I was reluctant to step into the house of the dead. "Do you know who is interred here?"

"I'm assuming Helene Buntman." Tinkie frowned. "Perhaps some of her family. The place is big enough to accommodate dozens of burials."

"Capone is buried in Illinois." I knew that much. "Why not here?"

"Maybe his family wanted him to be with them. He wasn't married to Helene."

I put my hand on the door. "That whole romance is sad. Helene had everything. Glamour, a movie career where she was treated very well, fame, excitement. Yet she was here on the Gulf Coast whenever Capone needed her. He built her a mansion and gave her the dream she wanted. But they never married each other."

"It's a great love story if you aren't Mae Capone," Tinkie said, rather sharply.

"His wife." I'd forgotten about her. As obviously Al had, too. "He never divorced Mae. In the end she took care of him when he wasn't mentally able to care for himself." I'd read about the syphilis and how in his last years he was rendered incapacitated by the disease. "I could never be that forgiving."

"Do you think Capone and Helene were lovers or just friends?" Tinkie posed an interesting question.

"I just assumed . . ."

She gave me the look that said assuming made an ass out of me. But once she'd planted the idea it took root and quickly grew. "They both had a sense of high adventure. Helene was so brave. And while she loved her movie career, she loved this place more. So much about their relationship speaks to friendship, though."

"I know you've researched Helene in the library, and we've talked to folks in town, but I really wonder how many people truly knew her. I mean, she became a psychic medium in her later years. That's just not something a lot of people do."

Tinkie was right about that. Madame Tomeeka, our school chum we grew up knowing as Tammy Odom, had not asked for her gifts. She'd begun having dreams that ended up coming true. Visions that foretold events. Messages from her spirit guides and those who had crossed over. It wasn't a comfortable gift for Tammy, but she had used it to do a lot of good. Had Helene also had the gift of truly seeing the future and the dead? Had that been the driving purpose of her life, rather than romance and love?

"I wish there was someone we could ask about the medium stuff," I said, sounding suddenly old and tired. "I searched everything the library had."

"We haven't asked Janet."

"You think Sandra's disappearance is somehow related to Helene's psychic endeavors?" After our latest Halloween case with a strange cult and human sacrifice, I really didn't want to dabble in the underworld.

"Look." Tinkie was on a roll and her eyes sparkled dangerously. "No one has ever come close to finding Capone's treasure."

"If there really was one," I threw in to try to keep this conversation on the rails.

"Hundreds of people have searched for it. Treasure hunters, ghost hunters, scientists, locals, scholars who've spent a lifetime digging into Capone. No one has found a single gold coin or dollar bill. Maybe the treasure is protected by some kind of . . . enchantment."

"Maybe there was never any treasure," I countered.

Tinkie held up her hands, palms out. "Okay, okay. I didn't mean to get you stirred up."

I didn't believe that either, but I turned back to the more fruitful points of our conversation. "If Helene and Capone weren't romantically involved, what would make a man build a place like this for her? He had strong feelings for her, whether they were platonic or romantic." That much I could concede. "And yet he left her here, buried all alone. That just seems wrong and sad."

Tinkie leaned against the wall beside the heavy door. "By the time he died, he didn't have a whole lot of say over what happened to his remains," Tinkie said. "They kind of had the best of each other. Helene got her dream of being a movie star, Capone got a fearless partner in his business. It never fell into the mundane or boring."

I realized Tinkie, too, was procrastinating about going inside. "Let's check it out." I pushed the door open and sunlight fell across the threshold of the burial house. It took a moment for our eyes to adjust to the darkness, but we found two beautifully carved alabaster vaults. Scrolls and fleur-de-lis decorated the base and corners of each. On one, the image of a glamorous flapper had been carved in exquisite detail. The other was unadorned, empty. Yet the marble slab seal was in place. I pushed at it and laughed. It would take a lot more than me to move it even an inch.

Tinkie walked forward and put her hand on the empty grave. "This is where Capone should have been laid to rest."

I wasn't certain of that, but I kept quiet. The local lore indicated she was correct, but Tinkie was a romantic. Often I was too practical, too cut-and-dried.

"We need flashlights," Tinkie finally said. "This place is dark."

I found a light switch on the wall and flipped it, but nothing happened. In all likelihood, the power to the mausoleum had been cut long ago. But the place was strangely clean and orderly. There was no dust on the sepulchers.

"Why would you run power to a grave?" Tinkie asked. "It's not like the people buried here will be doing any reading or needlework."

"I guess if someone wanted to come here to visit the dead, it would be nice not to be in total darkness." It sounded a little eerie once I said it aloud. I visited with my parents and kin often, but not at the cemetery where they were buried. I found them in the places where we'd laughed and loved.

I moved deeper into the room. The shadows in the corners could have hidden anyone or anything. And I had no real sense of how big the interior was. On a shelf at the head of the tombs, I found candles and a lighter. And a pack of cigarettes. I smelled them and realized they were relatively fresh. Unless there was some magical preservative in the vault.

Once I had the candles blazing, I examined the cigarettes. Unfiltered Camels. Someone was a hard-core smoker. When we had a little light from the candle, we found torches in holders in the wall and lit them. How people existed before electric light, I couldn't say. It was like living in a sepia world with no clear definition.

The crypt was rectangular, with only the two sepulchers, but there was plenty of room for others. Had Helene or Capone imagined that other family members would be there? The thought made me sad. To end up all alone after having lived a dream of glamour and success, adventure and freedom—it was melancholy. Anyone at any point could find themselves alone for the final chapter of their lives. The older I got, the more I understood that nothing was guaranteed, nothing inevitable, except death.

"Do you smell that?" Tinkie asked.

Her question almost made me gag, though I didn't smell anything. A charnel house equals bad odors, in my book. The combo kicked in my gag reflex. "What smell?" I finally managed.

"It's floral. Patchouli?" She moved toward the farthest wall, sniffing the air like a bloodhound. "It's incense."

Tinkie could identify at least a hundred high-end perfumes, so I didn't doubt that she had caught a whiff of something. I joined her and the musky scent made me think of warm summer nights in a garden. But where was it coming from?

I took one of the torches and set off to examine the darkest corners of the room. Tinkie grabbed a torch and came after me.

"Remember those old movies like *The Man in the Iron Mask,* where dashing heroes run around dank castle dungeons where people are tortured? I feel like we're living in one of those." Tinkie held her torch like a sword and advanced toward me in a playful way.

I struck a fencing pose. "You can be Olivia de Havilland and I'll be Errol Flynn," I teased her, trying to shake the dark mood off both of us. "'Rob from the rich, give to the poor.' It's a great motto."

"Look!" Tinkie said, poking her torch toward an ornate design on the back wall.

"Holy cow." In the flickering light of the torch, I couldn't make out all the details, but it was clearly a story of some kind, created in figures carved into the stone wall. I walked up to it and ran my fingers over the design, trying to feel what it might mean. My attempt at Braille didn't work. The figures didn't speak to me. But as I was tracing along the motif, I felt the back wall shift. I leaped backward, colliding with Tinkie.

"Hey!" Tinkie jumped back, bumping into me. Our torches locked together and for a moment, we reenacted a scene from *Highlander*, torches clashing like swords. Our shadows against the wall danced and flickered in what appeared to be a battle for survival.

"There can be only one," I said before Tinkie knocked the torch from my hand. It clattered to the floor, and when I turned around, the wall was moving on its own.

"Feet, don't fail me now," Tinkie said, heading for the front door. It slammed before she could get there.

"Damn." The word echoed in the still chamber of the dead.

24

Torn between the moving back wall and the closing front door, Tinkie and I threw ourselves at the door. Escape was the only thing on our minds. We discovered—too late—that there was no handle to pull the door toward us. No way to push it out the other direction. Our entrance into the tomb was effectively blocked.

"Try the back wall. Something was moving there." I sounded desperate, which was accurate. We clattered toward the back wall, jumping over the burning torches we'd left on the floor.

I picked one up and held it as Tinkie pushed against the wall. Nothing. We were trapped in the mausoleum and no one knew where we were. I took a deep breath and checked my phone. No signal. Whatever the place was made of had

blocked out all signals. I tried to quell the panic that wanted
to overtake me. "I guess dead people don't have a lot of use
for cell phones." I tried to make it funny but it only sounded
scared.

"You said this wall moved." Tinkie was being as reasonable as she could. "Show me. Maybe there's a way out
behind it."

"It did move." I put a hand on the relief carvings but nothing happened. I pressed down and up, tugged, and tried to
manipulate the cold stone. It had moved before. I hadn't
imagined it. "I don't know why it won't budge now, but it's
okay. They'll come looking for us."

"Unless they find Harold, they won't have a key to the
mausoleum," Tinkie pointed out. "Janet may have another
set, but I kind of doubt it. She doesn't strike me as a key
hoarder."

"The guys will figure it out. And Millie and Cece are on
the case. Our car is here. They'll know we have to be on the
grounds somewhere."

"Sandra and Daryl aren't."

Her logic only scared me more. "Stop it. We've been in
worse places and come out of it just fine. Remember, you
gave birth in someone's backyard. I thought you were going
to die then, too. But we're both just fine and Maylin is per-
fection."

"You're right." Her voice trembled. "I'm just more vulnerable because of Maylin. But she'll make me fight harder,
too. Who do you think closed that door?"

This was not a question I wanted to answer because it
didn't seem like the force that shut down our escape route
was human. I knew that wasn't logical, but we were in a
crypt, after all.

"Do you think it was the person who took Sandra and Daryl?" she asked.

"No."

"Then who?"

"Maybe Al Capone." I said it on a laugh, but my gaze searched the corners. "I heard he was very protective of his treasure."

"I feel like some poor shipmate left to guard Davy Jones's locker. Remember how there were always bones scattered around the pirate chest."

"Not a good reminder." But we laughed and the fear and tension broke. "Look, the torches are still burning. There's fresh air coming in here so it isn't a sealed facility. We just have to figure out where the air is coming from and how to make it big enough for us to get out."

"Sounds very reasonable—if we were rats or something that could squeeze through tiny places. After having that baby I'm not squeezing through anything."

"You're being silly. You didn't gain that much . . ." The look she gave me in the glow of the torch was demonic. Tinkie was sensitive about her size in both waistline and shoes. Since the pregnancy she was hypersensitive. "Hold the torches and let's keep looking."

Tinkie held both torches up as I worked on the wall carvings again. I fought the despair of being trapped in a tomb and concentrated on finding a way out. There had to be something that triggered the door or gave onto another escape route. Hadn't we been told that Capone always had more than one escape route? "What if this place was designed as a hiding place for the treasure?"

"A tomb?" Tinkie's nose wrinkled. "Ugh."

"Doesn't matter where it's hidden as long as the money spends."

"You sound like your aunt Loulane more and more every day, Sarah Booth."

The way she said it wasn't a compliment. "I know. It scares me, too."

"If I start sounding like my mama, just put me out of my misery on the spot."

Tinkie was still raw from the way her mother had callously ignored the birth of Maylin. Once again, keeping my mouth shut was the smartest thing I could do. My fingers traced along the wall, trying to move it.

Tired of holding up the torches, Tinkie leaned her elbow against the wall. When she put her weight on it, the wall moved and she stumbled. "Damn," she said, just about the most unladylike word she ever used.

"Push harder." I reached over to help put pressure on that particular section of wall, and slowly a portion of wall moved back, revealing utter darkness beyond.

"What do you think is back there?" Tinkie asked. She obviously didn't want to go in.

"Why don't you stay here in case this opening closes again," I said. "Someone has to get me out."

She put a hand on my arm as I slipped through the crack into the darkness. "I'll be right here," Tinkie said. She handed one of the torches in to me.

The flickering light was even creepier than the total darkness. I had no idea if I was in a room, a tunnel, a dungeon, or whatever. There was only black that seemed to drink the torchlight.

Tinkie poked the torch she held into the void and it helped

a little. I stepped away from the door, moving slowly, visually limited. There was something on the ground ahead of me. Something that didn't move.

"Tinkie, don't let that opening close," I called over my shoulder.

"I'm standing in the opening. I'll block it if I have to."

I moved closer to the form on the floor, a bad feeling creeping up my back. I recognized the shoes and slacks. I stepped closer, using the torchlight to check Harold's face. He looked like he was asleep, but in the torchlight his skin appeared gray, drained of all life.

To my relief when I touched his neck, he was warm. And he had a pulse. He wasn't dead, only unconscious. When my icy fingers touched his skin, his eyes opened and I almost wet my pants.

"Sarah Booth, where am I?" he asked.

"It's Harold!" I called back to Tinkie. "He's waking up."

"Why is he taking a nap in that place?" she yelled.

"Somehow I don't think it was voluntary."

"You can say that again," Harold said, sitting up slowly. "Where the hell am I?"

"In the hidden room of a mausoleum," I told him.

"Great. I can mark that off my bucket list." He sat up slowly, groaning and rubbing his head. "I think someone knocked me unconscious."

"What's the last thing you remember?" I asked him.

"I went out to my car to get my cell phone. Someone slipped up behind me and let me have it with something very hard."

"We need to get you to the hospital and get you checked out."

"Just get me out of this dark place. That'll be worth a lot." He took my hand and I pulled him to his feet.

"Tinkie, we're coming out."

"Thank goodness." Her voice was kind of wavering in the darkness. "I feel like this panel is getting ready to move. Hurry!"

I didn't need any more motivation than that and Harold was right with me. We rushed across the dark room and I slid through the opening first. He somehow managed to squeeze himself through it, too. We were all three clear when the panel shifted and closed.

I fell back against the wall and slid to the ground. I must have triggered something because the front door opened. Harold and Tinkie pulled me up as they raced to the sunshine. I feared the door would close and crush us until I fell panting on the grass. Tinkie found a large rock and put it in place so that the front door couldn't close fully.

We took a moment to inhale the fresh air and let the sun warm us. We could have died in that tomb. I would never admit to Tinkie how scared I'd been.

"Let's get Harold to the hospital," Tinkie said.

We headed to the car. It went against my instinct to leave the vault open, but I sure as heck wasn't going to say a thing about that. If thieves came to rob the grave, chances were they'd be trapped inside just like we were. I wasn't going back in there until I had power tools and a team of firemen or some safecrackers to blast me out.

It took Tinkie and I both to get Harold into the back seat. Tinkie sat with him to hold him steady. The rush to the car had taken all of his strength, and now his head lolled. I was worried about brain damage. A lump the size of a golf ball had risen on the back of his head. I had so many questions, but they would have to wait. I put the car in gear and tore out of the driveway toward the hospital, calling Coleman as I went.

"Harold's hurt. I have him. Meet us at the hospital, pronto. Can you call Cece and Millie?"

"Done and done. You're on speaker and Oscar knows the head of neurology in the hospital and is calling him right now. Harold will be okay. Don't worry. Just drive safely. We'll be there five minutes behind you."

Oscar's ability to move the medical system was apparent when we were met at the emergency room entrance with a stretcher, four orderlies, two nurses, and Dr. Brad Heitzman, world-renowned neurologist.

Harold, who'd fallen back asleep, was loaded onto the stretcher and raced through the double doors. He disappeared down a hallway with the medical team, and Tinkie and I were left standing there, paralyzed by fear.

I heard the clatter of stilettos and Cece joined us. Millie, wearing far more sensible shoes, arrived silently.

"What happened?" Cece asked.

Tinkie and I filled them in, and we took seats in the waiting room. Coleman and Oscar arrived, and we huddled together. We'd done this far too often in the past few years.

At last, Dr. Heitzman came through the doors, rolling his eyes. "Your friend isn't hurt, but he damn sure is hardheaded. He's determined to leave even though we should observe him overnight."

I knew Harold wasn't going to sit in the hospital. If he could walk, he was leaving no matter what any of us said to him. It was a toss-up as to who had a harder head, me or Harold.

As though in answer to that question, he came through the swinging doors to the waiting room, the only evidence of his assault and disappearance a bloodstain on the collar of his crisp white shirt. His clothes, though a little dirty, were neat and orderly. "I don't need observation."

Before we could respond, the emergency room doors flew open and Janet Malone swept into the area. "Harold! You're okay! Thank goodness!" She hurled herself at him and if he hadn't been okay she would have knocked him down.

"How did you know he was here?" Tinkie asked her.

"The nurses love my books. Of course they called to tell me my beau was here and being treated. Which is more than I can say for the detectives I'm paying." She cut a glare at me that could have singed my hair.

"We just got him to the hospital," I said. "You really weren't the first thing on my mind."

Harold's attention was diverted by two orderlies trying to wrangle him into a wheelchair. Janet pounced on us.

"Where was he?" she demanded.

Tinkie and I fell silent and looked at the floor.

"Well, where was he?" Janet demanded.

"In the crypt at the mansion," I said.

"What?" Janet spun in a full circle, looking at all of us. Coleman was talking with two law officers, but he was near if I needed to get him to control Janet. "Who abducted Mr. Erkwell and stuffed him in a tomb?" Janet's question was loud.

"We're looking into it," Chief Thibodeau said as he came through the doors. "Just stay out of the way and let us do our jobs."

"Your job is to satisfy me," Janet said, falling back into full bitch mode. "My taxes pay your salary."

"Janet, you're being unreasonable. Maybe you should think about what you're saying." Harold wasn't putting up with her attitude. I wanted to cheer but a look from Millie told me to shut my piehole.

Harold's words were as effective as a slap. I'd never seen an expression fall off a woman's face any faster. Her eyes grew round and she looked at him. "Chief, I apologize. Harold is right. That was totally unnecessary."

You could have knocked me over with a puff of breath. Tinkie grabbed my arm. "He's bewitched her," she whispered. "Damn."

"I believe he has."

Janet turned to us. "Did you find any leads on Sandra and Daryl in the crypt?"

We really hadn't, but I wasn't willing to give up until we had some floodlights, evidence collection, and forensic evaluation. "We need a set of the renovation plans for the mansion," I said. "We found some secret rooms and a passage to the garage in the house. In the crypt we uncovered a secret room where someone had left Harold, but there's bound to be things we missed. That place is huge."

"Harold, did you see who grabbed you? And what happened?" He'd been sleeping on the way here and I hadn't wanted to excite him. Now that he claimed to be fine, he needed to give us some answers.

"I didn't see anyone and I don't know how I got into that mausoleum. I didn't even know where I was. I was struck in the head, and when I came to I was in the dark. I tried to crawl around, but I got confused. The last thing I remember was being in the house. I'd gone out to the car to get my cell phone, which had dropped out of my pocket. I intended to take photos of anything unusual I came upon. I remember walking into the kitchen, and that's it. I came to a couple of times, but I couldn't hear anything at all. It's the closest I ever want to come to being buried alive."

"Did you see other people or hear voices at the house?" Tinkie asked.

"No one."

That meant Harold had been taken from the house across the yard to the mausoleum. Had he been dragged or placed in a conveyance of some sort? He'd been moved across the lawn, and no one had come forward to report it.

"Your car is parked in Gulfport at the ferry parking lot. You didn't go there?"

Harold frowned. "Hell, no, that makes no sense. None at all."

Someone had knocked Harold out, taken his keys, and moved the car. I assumed it was intended to send the rest of us on a wild-goose chase to Ship Island searching for Harold. If so, it had succeeded.

"I need someone to take me to my car." Harold looked at me, not Janet.

"Your car is at the Gulfport PD. They took it there to process it," Thibodeau said. "I'll call to be sure they're finished."

I checked my watch. "We'll just have time to get to Gulfport and return so we can give our official judgment on the trees."

"Those trees are incredible," Cece said. "It's going to be a tough decision. You take Harold to get his car and we'll head on to the library with Tinkie and see what we can do to help Ms. Perkins."

Cece knew the value of deadlines and was never late for anything. "Good plan. Harold and I will see you at the library, ASAP."

"The car's ready to be released," Thibodeau said, hanging up his phone. "And I'll contact the architect involved with the renovations at the mansion. We should be able to have them in an hour or so and I'll check for hidden rooms and such. The state crime lab is sending a team to collect more evidence."

"Janet, what are you going to do about the tree judging?" I checked my watch. "It's almost time to go to the library. They need to have the winners so they can announce them this evening at the soiree."

She put a hand to her forehead like Nell in a *Dudley Do-Right* cartoon. Any moment now someone was going to tie her to the railroad tracks. "I just can't do it. I can't bear to go on with this. Mary Perkins will understand. She can find someone to fill in for me."

In a way I was relieved because I knew Cece and Millie would do a fine job and do it on time and properly. They were heading to the library now.

Before I could get a word out, though, Janet turned on the tears and grasped Harold's hand. "Harold, could you stay with me for a while? I'm distraught."

Tinkie started to say something but stopped. She leaned into me to whisper, "Janet found the perfect way to twist Harold around her little finger. She needs him. That strikes Harold's Pavlovian white knight response. He's about to slobber all over himself to help her."

Harold did look well and truly caught in Janet's drama. "Men," I whispered to Tinkie. "You're good at manipulating them but Janet is even better."

"Harrumph!" Tinkie walked toward the outside door of the emergency room. Afraid that I'd hurt her feelings, I went after her, only to find her laughing.

"Well, you know it's true," I said to her.

"In fact, I do." She looked back at Harold and Janet making goo-goo eyes at each other. "Harold needs to marry. The way he looks at Maylin, I know he wants a child. And he'd be such a good husband and father. He's aged out of being a player."

We had all matured a little over the past two Christmases. "You don't know anyone local?"

"He knows everyone I do and none of those women interest him. The Gulf Coast isn't a bad drive. Janet has plenty of time to play, and Harold likes cats. Now, Roscoe may take a little while to come around to her twenty-seven cats . . ."

"Bay St. Louis is a great little town," I agreed.

"And it is the coast." She linked her arm through mine. "If he came here to visit Janet, we could come, too. You know, home away from home."

I had to laugh. No matter how we plotted, Harold would do as he wished. "Let's get busy. Harold is fine. Janet will take him to get his car and we can do what we came here to do. But since we have an hour to kill, let's go back to the mausoleum and see if we can find anything we missed."

"We have to be fast. We only have an hour."

Tinkie took up the challenge and got on the horn to our friends. "Cece, Millie, we need to talk."

In a matter of five minutes, they'd agreed to judge, I'd called Mary and made things right with her, and Cece and Millie were on the job at the library. My partner and I had just under an hour to finish sleuthing at the mansion.

25

At least five police officers were still at the temple of death, as I had begun to think of it. Oscar and Coleman pulled up right behind us, and I left my lawman to talk with the police. He'd have a lot more rapport with them than a private investigator from the Delta would. Tinkie and I walked into the crypt to find Thibodeau inside, overseeing the CSIs as they collected evidence.

"Anything interesting?" I asked the chief.

"Someone has been coming to this grave site for a while."

"Maybe it was Sandra? Who else would have a key or be interested?"

"Good questions. If we get any answers, I'll let you know. Sheriff Peters told us about the map he'd received for the ports of call for illegal liquor along the bay. I've sent some of my deputies with the coast guard to check out places where Sandra and Daryl might be hiding."

I was glad Coleman had brought in help. We didn't have time to look everywhere we needed. Plus, this case was really taxing the BSL general fund. Extra cops, overtime, special craft for water patrol—it was going to be a budgetary nightmare for Thibodeau, which is likely why Coleman was being so helpful. He understood trying to provide effective law enforcement on a budget.

"Sheriff Peters, could I speak with you?" A man in a business suit asked.

Tinkie and I were dying of curiosity, but Coleman and the man walked away. "Let's get busy." Tinkie tapped her watch. "Time's a-wastin'."

"If you get any folksier I'm going to start calling you Cornpone."

Tinkie only laughed. She headed to the back of the vault where klieg lights now illuminated the beauty of the tomb. The carvings on the back wall stopped me. I hadn't realized it because in the torchlight I could only see a small portion at a time. But now, my brain seemed to catch fire as I looked at what I'd thought were decorative scrolls. Not true. The images told a story, one that seemed to end tragically.

"Look!" I pointed at the wall. "What do you see?"

"Someone is really talented and had a lot of time to work on that design."

She didn't get it. "Isn't that a pirate and a treasure chest?"

She stared for a long moment. "I see it now. It's so stylized, I thought it was just decorative. That's amazing."

"Take a photo; we need some help interpreting this." I could make out that it was a narrative of some kind, but I wasn't certain of all the symbols or markings. Only the one in the end that showed a solitary death.

The library was aglow with Christmas lights. Tinkie and I rushed in the front door just as the clock struck the hour to judge. Cece and Millie were waiting for us with clipboards and the notes they'd made. We all four took a walk through the trees, writing down our private comments. We could have debated our choices all night long, but we were on a deadline. The librarians had to prepare certificates for the winners and they needed our answers.

"I can't believe Janet didn't want to do this," Millie said. "It's so beautiful. I'm thrilled to be part of it."

And so was I. As much as I tried to deny it, I was still a child at heart. Looking at the beauty of the trees and all of the work and imagination that had gone into creating them, I couldn't help but feel the wonder of the holiday season. I missed my family, but Coleman and I were starting our own traditions. As I snapped photos of the trees, I made a note of decorations that I would re-create at Dahlia House next year. I'd never been one to buck tradition, but some of the trees were so original and delightful. Adapting to change was a good thing—or so everyone told me.

Mary Perkins appeared at my elbow. "Are you ready to tally your votes?"

My friends nodded and we followed the librarian into a conference room.

"I've judged beauty pageants, decorated homes, Halloween costumes, and art," Cece told her. "This is the toughest decision I've had to make. So many of the trees are noteworthy and spectacular."

"We have a lot of talent here on the Gulf Coast and a lot of people working hard to raise money for the library. We're lucky," Mary said.

"I'm sorry about Janet," I added.

She shrugged. "I don't blame her. Despite how she behaves, I know she's worried about Sandra."

I didn't want to point out that Janet wasn't here because she was spending time with her new obsession, Harold. Mary was taking the high road and I didn't want to push her into a ditch.

"You ladies ready with the winners? As soon as you decide, we'll print the certificates."

"Give us another ten minutes." We still were hotly debating the most original tree. I loved one decorated with incredible papier-mâché magnolias and garlands of popcorn. Cece was all about the more modern tree made from driftwood and adorned with images from Walter Anderson, a fabulous Mississippi artist who used the natural world, particularly the Gulf, for his colorful creations. Millie had no dog in the fight for most original, but she was absolutely taken by a tree decorated with Barbie dolls for the best children's tree. It was original, but it kind of freaked me out. I was never a fan of dolls, but it was certainly creative.

"I'll be back in ten minutes. I don't mean to rush, but I have to help set up for the party tonight." Mary closed the door behind her as she left.

We debated the merits of our choices, and ten minutes later, we had a complete list of winners. Each of us was satisfied with the results.

We took the tally to Mary, and she thanked us as she got to work on printing the certificates and handing the ribbons to an assistant to put on the winning trees. "Ladies, the party starts at seven. See you here."

"Looking forward to it," Cece said. "The TV station that Sarah Booth ghosted called me and I'm providing coverage of the party tonight for them." She gave me an impudent grin. "Thanks for handing me the freelance job."

I rolled my eyes at her. She was correct that I'd forgotten all about the interview with the New Orleans station. I hadn't bothered to check my phone for a long time, and must have missed their call. Too late to do anything about it now. I had been rather preoccupied with Harold and everything else that had gone wonky.

"What are we going to do until it's time for the party?" Millie asked. "Is there something we can do to help with the case?"

We were already at the library so it was the perfect opportunity to do what I thought needed to be done. "We're going to interpret this." I showed her the photo of the back wall of the crypt.

"It looks like hieroglyphics of some kind. What will that tell us?" Millie asked.

"Maybe nothing. But the police are following the physical leads from the mansion. Coleman and Oscar are going over the floor plans and looking for any rooms or hideaways Tinkie and I missed. Maybe Sandra and Daryl are there. So this is what we can do, unless you have another idea."

"Sounds good to me," Millie said. "Maybe Mary can print this out in a large format for us. That would help."

"Let's get crack-a-lacking," Tinkie said.

"Right on, Cornpone." I had warned her. We were still laughing when Mary got an assistant to take the phone and print us each a copy of the photo of the back wall.

26

We researched symbols and religious imagery, but found nothing that matched the wall. I was deep in the stacks when my cell phone vibrated. I was surprised to see it was the number of the Beer and Bait, Daryl's parents' place. I'd heard on the news that the arson had resulted in minimal damage and the restaurant had reopened for business. I answered the call. Oh, I was eager to talk to Donnie Marcus, he of the blue flannel shirt.

I slipped out the side door into the parking lot so I could talk freely without upsetting my friends.

"Ms. Delaney," Mrs. Marcus said, her voice tense and upset. "I have to talk with you. Right now. I heard from Daryl."

"What?" Her news had blown my irritation right out of the water.

"He called me early this morning."

"Daryl called you? He's okay?" I was relieved but also annoyed. She'd waited all day to let me know.

"He said he wasn't hurt, but . . . he sounded scared." She was about to cry.

"Did he say where he was?" This wasn't the time for tears but for action.

"He couldn't say. He said they would hurt Sandra if he didn't do exactly as they wanted."

"Who is 'they'?" I looked around the parking lot.

"He couldn't say that either."

"Did you happen to record the call?"

"No. I don't do things like that."

I normally didn't record calls either. It had just been a slim hope. "It's okay. Did Daryl say if it was a man or woman who called him?" I needed as many details as I could get.

"It was a woman. He said she sounded local. And she meant business. That's what he said."

More details than I'd hoped for. "Mrs. Marcus, why did you wait so long to call me?"

"Daryl told me not to call anyone. Except Janet Malone. He told me to tell her to fire you and the other private investigator. And he said you had to call off the cops." A moment passed before she continued. "I did call Janet and she told me to call you and tell you that your detective agency is fired."

"What?" I couldn't grasp this. "Why didn't Janet call me herself?"

"I don't know. I only know that you need to stop looking for Daryl and the writer. Stop now. Not another phone call or question. If you keep on, someone is going to get hurt."

I didn't think she was threatening me, but I couldn't be completely certain. "Who's going to get hurt?"

She sobbed softly. "I'm afraid it will be Daryl. Whoever took him and Ms. O'Day doesn't like what you're doing. They said to stop all of it. Stay away from the mansion and Ship Island and all of it. Call off the police who are looking."

"I may not have the kind of power to stop the law from investigating," I told her, and it was true. Coleman would stop if I asked, but Thibodeau was like a horse with the bit in his mouth. He'd put a lot of effort and manpower into finding Sandra and Daryl, and I suspected he wasn't going to stop because of a threat.

"You have to stop them. Daryl said they would harm him. He made it sound like they would kill him if you kept prying into this."

"Did you speak with Sandra?"

"No. I didn't even think to ask."

"Are you sure she's still alive?"

"Yes. She has to be. Daryl said they would hurt him and her if you didn't stop."

"Mrs. Marcus, I found a piece of flannel at the inn where I'm staying. Someone wearing a shirt exactly like your husband's shirt was watching me and my friends. And one of my friends, Harold Erkwell, disappeared and was sealed into a tomb."

"What? Are you saying I abducted Mr. Erkwell? Or that my husband did? That's insane."

As the conversation continued, the light left the sky and darkness fell. In the winter months, there was no lingering dusk. Night came swiftly, and a chill raced over me as I stood in the dark lot alone. Soon the guests would arrive for the Christmas tree party, but right now, it was a bleak and empty time. Even the traffic on Highway 90, normally a busy thoroughfare, was sparse. Only a few headlights cut through the darkness.

"I'm not saying anything of the sort." I needed to interview her right away, but it was almost time to get dressed for the big Christmas tree party. I couldn't let Mary down by failing to be there. "I'll be out to talk to you first thing in the morning."

"Don't bother driving out here. Neither Donnie nor I want to talk with you. Someone tried to burn our place down right after you were here. We were lucky to be able to put the fire out before anything was damaged. I'm done with all of this. Just stay away and stop looking before you get my son killed." The line went dead.

If she was telling the truth, I didn't blame her. Someone had almost burned down her livelihood. And her son was missing. But until he and Sandra were found, I couldn't give up. Not even if Janet fired me. I wasn't the kind of PI to quit in the middle of a case, especially one where I felt all of us were being manipulated.

I had turned to go inside when I caught movement in a fringe of crape myrtle trees at the edge of the parking lot. A dark figure scurried away, dodging behind a donut shop. I trotted after the figure. An engine revved and a dark sedan peeled out of the parking lot beside the shop, pulling onto Highway 90. By the time I got back to the library and jumped into my car they would be long gone.

Janet might be giving up on the case, but someone else sure wasn't. And that troubled me.

We all rushed back to the inn to change clothes and be in the receiving line at the library when the party began. Folks were super gracious but curious about why Janet and Sandra had failed to show up to judge the trees. A few seemed to know that Sandra might be missing for real, but Mary kept the line moving so we didn't have to answer any really tough questions.

The library staff kept us supplied with wine, and the catered food was delicious. It was a real joy to hear the comments about the trees, and to talk with some of their creators. My friends were having a fine time. Only Harold was MIA. When I couldn't stand it any longer, I stepped into the library office area and texted him.

"Sorry, Sarah Booth. Janet is a mess. I didn't want to leave her" was the text he sent back.

"Just as long as you're safe."

"Someone is watching us" was his reply. That alarmed me.

"I'll send Coleman."

"Good idea," Harold texted. "Can you come?"

"Very shortly." I peeked out of the offices to see the party still in full swing. "Soon."

"Just be careful."

"Will do."

Weezie showed up, circling my feet, purring loudly. "What's going on with you, Your Highness?" Weezie was loving, but never fawning. She grabbed at my pants leg to demand my attention. I had things to do but I took a moment to stroke her beautiful tabby back and talk to her. I'd send one of the caterers back with a taste of shrimp dip for her. She was a gourmand kitty. Now, though, I needed to talk to Coleman.

I stood up to go and Weezie snagged my ankle, this time none too gently.

"Hey, I gotta go."

She looked deep into my eyes as her claws slowly pulled at my good black pants. I could see the material puckering as the kitty deliberately tugged. I knew I should have worn jeans.

"Weezie!" I bent down to extract her claw and she darted away under Mary's desk. I knew that was where the librarian kept her store of cat delectables, so I crawled under the desk to find a can of something. Weezie was likely feeling neglected by the commotion out in the library where everyone was having a good time. Mary wouldn't care if I doled out a little holiday treat to the kitty.

As I reached for a can of food, Weezie's claws caught the top of my hand. She dug in lightly. Enough to hold my hand in place. Weezie could be moody, but she'd never been aggressive. Something was up. I got my phone out of my pocket and turned on the light to examine the area under the desk.

The glitter of a jewel sparkled back at me and I reached under the edge of a box to retrieve an earring. It was delicate and beautiful, and looked expensive. It also looked familiar. It was very much like a pair that Sandra had been wearing during the great book brawl at the local downtown store. How had it ended up under Mary's desk?

A curl of dread made my stomach contract. I'd confided in Mary. I'd told her my plans and what I was thinking. Had I put my trust in the wrong person?

27

The party was in full swing when I returned to the library with the earring in my pants pocket. Tinkie and Millie were doing the swing to a wonderful little band that had struck the perfect note with fantastic dance tunes from the 1950s and 1960s. The lighted Christmas trees created a unique and colorful atmosphere. Chatter and laughter rang out. It was hard to believe skullduggery was afoot.

I searched the library but didn't see Coleman or Oscar. I texted my guy, and suddenly felt a hand on my shoulder. I almost screamed.

"You're nervous. What gives?" Coleman was amused and concerned.

I drew him behind a bookshelf and showed him the earring. "I think this is Sandra's. It was under Mary's desk."

"And?" He raised an eyebrow.

"Do you think Mary knows anything about Sandra and Daryl and what happened to them?"

He considered it. "It's not impossible, but why? How would this benefit her?"

He had a point. She had means and opportunity, but what could the motive possibly be? Then again, Weezie had been so persistent. But Weezie was Mary's beloved cat. Weezie wouldn't betray Mary. My head was spinning by the time I stopped my thoughts. "Okay, ignore the earring for now, but can you go over to Janet's and make sure Harold is okay?"

"Sure. You think something is wrong?"

"Harold sent some text messages that indicated someone was watching them at Janet's house. And I saw someone outside the library. It could have been a local walking by, but I don't think so." I focused on what had made me instantly suspect the figure. "They were . . . furtive. That's not a lot to go on, I know."

"I'll check on Harold and Janet, but you have to promise me you'll stay here in the library until I get back."

I didn't really have a choice. After I watched Coleman drive away, I went back inside to chat with all the wonderful people who donated to the library to keep it going. And to keep an eye on Mary Perkins. Coleman was correct in that Mary had no motive I could see to want to kidnap Sandra and Daryl. For all of her contrariness, Sandra was a big donor to the library. And Mary adored Daryl. She'd practically raised him in the library. Still, why was that earring on the floor? It was valuable, which led me to believe Mary didn't know it was there. And then it hit me. Was Mary be-

ing set up by someone to take the fall? This led me straight
to thinking that Sandra and Daryl were in serious danger.

I grabbed a glass of wine at the bar. My brain was on fire
with worrisome thoughts.

"What's wrong?" Cece slipped up to my side. "You look
like you might explode."

"I might." I ran down the last scary thoughts and was
gratified to see my anxiety resonate with my friend.

"Everything you say makes sense, except that I don't
think Mary could harm a fly."

I looked at her. "Remember, she's a librarian. If anyone
could pull off a perfect crime, it would be a librarian. They
know how to research and have the resources for it."

"Excellent point," Cece said. "But Mary?"

I felt as if I were betraying my friend even to suspect her.
"I've only mentioned this to Coleman so far, and he had the
same response."

"Uh-oh, here comes trouble," Cece said, turning her
back on a woman who was barreling toward us.

"You're two of the judges," the woman said angrily.

"Yes." I pasted on a smile.

"Well, you're dumber than a sack of rocks."

"Okay," I said brightly.

"I'm not complimenting you, you bimbo," she said.

"And who are you?" I was still twinkling away, trying
to edge her out of the middle of a cluster of partygoers who
were giving us curious looks.

"Mrs. Clarence Osteller the fifth. That handsome, talented man over there at the bar is my husband."

I was sure that meant something, but not to me. "What
can I do for you, Mrs. Clarence?"

"Don't call me that. My name is Tilly. Or Mrs. Osteller is what I would prefer."

"What can I do for you, Tilly?" I glared at Cece, who'd edged away and was watching with amusement as I tried to handle this society ninja. It was clear I had offended her and she was going to make me pay in public.

"Do you have an art degree?" she asked imperiously.

"No."

"An interior design degree?"

"No." Did such a thing exist any longer? "Is that a real college degree?"

She ignored me and kept pressing. "Fashion? Fabrics? A certificate from the Bebe Bazelton School of Design?"

"No, no, and no."

"How are you qualified to judge Christmas trees?"

"Because I volunteered to do so." I understood. She didn't like the winning trees we'd picked. "Which one is yours?" I asked.

"The blue one with silver ornaments. Everyone in town knows that's my tree and it's won for three years in a row. The Osteller Ministry and Foundation. It perfectly reflects the spirit of Christmas. Just as our tree always does."

I waited.

"Which is why it should have won."

And there it was.

She leaned in closer. "If Sandra O'Day and Janet Malone or someone with some class and taste had been the judges, my tree would have won."

"I'm sorry you were disappointed, but we selected the trees we thought best fit the categories. Better luck next year."

She stepped right into my personal space, her face inches from mine. "I want that first place prize."

Cece had finally started paying attention. She came to my assistance. "I was also a judge, and your entry didn't win. Them's the breaks, Mrs. Osteller." She linked her arm through mine and started to draw me away.

"Get back here. I'm not done," Tilly said.

"Oh, yes, you are," Cece said. She nodded at Tinkie and Millie, who'd come up to join the fracas. "Mrs. Osteller the fifth doesn't like our selections."

"So these are the other judges?" Tilly sniffed. "It figures. Plebian attire, overdone makeup, cheap shoes. No wonder none of you recognized the superior tree. My husband warned me the judges who failed to recognize the superiority of my tree would be low class. He was right. They wouldn't let Hester judge." Her lip curled. "And yet they picked you."

I almost started to laugh. Almost, because this was the craziest conversation I'd had in a good long time. But it wasn't really funny at all. It reminded me that people took things very seriously. Even tree decorating.

When Tilly stepped back, I stepped forward, stopping an inch from the old dragon. "Merry Christmas. Now excuse me, I have things to do." I grinned wide.

"You are intolerable."

"I know." I stepped back, ready to end the silly tussle, but she grabbed my arm and her bony fingers were surprisingly strong.

"No one in this town disrespects me. Or bad things happen to them."

Maybe I was already a little anxious, or maybe she really

did remind me of the Wicked Witch of the West, but she almost took my breath away.

"Move along," Cece said in a voice that brooked no disagreement. "You're a joke, lady. You didn't win and nothing will change that."

Mary Perkins had caught wind of what was happening and she came toward us with two other librarians and several volunteer staffers. They surrounded Tilly and herded her away while chatting gayly and laughing, pretending they were going to look for more wine in the kitchen.

"There's one of those ladies in every Southern town," Cece said once we had shifted into a corner of the library where we could talk. "They think they run the world. Karen on the loose."

I had to laugh, even though I was still annoyed. "She's just used to getting her way," I said. "The locals probably give her what she wants just to keep the noise level down."

"Probably," Millie said, "thereby contributing to a serious case of entitlement."

"I wonder what that ministry she mentioned is about?" It didn't seem very Christian of a minister's wife to complain about not winning a contest.

"I don't think I want to know," Millie said. "But let's schmooze some more and then Cece and I will head out to check on Harold. I just don't trust our steamy romance writer with our most eligible friend."

And I didn't completely trust the librarian, either. The earring was burning a hole in my pocket and I really wanted to confront Mary about it. That would not be wise. The best thing was not to let Mary—or Janet—know I suspected them of anything.

My friends and I circulated through the partygoers, talking with folks about the entries. I saw Mary Perkins walk out the side door, probably heading for a smoke—unless she was up to something else. I eased away from a group of twentysomethings with great ideas for next year and slipped out the door.

I heard voices coming from the side of the building, a man and a woman, arguing. I couldn't understand what they said, but the words were heated in tone. I shifted closer as fast as I could.

"You have to tell me," the woman said, and I realized I'd heard her voice but couldn't place her.

"Don't push it," the man replied. "Or you'll end up hurt."

"You must—"

"What's going on out here?" Mary came from around a corner of the library and sprinted across the parking lot. "Who are you? Stop!"

Both the woman and the man took off running in opposite directions. Mary went after one and I ran after the other. My hot pursuit ended about two hundred yards from the library when I stepped in a ditch filled with water. I went down like a floundering buffalo.

I started to cut loose with the vilest curse words I knew, but the library back door opened and several people came out. My friends separated from the herd and came toward me.

"Sarah Booth, what on earth are you doing out here?" Millie asked. She was tut-tutting as she called out for something to blot me with and warm me up.

"Forget cleaning her up. Let's just take her back to the inn," Tinkie said. She grabbed my arm. "What the heck were you doing, running around out here in the cold in those pants and that silk blouse? You're soaked and are gonna catch your death of cold."

"I'm fine." I had to grit my teeth to quell the chattering. "I was chasing someone," I said. "And Mary Perkins is out here chasing someone else."

Oscar had joined us, and Tinkie turned to him. "Find Mary. She's out here running around, too."

I pointed east, my teeth clacking and my arm shaking. "She went that way."

28

Mary had totally disappeared from the library, but her car was still in the lot. We left Oscar to wait at her car to be sure she returned safely. Tinkie took me to the inn, and Cece and Millie—who were beside themselves with glee at the assignment—had gone to Janet's to check on her, Harold, and Coleman. They would join us at the inn. I could have called Coleman to come to our room, but the girls had begged me not to. They were desperate for an excuse to check in on the couple and had promised to be alert to any danger.

"They're going to drive Harold to madness," I whispered to my partner.

Tinkie only rolled her eyes and waved them on their way. If mischief was on the loose, we needed to know that everyone was safe. Besides, Harold and Janet deserved a little

aggravation. And Cece and Millie had earned a little pleasure after stepping in as judges. As for Coleman, I wasn't
worried. Yet. But he'd been gone longer than it should have
taken him to do a wellness check on Harold. If he'd been
at the library, he might have been able to catch the person
I was chasing.

We were pulling into the inn parking lot when I turned
to Tinkie. "Could you let me out and go check on Mary?"

"Sure thing. Oscar is at her car. If something were wrong,
he would have called."

"I know, but she was really sprinting after that person. I
just want to be sure she either caught him or made it back to
the library safely. If she isn't at the car or in the library cleaning up, please drive around and look for her. She could have
sprained an ankle. For such a small town, Bay St. Louis has
a lot of action going on." I didn't want to think that Mary
might possibly be meeting with a villain or evildoer. I really
liked Mary, and we shared the common bond of Weezie.

"And what about you?" Tinkie asked, instantly suspicious that I was up to no good. "What are you going to do?"

"I'm going upstairs to take a hot, hot shower and put
on sweat clothes, fix a drink, and then plot my next move.
Coleman should be home any minute once Cece and Millie
start yakking at Janet's. Assuming all is well with Harold,
we'll move forward from there." I didn't normally lie to my
friends, but I needed to do something, and I needed to do it
alone, quickly, and quietly.

"That's true. Coleman won't be able to keep a straight
face with those two yanking Harold's chain. Okay, get out.
I'll wait here and watch until you make it inside."

I opened the car door and then lightly grasped my partner's hand on the steering wheel. "Thank you, Tinkie."

"You're welcome." She laughed. "You're too serious. Lighten up, or I'm going to worry."

I sang one verse of "Rocking Around the Christmas Tree" until Tinkie put her hands over her ears and started moaning. "Hey, do you think Harold is really smitten by Janet?"

"Time will tell," she said. "Now get in that shower before you seriously freeze to death." Her eyes lit up. "Then again, if that happened I could take you to the pier and stand you up as an ice sculpture."

"Thanks, but no thanks." I got out and closed the door. I trotted across the lot and up the stairs as fast as I could go with frozen feet. When I opened the door of my room, Tinkie tooted the horn and drove off.

I rushed inside and called an Uber, turned on the shower full blast, and stepped in as soon as it was hot. I didn't waste a second. In ten minutes I was dry, in warm clothes, and headed out the door. The Uber was waiting for me on the main street in front of the inn office. I gave the driver the address of the mansion. Tinkie would be fit to be tied, as would Coleman. But there wasn't a minute to waste.

As the car pulled up in front of the mansion, I hesitated. Up on the hill, the big house was dark and forbidding. When it was lit up, it had a certain grace and beauty to it. Wearing the finery of Christmas, it had looked magical. Now, alone and dark, it held an edge of danger. I had a sudden and unpleasant thought of the old hotel in Stephen King's classic, *The Shining*. Were there ghosts of prohibition players and the Dixie Mafia partying inside?

I considered calling Coleman or any of my friends and waiting for their arrival. It made sense to do that. But I was driven to move forward. *All work and no play makes Sarah*

Booth a dull girl. I could almost see the typewritten words on the page.

"Beat it, Stephen King," I said.

I handed the driver a ten for a tip and began the gentle climb up the driveway. My intention was to go to the mausoleum, but my feet took me to the house. My fingers searched my jeans pocket for my phone. Just feeling it gave me more confidence. I could always call for help. Bay St. Louis was a small town.

Before I got to the front door I stopped and checked my phone to be sure I hadn't missed any calls from Coleman, Tinkie, or the rest. Nothing. I went to the door. I still had the keys to the mansion, and I opened the front door easily. When I was inside I was tempted to turn on the lights, but something held me back. The truth was, I didn't have a clue what I was doing there. I'd followed a hunch. Not just a hunch, but a compulsion.

I stood in the foyer, listening to the house that had seen so much history. Glamour, intrigue, passion, disappointment, schemes, and crime had lived within the walls. And possibly two recent abductions.

I felt the earring in my jean pocket. I'd transferred it from the black pants I'd probably ruined in the ditch. Why? I didn't know that either. It was almost as if I were being directed by an external force. I was a great believer in intuition, but as a private investigator, I'd learned that evidence was the pot of gold. A gut check or feeling might end up being a good lead but only evidence could solve a crime. I had no real reason to be skulking around this house.

Noise at the top of the beautiful stairs made me freeze in my tracks. Someone else was in the house. And they weren't going to a lot of trouble to hide that fact.

There was the sound of footsteps—high heels. It was the clackety-clack of a woman in fancy shoes. I looked up the staircase and gasped. A spotlight came on, illuminating the top of the stairs. An elegant woman stood there in a black, cleavage-revealing tulle gown and enough diamonds to light the room. She came down the stairs, her eyes wide and slightly demented.

"All right, Mr. DeMille, I'm ready for my close-up," she said with grand drama, her eyes wild and crazed. She looked at me. "You can call me Norma, dear, and bring me a drink."

Oh, I was gonna get my dang ghost. "Dammit, Jitty, what are you doing here?"

"This is the perfect staircase for my Gloria Swanson scene. I adore that movie. I've watched it a hundred times. I can recite all of Gloria Swanson's lines. She was the best, wasn't she?" She did a pirouette and swept up to me. "Care for an autograph? I'm quite the celebrity, you know."

"I care to give you a bump on the noggin!" I was tempted to ka-bong her, but she wouldn't notice. "Why are you always showing up and scaring me?"

"What would you do without me?" she taunted. She was pure devil—in a black dress.

"Age gracefully, without a heart attack."

"You're always claiming I endanger your health, but you're the one running around town swimmin' in ditches in forty-degree weather."

"Why are you here?" She wouldn't answer but I always asked.

"I'm here for you, Sarah Booth."

"Explain, please."

"If I told you I'd have to kill you." Her impudent grin made me laugh.

"Jitty, you're slowing me down." I looked around the house. "I need to find something and get out of here."

"Find what?" She settled on top of the stairs, her diamonds sparkling in the moonlight coming through a window. "What could be here that would help?"

"I don't know." Jitty was the one person I didn't have to lie to. "I don't really know what I'm looking for. Maybe it's in the crypt."

"You've almost been shut up in that place once already. Maybe wait until you have a partner here to make sure the door can be opened. Someone like . . . Coleman! Seems to me a little canoodling in a tomb might add some kink to your—"

"Don't you dare say it!"

"You're just afraid to unleash those dark passions."

"Dark passions my as—elbow! That place is just creepy and dangerous." It had been unnerving, even with Tinkie beside me. Alone, it was too big of an ask of my superstitious self.

I stepped around Jitty and started up the stairs. I had no clue where to go or what to look for, so I just followed the same compulsion that had brought me to an empty mansion at near midnight. At the third floor, I entered Sandra's office. My fingers touched the earring in my pocket. Why was I there?

"Better get a move on. You gonna be reported for trespassing." Jitty had abandoned her glamorous movie queen persona and was back to her normal self, wearing Christmas leggings with Santa Claus and Rudolph on them. When I wore them, Santa's face was kind of distorted, but Jitty was svelte and slender. One more reason she annoyed me.

"Thanks, Jitty." My intuition had led me there, but my

brain hadn't conjured a plan. "You're right. I should just leave." The room was so chockful of books and files and drawers and cabinets I'd never find anything useful. And we'd already looked in all the obvious places.

"Keep in mind, darling, that money, passion, and revenge aren't the only motives for murder."

I swung around to face her. "What else?"

For one brief second, she was Gloria Swanson again. "Vanity." There was a popping sound, like a champagne cork, and she was gone.

I turned on my cell phone light, annoyed with myself for not bringing a better flashlight. I had a Q-beam in the trunk of my car, along with a gun, but Coleman had my car. A book title caught my eye. *The Glamorous Stars of Film.* I pulled it out and something else hit the floor.

I picked up an earring matching the one in my pocket. Now it was time to get out of the house.

29

Sirens wailed and wobbled toward the mansion, reminding me that, technically, I was trespassing. I hadn't called the police, but someone had. There wasn't another house nearby. I had two choices. Stay and talk to the police or slip out of the house and head back for the inn. The night was cold, but I was warmly dressed and I could hoof it back to my room. I slipped down to the first floor and ducked into the bedroom where Tinkie had found the passageway to the garage. There were bound to be other exits, but I didn't have the time or inclination to hunt for them.

I had both earrings and the book of movie stars, and I took the coward's way out. I ran for it. Through the hidden door and into the garage. The smell of exhaust almost knocked me to my knees. Sandra's classic T-bird with the

hardtop in place was running—had been running—and the
fumes had accumulated in the garage. Who would do such
a thing? And why?

I ran around to the vehicle to turn it off when I realized it wasn't empty. Someone was in there. The person was
slumped over into the passenger seat and I reached in to
turn the car off. I shifted the female body to see if the person
was alive.

"Mary!" I stepped back. It was Mary Perkins and she was
barely breathing. I opened the garage door wide just as a patrol car and ambulance whipped in to block any attempted
escape. The officer had no worries. After inhaling all that
poison, I wasn't able to run anywhere. I sank on the grass
beside the garage and gave in to a coughing fit. "Car! Car!"
Sounding like a crow with a lisp, I pointed into the garage.
"Someone in car!"

My cell phone began ringing and I fumbled in my pocket.
I was so light-headed I thought I might pass out, but I concentrated on collecting myself. After a few deep breaths of
clean air, I felt much better and looked up just in time to see
two medical rescue officers carrying Mary out. An oxygen
mask covered her face, but the EMT gave me a thumbs-up
to let me know she was alive.

"We think she's going to be okay," he said. "You got to
her just in time." They pushed the stretcher inside the ambulance and slammed the doors.

The phone rang again and Coleman's questions were not
unexpected. "Are you okay? Where are you?"

I loved that he was checking on me. Had I run into the
person who tried to kill Mary, I could have been in dire
shape. "I'm fine. I'm at the mansion. I found Mary Perkins.
I just hope it was in time."

"We've been looking for Mary, and you." Coleman was already driving while we talked. We hung up as he pulled up the driveway. He was out of the car and had me in his arms in record time. "Are you hurt?"

Even though I knew he had absorbed the ambulance, squad cars, and commotion, he was totally focused on me. "I'm fine. Mary Perkins was in a running car in the garage with the doors closed. Someone tried to kill her."

Coleman helped me to my feet. "This has gone too far. I want to talk to Thibodeau."

"So do I." He wasn't leaving me out of this conversation. I needed to tell the chief what I had touched and how I happened upon Mary. Luckily, I had a key to the mansion so I hoped a charge of trespassing was not in my future.

Thibodeau waved the ambulance down the driveway with a squad car for an escort. He turned to me and drilled right in with his questions. I told him about everything except the earrings. As I was talking, I noticed the book about movie queens on the lawn. I'd clutched it even as I ran out of the garage for my life. As soon as I finished with the chief, I'd retrieve it.

Two officers came out of the garage and signaled Coleman inside to examine the car. I stayed with the chief, wisely deciding not to push it.

"How did you happen to be here at the mansion?" Thibodeau finally asked the question I'd been hoping to avoid.

"Someone at the library party said something that got me thinking. I realized I needed to look harder for clues to the whereabouts of Sandra and Daryl. The mansion was the logical place to look. The last time I was here, I got trapped in the mausoleum, so . . ." I shrugged. "There's so much stuff in this house, clues could be anywhere. And I have a key." I held it up. "I wasn't trespassing."

The look he shot me told me how little he believed that statement. And also that he didn't care. "So you came here after falling in a ditch full of freezing water *and* you left all your friends and Coleman behind?"

"I had a compulsion." I lifted my hands palms up in the universal sign of surrender. "I don't understand it myself. But it's a good thing I did come here. I mean Mary . . ."

"Some people would see that coincidence as . . . more than coincidental."

I nodded. "I can see that. But then why would I rescue her if I was trying to kill her? And why would I have a burn on to off Mary?"

"I don't have a clue," he said. "Not about Mary and this, or about where Sandra and Daryl are, or who may have taken them. Nothing about this makes sense. But I promise you, I won't quit until I have those two back here safe and sound and the responsible people in jail. No matter who they are."

Mary Perkins was normally my source of info on the locals, but I had to ask Thibodeau about the liege lady of the town, Tilly Osteller. "What kind of ministry are the Ostellers involved in?"

He sighed. "It's a prosperity church. They have a mega-facility north of I-10 not so far from where the Marcuses live. They were on the beach until Katrina blew them inland. A church member donated over a hundred acres for the new church and entertainment facilities. As I understand, the complex has a movie theater, bowling alley, all the amenities for praising the Lord. Locals call it Six Flags Over Jesus."

His sarcasm tickled me, but I was more interested in learning about the Ostellers and the church. "Is Tilly from an old family?"

"Yes, she is. Her great-grandfather was in the seafood business. He ran shrimp boats out of Biloxi, Gulfport, and here. At one time I think they ran the ferry to Ship Island. Tilly hated the fishing industry and the water. She is . . . too refined for that kind of life and work." To his credit, he kept a straight face. "When Clarence came to town, preaching at the local Methodist church, Tilly was at the head of the line to date him."

"This was what, thirty years ago?"

"Maybe more. I think Tilly was very young when they married. They left town for a while, but then came back and started their church. I'm not sure what they believe except that Jesus wants everyone to be rich. Especially them."

"And Clarence?"

"From Chicago, I think. But his family was from here, back in the twenties and thirties. He's a dapper dresser. Has a real flair for fine living. You saw him at the library. Charismatic." Thibodeau hesitated. "There were rumors . . ."

"Of what?"

"That he was involved with an unsavory element."

"Seriously?" This was a great lead.

"Look, he doesn't need illegal connections. The man rakes money in every Sunday. He has a radio broadcast and a TV show on cable. He's good-looking and polished, and a number of wealthy widows chase him even knowing he's married to Tilly."

"And how does she take that?"

Thibodeau shrugged. "As long as the money rolls in, I don't think she really cares."

"Was Sandra O'Day one of those women in hot pursuit?" Of all the things we'd checked, we'd failed to think about a religious motive for the abduction. Or a jealous spouse or lover. I'd been far too focused on treasure, rivalry, and jealousy.

"I don't know," Thibodeau admitted. "I've honestly done all I can to stay clear of Sandra and Janet. They are such total pains in the butt. I would just head in the opposite direction when I saw them coming."

"And Mary told me Sandra was politically active and had made a few enemies in that arena."

"And a lot of friends who gave her solid support. Heck, I agreed with a lot of the issues and policies she talked about. She said she was going to campaign for a seat on the school board and she could give the current seat holder a run for her money. In fact, I heard she'd ignited Janet's social conscience, too. Janet may be nuts, I mean, twenty-seven cats? But she's also bright and has had exposure to a lot of things that could push Mississippi to a better future instead of wallowing in the past." He sighed. "And I've learned she can be fun and funny. She can help Bay St. Louis if folks let her."

"If politics were involved in the abductions, which woman would more likely be taken?"

"It's a hard question. The goal may be to make Janet suffer. For all the catfighting between the two, an astute observer could have seen they cared about each other."

It was early in the morning and I was very tired. It had been a long day. I realized, standing in the cold, how much easier it was to work a case in a community like Zinnia, where I knew the lay of the land. Background was everything, and I was at a disadvantage with Sandra, Janet, and the wild dark past of coastal Mississippi. I tried one more direction.

"Tilly Osteller's family. They were in the fishing business. Were they also associated with Al Capone?" It was a wild guess.

"They could have been." Thibodeau nodded his head. "They easily could have been. I'll have to check the time frame but that's very likely, and it would explain the money Clarence had banked to start his mega-church. We all assumed that it was insurance money from the church on the beach that Katrina blew away, but even after what that new complex cost, Clarence is still flush with cash."

Tinkie could easily get Harold or Oscar to check the financials on the Ostellers and her resources would be faster than anything Thibodeau could employ. "Did Mary Perkins know anything about the Ostellers? Beyond their involvement in the tree competition?"

He shrugged. "I suspect they support the library with donations and help fund social events. They have a lot of money and they wield a lot of influence locally."

Which begged the question of what the Ostellers might have as an end goal. And, even more important, were they somehow tied to the history of Bay St. Louis, Helene Buntman, Al Capone, and the mansion?

Coleman came out of the garage and put his arm around me. "I'm going to take Sarah Booth home if you've finished asking her questions," he said.

"Sure thing. I know how to reach her if I need her. And by the way, y'all did a good job on the Christmas tree judging. Will you be staying for the big parade?"

"We hope to," I said before Coleman could answer. "Right now we need to swing by the hospital to check on Mary." The paramedics had assured me she was going to recover, but I wanted to see for myself.

Coleman kept his arm around my shoulders as we went down the drive to the Roadster. Coleman had thankfully put the top up since the temperature had dropped significantly. That was winter on the Gulf Coast. Balmy one minute, cold the next.

He got on Highway 90 and drove past the darkened library to the hospital. We easily found Mary's room and Coleman waited outside while I checked on her. She was awake, but still feeling pretty low.

"Did you see who did this?" I asked her.

"No. I was chasing that figure. I ran around the donut place and someone in the shadows hit me in the head. I went down hard." She held up her hands to show the abrasions on her palms. "When I woke up, he was throwing me into a car."

"So you saw him then?" I couldn't help the hope that rose.

"Not really. The garage was dark and I was woozy. My head was throbbing, and blood had gotten in my eyes."

"What happened next?" I was disappointed she hadn't even caught a glimpse, but that wasn't out of the ordinary. After a strike on the head it took awhile to realign with reality.

"I'm not certain. I came to in the car, but I couldn't get the door open. There were fumes everywhere. I blacked out again. The next thing I remember is being with the paramedics in the back of an ambulance. They said you rescued me."

"I found you, but the EMTs rescued you. If I'd stayed in the garage any longer, I would have been a victim, too." It had been a close call for both of us. I was just relieved Mary was going to be okay.

"What were you doing at the mansion?" Mary asked.

"Looking for clues as to what happened to Daryl and Sandra. My last visit there I was locked in a tomb," I reminded her. And then released, which made even less logical sense. "I talked with Tilly Osteller at the library tonight. After I fell in the ditch chasing one of the two people we saw outside the library, it occurred to me that I might have overlooked something. I had a strong urge to check the mansion. And I'm glad I did."

"Me, too. I would be dead."

That was a gruesome thought. My hand strayed into my pocket and I touched the earrings. I opened the door and checked the hallway. No one was coming, at least not right now. "Mary, I found one of Sandra's earrings under your desk. Weezie led me to it. That's really what sent me to the mansion. I thought maybe it was a clue."

She sighed. "You thought I might be involved in the abduction."

"Maybe." I wasn't going to lie.

"And you think Weezie would betray me?"

I had to smile at that. "I was a little shocked." Weezie was not a two-timing cat. Mary was her person.

"Maybe she was sending you to rescue me." Mary had regained her humor and wit. And possibly the right answer to her cat's behavior. "Think about it. She led you to the earring and that's pretty much how you ended up at the mansion."

Mary had several good points. "Weezie *was* determined that I find the earring. I believe Sandra was wearing them the night she disappeared." I pulled it from my pocket and put it on the hospital table in front of her. The diamonds sparkled.

"Yes, she was wearing those earrings." Mary picked it up and examined it, then put it back on the table.

"Any idea how it got in your office?"

She shook her head. "I don't. Of course Sandra's been in my office dozens of times, but the day she disappeared, no. And she had the earrings on at her house for the beginning of her party."

"Which would mean someone took the earring from her and put it in your office. Or that Sandra herself visited your office and left it for you. Who all has access?"

"Everyone in town. Anyone could have planted it there. During the tree judging party people were going in and out, some using the staff's private bathroom if the public one was busy."

She was right. It could have been anyone. "I found the other earring in Sandra's study, before I found you. I didn't get much of a chance to look thoroughly for other clues."

"Why not?"

"I heard sirens coming my way and I panicked. I thought the police were coming because I'd been seen sneaking into the house. That's why I slipped out through the garage. That's why I found you."

"Who called the cops?" she asked.

Another good question, and one I'd failed to ask Thibodeau. I'd take care of that before I left the hospital. "I don't know. They were in the driveway when I opened the garage door. That's how they were able to help you so quickly."

"Someone is pulling our strings," she said, anger flickering in her eyes. "I think they intended that I be found before I died."

"Was Daryl Marcus in your office recently?"

"I can't say. Daryl has a key to the library and my office.

He's always allowed in there because he does research for Sandra at all hours. He and Sandra are huge donors."

I nodded. "Daryl loves you. He wouldn't want you seriously harmed, would he?"

Instead of answering, Mary asked, "None of this makes sense. None of it. Not the disappearances, the strangers showing up to spy on us." Her anger grew. "What's the point of this charade?"

30

When I left Mary she was frothing at the mouth to get out of the hospital, determined to find her own answers. Coleman and Thibodeau were still talking so I joined them near the emergency room exit.

"Chief, who called you to go to the mansion?" I asked.

He frowned. "I assumed it was you."

"No. I'm glad you showed up, but I didn't call."

"Excuse me." Thibodeau stepped away as he hit his radio. I could overhear him as he asked the dispatcher to find out where the emergency call had originated. It didn't take long. He came back to me.

"Someone in the house called for help. The call originated from the O'Day landline in the mansion."

My first thought was to wonder who still had a landline,

but then reality hit. Someone had been in the house at the same time I was. Someone had been inside, slithering around and dodging me, and that person had called the police while I was searching Sandra's office. To get me arrested for trespassing or to prevent Mary dying? I couldn't say for certain.

Goose bumps rippled over my body. Mary was right. We were being played left and right by someone who was a master puppeteer. And I didn't like it at all. It was someone on the scene, watching and paying attention to everything we were doing. Why? What was the benefit of this?

I hooked my arm through Coleman's, told the chief adios, and led my man out the emergency room doors. "Let's go over to Janet's house. I guess everyone is there now."

"I told them I'd bring you back." He opened the car door for me and in a moment he was driving toward the writer's house.

"What happened to you? You went to check on Harold and never came back. Is he okay?"

Coleman's eyes narrowed. "I don't know what's going on with him."

That sounded ominous. "Has he fallen for Janet?"

"He acts like it, but there's more to this than meets the eye."

"Is he playing her?" Harold was always up to help Tinkie and me, but he was never duplicitous. Or hardly ever, though we'd discovered he was a damn fine actor when he needed to play a role. We had asked him to seduce information out of Janet. I couldn't help but wonder if he was playing a lovelorn swain to benefit us.

"I honestly can't tell," Coleman said. "If he isn't soliciting info from her, he fell mighty hard, mighty fast. He hangs on to Janet's every word. That's not Harold to me. He met her what, a day ago? And he's over at her place right now in a smoking jacket sipping martinis on her patio on the roof. She does have a magnificent telescope up there. It's the perfect place to celebrate the solstice."

We pulled up into Janet's driveway. When we were at the house, Coleman cut the lights and killed the engine. In the beautiful starlit night I could hear the water's lullaby only a hundred yards away. Janet was brave to live right on the bay, but Mary had explained that her house had been designed to survive hurricane force winds. While the Buntman mansion claimed the highest ground in Bay St. Louis, Janet's house was well above sea level.

"Just keep an eye on Harold, please. If you think he needs an intervention, we can do that." I didn't want to interfere in his love life or stargazing, but I also didn't want to see my friend harmed.

"Harold's a grown man, he—" Coleman didn't finish. He slipped out of the car through the window without opening his door. "Stay here. Don't open the door or the interior light will come on."

"What?" I asked.

"There's someone down on the beach behind that sand dune and the sea oats. Looks like he's spying on the house."

I swiveled to look but saw only the glitter of moonlight on the water. "I don't see anything."

"Someone is there. I saw them."

"It could be her creepy, nosy neighbor. The cat hater."

"Could be, but whoever it is, he's going to explain it to me."

I handed him my gun from the glove box. I had no intention of being left behind, but Coleman was far more experienced with a gun.

"Stay here."

"Sure."

He didn't linger to argue. He was just suddenly gone. Coleman had that ability, which I coveted and admired. I couldn't hear anything but what I took to be the normal sounds of night on the bay. There were a few birds calling and the water shushing. Not a single sign of a car on the road.

I hurried down to the beach to see if I could pick up Coleman's trail. I couldn't use my phone light to check for tracks, and I realized that I could really make matters much worse if I pushed onward. Coleman always told me that I could make things more dangerous by splitting his focus from finding the culprit to protecting me. For once I decided to do what he asked.

I dropped onto the cold sand behind the dune and waited, listening hard. The bay sang softly against the shore, and the cold, clean smell of the beach wafted on the breeze. We were far enough from the downtown area that the water and breeze smothered any music from the bars. Overhead, a waxing moon hung low. It would likely be full for Christmas, the last moon of the year.

The sound of heavy breathing drifted to me. I tucked myself deeper against the dune and peeped over the top, through the sea oats. A man was running along the beach in the deep sand. Or it *looked* like a man. I couldn't really tell because whoever it was wore a bulky coat. They ran fast, like a sprinter, and seemed light on their feet.

"Stop!" Coleman was on the hard road some seventy yards behind, but gaining. We were going to have an answer about our stalker very soon. I stood up and trailed behind the two running figures.

The person in the sand cut across a dune and up to the

pavement where they put on a burst of speed. They both had to be tired. They'd been running for a while. Coleman was keeping pace with the figure, but no longer gaining.

Headlights pulsed on in the dark night and a powerful engine came to life. I could make out the outline of a sedan, and the lead figure jumped into the car, which quickly turned around and took off down the road.

Coleman was only fifty yards away, but not close enough to catch the fleeing vehicle. He jogged to a stop and watched the red taillights disappear down the highway toward Waveland. There was no chance of catching them. By the time we got a car, they'd be long gone. Nonetheless, I jogged back to the Roadster parked at Janet's house and drove down the road to pick Coleman up. He had to be exhausted. He'd run like a scalded politician.

"I almost had him," Coleman said as he got in the passenger seat.

"Almost. Did you get a look at him? Could you tell who it was, or if it was a man or woman?"

"I couldn't tell. Whoever it was is fast, though. They're athletic."

Just our luck to have an athletic Peeping Tom spying on us. "I just wonder what they were hoping to see at Janet's. This isn't the first time someone has been watching her place."

"Do you feel she's being totally honest with you?" Coleman asked.

"I don't know. It doesn't make sense to waste money hiring us if she's going to lie to us, but so little of what goes on with Janet or Sandra seems to make sense." I parked in the driveway and we got out, aware that little kitty eyes glowed back at us from two dozen places. They were on the

porch, under shrubs, on top of columns, on windowsills—
everywhere. "That could have been someone trying to mess
with Janet's cats. One of her neighbors is determined to
harm them, I fear."

"If that's the case, once this disappearance is resolved,
I'll sit out here and set a trap for that person. Harming
helpless animals is never okay. Never. I'm always glad to be
sure those cretins get the punishment they deserve."

I gave him a big, mushy kiss before we entered the house.
"You are my hero." We opened the door and stepped into
Grand Central Station.

Janet was on the telephone, arguing vehemently with
someone. Tinkie was on another phone, also arguing. Cece
was transmitting photos and video back to Ed Oakes at
the newspaper, and they were periodically having a yelling
match. Harold was at a computer, furiously typing. Everyone looked up as we entered and started talking at once.

Coleman held up a hand to silence them. "What's going on?"

"You won't believe this. Those records from my parents'
attic," Janet said, putting a hand over the phone to muffle her
response. "Harold is tracing some of the funds that Al Capone had invested and that no one but my great-grandfather
knew about."

"There's money?" I asked. I hadn't really anticipated this.

"Possibly a lot of it," Harold said. "I'm still trying to
track it. Samuel Malone was a genius at hiding the financial
trail. No wonder Capone trusted him. This is . . . big!"

"Offshore accounts?" I asked.

"That and god knows what else, but with computers, I
think I'll be able to follow the trail."

I looked at Tinkie and she mouthed the words, "The Capone treasure is real!" Her eyes sparkled with excitement.

Was this the reason for the spying and attacks, the kidnapping and shots fired? Did someone else know the records were in the house? I thought of the man shooting at me. But that didn't really make sense, because the boxes of files had been there, in an empty house, for at least two years. There were no guards, no security, not even one of those damn doorbells that recorded people poking around. Anyone could have easily broken into the house and obtained the records at any point in time—without confrontation.

"Any clue to where Sandra and Daryl are?" I asked.

The silence that met my query was not what I wanted to hear. But it was exactly what I expected. We'd found a treasure—perhaps—but no indication of the two missing people.

I maneuvered over to Harold and leaned close. "Who has the right to these funds, if you do track them down?"

"It depends on how the financial accounts are structured," Harold said. "Possibly an heir of the Capone family. Possibly Janet. I won't know until I find the accounts and discover how they were established."

"Do you know how long it'll take you to find that out?"

"If I were at the bank, where I could launch an official query, it would go a lot faster, but I'm doing what I can. I don't think there's that much rush from Janet's point of view. She doesn't seem really interested in the money." He chuckled. "She's very rich, Sarah Booth. Her books sell like hotcakes, and since Sandra disappeared both of their books are hitting record sales. Janet's new book drops tomorrow and the preorders are well over three hundred thousand copies. If this turns into a media feeding frenzy it's going to be a huge financial windfall for both authors with movie deals likely and possibly even merchandising."

That was a staggering amount of money.

"Sandra's new book is running up the same kind of sales publishers dream of. Rumors are flying in the publishing world about what's going on with Sandra's disappearance, and it's created huge demand."

"But no one has really done any interviews or anything. How has word about the abduction leaked out?"

"As Janet explained it to me, publishing is a very tight-knit business. Everyone knows everyone else, and the booksellers are snapping up copies of these books left and right. Janet is giving a big press conference tomorrow. Media from all over the place are covering it. The cork is about to blow."

It sounded like even more of a headache for those of us looking for Sandra, but it might also flush the abductors out. I could at least hope for that, because I could no longer keep this story under wraps.

31

When Janet was done with her phone call, Coleman and I took her into the kitchen and told her about the man we'd seen out on the beach. We didn't want to needlessly scare her, but we felt she needed to be aware.

"I am so done with this," she said. "It feels like some mean person is just waiting for an opportunity to do something awful. Why would anyone be stalking me?"

I didn't mention anything about her cats—or the man who'd been spying and had broken into the inn, terrorizing the two sisters. Or the person who'd fired at me at Janet's parents' house. Or the person who'd tried to torch the Marcuses' business.

"Do you think this person was trying to harm my cats?" she asked.

"I don't know. At least the cats are contained behind a high fence." That didn't mean they were totally safe, but there was no point making her worry more right now.

"Did Sandra have any clue about the financial records in your parents' attic?" I asked.

"Why do you ask?" Janet responded.

"She's hinted that a treasure exists. You both have. You've drawn attention to the old legends and rumors about Helene and Al Capone. It's possible someone believes there's wealth to be had."

"I don't know what Sandra knows." She sighed. "When we were growing up we were always playing up in the attic. There were great old clothes and things we could dress up in. No one supervised us, and we were free to act out scenes from a past we made up based on gossip and tall tales. Sandra loved it up there more than I. Even when I'd leave and go play a game out in the yard, she'd stay up there." She clicked her tongue. "She could have found something."

I didn't think a child would have the sophistication to unravel the records Harold was pursuing. I didn't really know Sandra, though. She could have been a savant. "I hear your books are really selling. Does anyone in town know anything about your finances?"

"Not really. My main banking is done in New Orleans because I don't want to become a source of local gossip or speculation."

"But your books are doing well? And Sandra's, too?"

"Our publishers are very pleased. Very."

"After your release tomorrow and the interview you've got scheduled, they'll be even happier. Are you going to mention that Sandra is missing?"

"I haven't made a decision." She met my gaze. "There's

no reason to try to pretend this whole mess hasn't helped sell books. Sales are spectacular. For both of us. But I'll tell you the truth. The only thing that could be better would be for Sandra and Daryl to show up. A real Christmas miracle. Now that would force the publishers to run the presses at warp speed to keep up with the Christmas demand."

"If they're going to make a surprise appearance, they'd better get busy. Christmas is right around the corner."

"I know." Janet became solemn. "I can't imagine the holiday without at least one big book fight with Sandra. That would just be wrong. It's become part of our tradition. Last year she pushed me off a boat in the bay. Book sales soared." She brushed a tear off her cheek. "Sandra and I are bonded. To each other, to the past, to a time when we shared our dreams and fears. I'd give anything to have that back."

More proof that all relationships are very complicated. "You need to put cameras up outside your house and property."

"Oh, I have some."

Well, just great. Damn great. She could have told me that a week ago. "Can I see the recordings?"

"Why?"

"I told you. Someone is watching your house."

"It's that old busybody Impotent Isaac or Jerk-off Johnny. He's always going on about how my cats are killing the endangered beach birds. I've explained that the cats are contained in my yard, but lately he's been filming my yard to prove the cats are killing birds on my lawn. The man is a kook."

"But that doesn't mean he's harmless. Do you know where he lives? His real name?"

"I assume he lives around here somewhere. Maybe he

has a beach hut where he lives with the brown pelicans and delivers babies. Who the heck knows? He's just a harmless moron. He knows if he tries to do anything to my cats I'll take action."

Well, at least I didn't have to worry about Janet's cats. She was on top of her wacky neighbor. If he was the peeper, she knew all about him.

"Can I see the footage from the doorbell?"

"Sure. Tomorrow morning I'll get one of the staff to pull it up for you. I don't know how to use any of that technology. That's what they're paid for."

I knew it was pointless to try to force her into doing anything tonight, and I was tired. I called the hospital to check on Mary and was relieved to hear she was spitting mad about being held overnight but would be released in the morning.

Harold would have more complete reports on the financial statements by then, too. The banks that he needed to access were all closed. Most everything was shut down until business hours. The smart thing to do seemed to be to withdraw and go back to the inn with Coleman. I'd sorely neglected him on this holiday trip. Maybe a dawn swim in the heated pool. Maybe an eggnog toast in our room. Maybe just three minutes of conversation and a dive into bed. I was ready for all of the above but leaning toward the eggnog. The night was slowly ticking away and I had a bad feeling that our case was going to come to an unhappy conclusion.

I awoke at three thirty-three in the morning. Coleman was fast asleep with a slight smile curving his lips. I tried to fall back into slumber, but it was pointless. My brain was on fire with unanswered questions and anxiety. There was no indication that Sandra and Daryl had been hurt except for the minimal amount of blood in the mudroom sink. But something was gnawing at me. The "found" accounts of money, the whole Capone treasure, the crazy cat-hating neighbor, the attempted arson at the Beer and Bait. This case had spread out over a wide territory, and I couldn't stitch any of it together.

I quietly dressed and picked up my boots. I'd drive to an all-night service station or Waffle House and grab some coffee or maybe just take a ten-minute ride down the beach, enjoying the Christmas lights on some of the big homes. I'd done that one year with my parents when we'd treated ourselves to a holiday at the White House Hotel, and it had been magical.

I took a seat on the cold steps while I slipped on my boots. Peering through the live oaks, I caught a view of the bay and marina. The vista before me was serene and magnificent— with the boats lighted and floating on the soft swells. It was impossible to believe that bad people were at work. But they were.

I eased down the steps and got in my car. The Roadster came to life with a touch of the key and I wheeled out of the parking lot and drove down the road toward Waveland. With the water on one side and the older beach homes, dec- orated with bright lights, on the other, I felt like a ghost of Christmas past floating about the sleepy town, watching over the many children who couldn't wait for Santa to make an appearance.

The streets of Bay St. Louis were totally empty, giving the town a magical quality, like a witch had cast a spell and all the citizens dozed. But the lights were on, and I rolled my car window down as I found a radio station that was playing all of the old Christmas standards nonstop. I remembered how my father and I would walk the main street of Zinnia, singing carols during the days before Christmas.

The moon hung over the bay with a million stars twinkling. I drove by a rib place where a fake, life-size pig brought home the concept of barbecue. It was a bit disturbing to me, much as the advertisements of animals asking humans to eat them bothered me. I somehow didn't think pigs, cows, chickens, or fish wanted to be eaten any more than Hansel and Gretel did in the fairy tale. Nonetheless, the pig was a fine-looking porker.

I drove on down the road, leaving behind the lights of Bay St. Louis. This stretch of highway was isolated and I slowed and finally stopped to enjoy the magnificence of the beach untainted by any human influence: the water, the moon and stars, the sand, the sea oats waving in a gentle breeze. Through the open car window I could hear the water, whispering and sighing. Too many years had passed since I'd camped out on a beach near the gulf or a bay. When the weather warmed, Coleman and I would rectify that.

I hadn't left a note and I didn't want Coleman to worry if he woke up and found me gone, so I turned around and drove back toward the lights of the town. BSL was a big tourist attraction, but like most small towns, things settled into quiet in the predawn hours. The neon burned bright, but the bars and restaurants were closed. As I came upon my favorite pig, I noticed someone walking down the sidewalk in a full-length cloak with a hood. The high heels told me it was a woman. Why would any person be out at this hour walking in those shoes?

The way the hood was pulled over her head, shielding

her face, it was almost as if she didn't want to be recognized. Curious, I slowed and drove beside her. The window was already down so I called out to her.

"Ma'am, do you need some help?"

She kept walking.

"Lady, are you okay?" There was something unsettling about her, and my right hand clutched my cell phone just in case I needed to call backup.

She kept walking without acknowledging me.

"Hey! Stop!" I pulled a few feet ahead and stopped the car and got out. "Who are you?"

She flipped the hood back and I inhaled sharply and took a step back. Hedy Lamarr stared right into my eyes. I instantly saw that her beauty had never been exaggerated. She was luminous and mysterious.

"Jitty, what are you doing? What is it with you and these movie queens?" I knew the movie star hadn't come back to life so it had to be my haint, doing her normal routine of tormenting me.

"None of us are just one thing. Remember that." She spoke eloquently with just a trace of an accent. As I recalled, Hedy was born and worked in Austria before she was discovered by Metro-Goldwyn-Mayer studio head, Louis B. Mayer, while traveling from Paris to London. He offered her a movie contract and she came to Hollywood as a star. Hedy was an actress that I'd long admired, and so much more than just a pretty face.

"You were an actress and an inventor."

She only smiled, but didn't respond.

I only knew this because I'd been fascinated by her. I'd done one of my major college papers on her. She was mysterious, and for a famous film star, little was actually known about her during her time in Hollywood. It was later that her scientific genius was revealed. "During World War II, you and that composer, George something, developed a radio guidance system for torpedoes that the Axis powers couldn't jam. You were instrumental in saving many Allied lives and defeating the bad guys."

Her face brightened and I could tell she was thrilled that I knew about her inventions, but she didn't say a word.

"We use that technology with Wi-Fi today, I think." Technology was a weak point for me, but I thought I had read that somewhere. "You helped the Allies win the war."

"The march of evil had to be prevented. I was happy to play a role in it. If Hitler and his pals hadn't been stopped . . ." She didn't finish the sentence and I wondered what scenes of chaos and destruction she was witnessing in her memory.

"No one ever really talked about your inventions when you were a movie queen."

"The world wasn't interested in a female inventor. My role was handed to me, and it was one many coveted. I was an actress who worked a different kind of magic. I took an audience on a journey into time and imagination. My acting forced my scientific brain into the back seat of the automobile."

"Did that bother you?" It would have truly pissed me off.

"Times were different then, Sarah Booth. Women were fighting for basic rights. Honors and scientific acknowledgment didn't seem as important as the right to own property and the right to vote."

"Your beauty and acting ability worked against you." It was true. Had she been ugly or untalented, she might have gotten more credit for her scientific work.

"What matters the most, Sarah Booth? Doing the work or getting the credit?"

Jitty was coming through loud and clear and I didn't need Wi-Fi to hear her. "I know what you're saying, but I say, why not both?"

"Do what must be done. Don't let trappings deceive you."

This, then, was at the heart of why Jitty had chosen to appear as the Austrian actress. "I'll do my best."

"Look for it." The seriousness of her face and voice unsettled me. *Fierce* described her perfectly. Which meant she wasn't just tormenting me for fun. There was more at stake here.

I glanced down the empty Main Street of Bay St. Louis and took a breath. "Can you help me find Sandra and Daryl? I'm getting really worried now." It was true. Too much time had passed for this disappearance to be merely a joke.

The vision of Austrian beauty faded and morphed and my lovely haint, Jitty, stood before me in the dark green hooded cloak. "You know I can't tell you nothin' about what I know from the Great Beyond."

Oh, I knew the rules. I didn't like them but I knew them. "Do you have a message from my mama and daddy?" Sometimes Jitty had a special delivery tidbit.

"They love you. Oh, and your mama said to tell you to be sure and get home for Christmas dinner. DeWayne has some home fires to stoke on his own."

Now that was news. DeWayne was always obliging about keeping the horses and pets, but if Jitty was telling the truth, it seemed he might have someone he wanted to share his Christmas Day with. For a moment I lost the thread of my case and fell into total gossip mode.

"Who is DeWayne sweet on?" I asked Jitty.

Instead of answering, she threw off her cloak to reveal a belly dancer's costume. Music swelled behind her and she began to dance as she had in her most famous movie, *Samson and Delilah*.

On the clash of her finger symbols, she disappeared in a swirl of gauzy material. Before I could blink, a hand reached out of the whirling gauze and snatched up the fallen cloak. Then Jitty was gone.

I found myself alone on Main Street. There was the gentle lull of the water, just behind the barbecue place where I stood. The long bridge across the Bay of St. Louis was even quiet. I hadn't seen car lights in a while.

Right in front of me was the pig.

I'd admired the animal since I first saw it and I decided to take a selfie of me sitting astride it. I had on my red muffler and there was a Christmas hat in the backseat of the car so I retrieved it and plopped it atop my head. I wrapped the scarf around my neck. It took a little effort to get on the pig, but I managed. Waving the end of my scarf with one hand I snapped the selfie. Maybe I'd use this for next year's Christmas cards.

I was about to slide off the pig when the whoop-whoop of a police siren came from behind me.

"Hands in the air," an officer said over a loudspeaker.

He had to be talking to me. I was the only person out and about. I lifted my hands.

"Get off the pig," the voice said.

The problem was that I couldn't slide off the pig if I had to keep my hands in the air. I wasn't going to yell that out loud. I just waited.

In a moment a police officer got out of the car and came toward me. "I said get off the pig," he said.

"Can I put my hands down?"

"Okay."

I grabbed the pig's ears and slid to the ground. When I turned around to face the officer, I saw Thibodeau. He wasn't even bothering to hide his amusement. "Does Coleman know where you are?" he asked.

"No, I didn't tell him I was going to ride a fake pig."

"Probably a good thing," he said. "What are you doing?"

It was a long story and involved way too much Jitty, so it was best to come up with a lie. "I saw the pig earlier and I wanted a photo for a Christmas card next year."

"Good thing I have an excellent snapshot of you," he said, showing me his phone. I saw the photo and burst out laughing. My hands were in the air and my expression was one of astonishment. It was hysterical.

"I'll send you a copy," he said. "Now you should head back to the inn before your boyfriend realizes you're running wild on the streets of Bay St. Louis." Thibodeau laughed out loud.

"With a pig, too." I had to laugh.

For a moment we both just laughed together, a release from the constant worry of the past few days. I said my adieus and headed back to the inn, hoping daybreak would bring some answers I so desperately needed.

32

Coleman met me on the steps of the inn. He was bundled in his pajamas and a blanket. Obviously he was waiting for me to return.

"I'm sorry." I sat beside him. "I just meant to take a short drive. I should have left a note."

"I knew."

I gave him a look. "Knew what?"

He sighed. "I never told you, Sarah Booth, but I have a little help at times with solving my cases."

"What do you mean?" My heart was beginning to race. Was it possible that he already knew the secret of Jitty?

"Sometimes I just know things. And I knew where you were."

"How?"

"Trained intuition and a lawman's instinct."

"You're playing with me." I hoped both that he was and he wasn't. What a relief it would be to tell him about my special talent—conjuring up a dead woman from the 1800s. If I could share Jitty with him— "Where was I?"

"Riding a pig on Main Street. I just hope no one saw you."

He said it deadpan, without a shadow of doubt. I was floored.

"What possessed you to climb up on that pig wearing a Santa hat?"

"Uh, maybe I was thinking it would be a funny Christmas card for next year?"

"I'm just glad no one else saw you."

So, his psychic talents were fallible. He didn't know Thibodeau had caught me. "Well, someone might have seen me."

"If it was the law you'd be under arrest. You know it's illegal to have that kind of interaction with porcine creatures."

"What?"

"You can't go around abusing pigs, Sarah Booth. There are laws."

"I didn't abuse—" I stopped and stared at him. There was way too much amusement in his eyes. "Thibodeau sent you the picture, didn't he?"

"Maybe."

"I'm going to kill him."

Coleman threw his arm around me and dragged me under the blanket he was wrapped in. "You want to ride with the big pigs you gotta learn to cover your tracks."

There was no point fighting. Coleman was stronger, and he had me. It was best to yield with what little dignity I had left.

"Let's grab some breakfast on the beach," I suggested.

"There are some places open now." Daybreak was just around the corner.

We stopped at a local mom-and-pop diner and had green eggs and red grits for a holiday breakfast. No bacon. The pig was now my friend. After we ate, we strolled down to sit on the beach and watch the sun climb over the horizon.

"I don't know what to do about my case," I told Coleman. "I don't have a clue where Sandra and Daryl might be. I'm afraid someone is going to harm Janet before we figure this out. How could such a simple case be such a tangle?" I told him about the phone call from Mrs. Marcus and about telling us that Janet had fired us, which I knew to be untrue.

"You don't think it could be—"

I covered Coleman's mouth with my hand. I knew what he was going to say. "Do not speak her name. I mean it. You'll conjure her up."

He nodded and I dropped my hand. Gertrude was a former bed-and-breakfast owner in Zinnia who had decided—wrongly—that years ago my mother had betrayed her. She'd gone off the deep end with plots of revenge against me. Months would pass without a sighting of her, and then suddenly she'd be in my grill with murder on her mind.

"Sorry. It's just that this whole thing reeks of someone like her."

He was right about that. Gertrude was a master of criminality. But I didn't want to think about her and the things she'd done that changed my life dramatically. The past, as Jitty often told me, could teach us lessons but it could not be changed. Living in an alternate universe, where events could be reordered or outcomes mitigated, was the best way to break your heart every single day. My aunt Loulane had warned me that those who sought to escape the past never fully lived in the present. It was a harsh lesson for a grieving child, but one that had served me well.

"Should we wake up the rest of the gang?" Coleman gently drew me back to an awareness of the moment. "You looked like you were traveling a lonely road."

"I was. Just missing Aunt Loulane and my folks. But here and now is the best. I want to be right here." I kissed his cheek and jumped to my feet, offering him a hand. "Let's get those slugabeds up and moving."

On my journey to breakfast, I'd also noticed that Harold's car wasn't in the parking lot. I hadn't mentioned it, but when Tinkie insisted on knocking on his door, I knew no one would answer. She turned to Coleman and then me. "You knew he wasn't here."

"Maybe," I said. "But we need to call him. I'm hoping he has some answers for us about those financial records today."

Tinkie checked her watch. "The banks will open in another half hour. Let's grab breakfast at that diner on Second Street."

I leaned into Coleman. "Let's pretend we're hobbits and have a second breakfast."

"Good thinking."

As the gang trooped down the stairs, Coleman and I took the last position. My case might have been going to hell in a handbasket, but my friends were extraordinary and I loved the way they chatted and teased one another as they drifted to their cars.

By the time breakfast was finished, the banks were open. We headed back to the inn and helped ourselves to fresh orange, mango, and peach juice that Ellie left out around the pool for all her guests. When it was nine twenty, I picked up my phone to call Harold. Before I could dial, the phone rang.

"I have some exciting news," Harold said in a terse whisper. I put my phone on speaker as everyone gathered around. "I have to talk fast before Janet gets up."

"Go!"

"There are offshore bank accounts with at least three million dollars in them. It appears Capone opened the accounts and left Samuel Malone in charge of them. Capone died and Samuel never did a thing with the accounts. There are probably instructions somewhere in those boxes of records. We have to find them."

"Does Janet know what Capone intended?"

"She says she doesn't know anything about this." Harold sighed. "I really like her, but I'm not sure she's trustworthy. I thought it best if we resolved this before I told her."

I agreed with Harold's thinking, but I was concerned that Janet had a right to know what we'd found in her family home. I looked over at Coleman and thought I could see that same worry in his eyes. "We have to tell her soon. Very soon."

"Agreed," Harold said. "I need to get away from Janet and make some international calls first."

"We'll go run interference for Harold," Cece said. "I want to interview Janet anyway, and she has that big press conference coming up. I can give her some advice on how to play it so the story stays in the headlines for several days. Tell Janet we'll be over in fifteen."

"Will do. And thank you. I don't want to mess this up with Janet. She's a special lady. And here she comes. Later." He hung up.

Tinkie put a hand on my shoulder. "And we need to stop by and check on Mary. I'm pretty sure she'll be at the library."

"True." That left Coleman and Oscar.

Coleman's grin was pure devilry. "Thibodeau was going to send officers out on the route that Capone used to deliver liquor around the bay. I want to talk to him about that. And he was telling me some wild story about a pig."

"What pig?" Cece asked.

I glared at Coleman. "Oh, I have a photo for the newspaper," he said. "A Christmas photo involving a pig and Sarah Booth."

I was going to have to kill that man. That would be the only way to stop him. He hit something on his phone and all around me telephones dinged. My friends checked their phones and burst into laughter.

"What in the world, Sarah Booth?" Cece asked. "You look demented, riding that big pig, wearing a Santa hat, and waving your hands in the air. It's like some kind of fake hog Christmas rodeo."

"Sarah Booth, were you drunk?" Tinkie asked.

"I was not drunk. I only wanted to take a selfie for my Christmas cards for next year."

"Seriously?" Millie said. "Your mama would not approve. You do look like you're more than half a bubble off plumb."

"I think she looks fetching," Oscar said. "Now, everyone, get about your business. We have work to do."

We went up to our room to gather what we'd need for the morning, and I caught Coleman alone. "Who does that money belong to?" I felt a deep burden to tell Janet what had been discovered.

"As Harold said, it will depend on how the accounts were set up. If Capone owes the government, it may be theirs. He did time for failing to pay his taxes, remember."

"But he did the time. Would he still owe?"

"You need a lawyer to answer these questions."

"That's a lot of money. More than enough to kill for."

"But how does this impact Sandra O'Day?" Coleman asked. "Samuel Malone is related to Janet, not Sandra."

He was right about that. "Okay. Get with Oscar and see if Thibodeau will give you any information."

Coleman's naughty boy grin played across his face. "He's already given me plenty to work with. Such a fine picture of you, Sarah Booth."

"You can tell Thibodeau for me I'm considering a lawsuit for damages to my reputation."

Coleman laughed out loud as he stepped out of the room and stood by the door. "Holiday pig riding is likely a step up in the opinion of a lot of people."

"Watch your back, big boy. I'll get you for this." I put on a nicer sweater and was ready to retrieve Tinkie and check on Mary when someone knocked on my door. I opened it to find a young man shifting his weight from foot to foot. He thrust a padded envelope at me. "Are you Sarah Booth Delaney?"

"Yes."

"Janet said you wanted this recording from the doorbell camera."

He didn't wait for me to thank him before jogging off.

I walked over to Tinkie's suite and knocked. When she let me in, I gave her the thumb drive to check on her computer. Janet had been as good as her word.

I held little Maylin on my lap and breathed in the sweet

smell of clean baby as Tinkie scrolled through the blurry and grainy images that mostly consisted of cats walking back and forth in front of the door. With the exception of one fine, fat opossum.

Tinkie and I both were growing impatient when a human form appeared. The person crept up to the east side of the house. For a moment he disappeared from the camera, then reappeared by a large window, definitely peeping inside.

The interior light of the house illuminated his profile and I knew instantly who it was.

"That's Clarence Osteller, the preacher man."

"No-o-o!" Tinkie said. "A Peeping Preacher?"

"Yep." I ignored her sarcasm. "The question is, does he have a thing for Janet or for her money?"

"Good question. Let's ask him. Do you think he's behind all of this?"

Because I disliked him and his foolish wife, I wanted to believe it was him, but it didn't really make logical sense. Sandra and Daryl had nothing to do with his infatuation with Janet, if such was the case.

"Let's hit it and find out," I agreed. "We can pay a visit to the right reverend before we see Mary."

33

The boys had taken off in the Cadillac, leaving the Roadster for me. I was getting behind the wheel when I noticed the book of movie stars I'd found at Sandra's. When Coleman retrieved me from the mansion last night, I'd been so worried about Mary, the book had slid down the side of the passenger seat. I picked it up, eager once again to examine it.

"A book?" Tinkie said as she maneuvered into the passenger seat. She held out her hands and I gave it to her.

"I found it at Sandra's. I just borrowed it. I wanted to see if Helene Buntman was in it. Maybe something about the mansion or Capone or the secret passages. I was hoping for just about anything."

"I'll look while you drive," Tinkie offered.

"Thanks. That would be double the use of our time."

I used my phone's GPS to find the Osteller church. As Thibodeau had told me, the property was north of I-10—a lot safer from hurricane damage when the next big one blew in.

It wasn't a long drive to get there, and the gates were wide open, inviting everyone in. The campus was a real Disneyland, complete with an ostentatious church and all the entertainment benefits of the Magic Kingdom. Kids were taking tennis lessons on high-quality courts, there were ball fields for football and baseball, and a gymnasium with several courts for basketball. It reminded me of a country club. For God. If God had any use for country clubs.

"This is some setup," Tinkie said, lowering the book to her lap as she took in the buildings we passed.

"Yeah, prosperity gospel must pay pretty darn good. I wonder what they do for the poor."

"Teach them to golf?" Tinkie asked, pretending it was an innocent question. I grinned and rolled my eyes.

"Okay, Osteller's office is over there. By the Lamborghini."

"Oh, the wages of sin," Tinkie intoned. If she didn't cut it out, she was going to be a handful. Tinkie wasn't opposed to wealth, but she was definitely opposed to fleecing people with false promises or frightening them with hellfire to force them to donate.

We parked and walked to the front door. I'd expected some kind of security check, but no one stopped us. The lobby of the main office was a soothing blue. Soft music played. No one manned the receptionist's desk, but that didn't slow us down. We went down a hallway, opening every door until we came to a massive mahogany door with Reverend Clarence Osteller's name on it.

I started to knock, but Tinkie twisted the knob and walked in. Osteller was sitting at his desk, his back to us. He was on the phone.

"So it's going to be the Packers and the Saints. Put my money on the Saints. Same as usual. Oh, and Tommy, you should act on that stock tip I gave you yesterday. Tomorrow will be too late."

We stood quietly, but a sixth sense must have alerted him to the fact he wasn't alone. He swiveled around and started to his feet, his expression filled with horror and then anger. "I have to go," he spat into the phone and tossed it on the desk. Then he turned on us. "How the hell did you get in here?"

Tinkie pointed at the door. "It wasn't difficult."

"What do you want?"

Tinkie moved closer to his desk and took a seat in an overstuffed wing chair. She pointed at a second one. "Take a load off, Sarah Booth. We're going to have a long chat with Clarence."

Normally Tinkie preferred persuasion and flattery to strong-arming someone, but she was livid. Charlatans got under her skin in the worst way.

"You're going to stand up and walk out of here or I'll call security." Clarence rose to his feet and leaned forward on his desk to look directly into Tinkie's eyes.

She reached over and unplugged the phone on his desk. "What have you done with Sandra and Daryl? They better not be hurt or you'll be a sought-after commodity in prison. So many men there needing salvation."

"I have no idea what you're talking about." He was indignant, but he sat back in his chair. Tinkie had won the battle on that one. The winner of the war remained to be seen.

While she handled the questioning, I watched Osteller closely.

"We have video footage of you peeping in the windows at Janet Malone's house."

Osteller swallowed hard, a dead giveaway that Tinkie had him by the short hairs. "I wasn't peeping. I wasn't. You can't say that. That's defamation and I'll sue you."

"I'd dig that," Tinkie said with a flippancy that forced me to hide my smile. She was on a tear. "Think of the publicity Delaney Detective Agency would get from a lawsuit like that." If Tinkie smoked cigars, she would have lit one at this moment. "Ask for a million in damages, please. Less than that and the national media doesn't pay attention."

"There's something very wrong with you." Osteller had forgotten I was in the room, he was so focused on Tinkie. "You are corrupt. You are filled with evil. The venom of Satan runs through your veins."

"I know," Tinkie said. "Wanna see me shoot fireballs from my palms?"

I almost choked stifling the laughter that welled up, but I watched Osteller. His hands were slowly moving from his lap toward his desk. I wasn't psychic but it didn't take a lot to figure out there was likely a panic button—a means to alert his security he needed assistance.

There was an umbrella in a stand right beside his desk. Perfect.

"You are a blasphemer!" He glared at Tinkie. "I think you're possessed by a demon."

"At least it's not the demon of greed," Tinkie said. "Now

tell me where Sandra and Daryl are. You're obviously very interested in Janet. Is it her hot body or her money? And you'd better answer fast or I'll hold my own press conference."

"My wife Tilly is all I need in the companionship of a woman. The only thing Janet could offer me is in the financial column." His smile was self-satisfied.

"So you admit you were spying on her in an attempt to gain some type of leverage?"

Osteller leaned forward and I knew he was going for the panic button. "Yes," he said, "and you're not going to do a thing about it. Janet lives like she's above the social mores of this community. She does exactly what she wants and never pays a price. I'm going to fix that."

I stood, grabbed the umbrella, and brought it down on top of his desk in one quick, fluid motion. It startled him so badly that he pushed the chair back and slammed into the wall behind him. For a moment he was either stunned or just disbelieving.

Tinkie held up her phone. "And I have you recorded, Reverend Osteller. Confessing to peeping and also intending to scam Janet out of her money. So maybe you'd better stop being an idiot and cooperate."

"That's illeg—" He looked at me and I shook my head.

"As long as one party knows a conversation is being recorded, it's legal."

Tinkie had just won the war. Not a shot had been fired.

Twenty minutes later, I believed we knew everything Osteller knew. His concern for his reputation and saving his own skin far outweighed even his greed. He'd been peeping at Janet's house, hoping to catch the novelist in some act that would allow him to blackmail her for money. He'd successfully disguised himself as Claude Wells, Janet's cat-hating neighbor. He even had the vest with net pockets and binoculars.

"How did you gain entry to her yard?" I asked. "That fence is high."

"There's a tree. I climbed it and dropped into the yard. Same way out with another tree."

The concept of a religious leader climbing trees to spy on a woman made me shake my head. I'd be sure and alert Janet, though. She should know that a preacher, pervert, and blackmailer had his eye on her.

Tinkie looked at me and I nodded. We'd asked Osteller every question we could think of, and I sincerely believed he didn't know anything about the disappearance of Sandra and Daryl. But I had one more line of questioning.

"Have you tried to pull this blackmail crap on Sandra?" Though Sandra's house was bigger and in a more open situation, there was no fence and no security.

Tinkie sat forward and he pushed back away from her. "Come on, Osteller, we have things to do. Just answer the question."

Osteller was completely broken to Tinkie's will. He looked at her and then down. "I may have done some . . . things."

"Like what?" Tinkie asked.

"I may have left her a note or two, implying she was being watched. Just to make her more receptive to the Lord's protection."

"You're just a regular Elmer Gantry," Tinkie said. "Did you act on those threats?"

"No. It was just talk. I swear. I don't think Sandra was

fazed at all. Even though I called on her several times, I never got past the front door."

"What about your connections with the local criminals?"

The color left his face, and he gripped the edge of the desk. "Don't go there. I mean it. That's dangerous for you and for me. The past is very much alive for some people, and they want it left in peace." He slumped back in his chair. "When I was over at the Buntman mansion one night, hoping to get some video of Sandra and that young man who follows her like a puppy, I saw someone on the grounds."

"Who?" Tinkie and I asked simultaneously.

"I don't know. I wasn't close enough to see any features. It was dark and the person was skulking around the house. Not a big person, but someone who moved quickly. They left something at the garage door and then took off. By the time I got to the garage, they'd disappeared into the shrubbery."

"What did the person leave?" I demanded.

"A note. It warned Sandra to back off the book she was working on."

"You read the note. Did you take it?" I asked.

"Yes." He swallowed. "I took it. In a way, I may be responsible for the fact that she and Marcus are missing."

"Where is it now?" Tinkie asked.

"I destroyed it. But I can tell you what it said. 'Abandon the book about local events or pay the consequences.' I memorized it before I burned it. Oh, it was typewritten. In big type."

"When did this happen?" I asked.

"Just before she disappeared. I was planning on telling her about it at her book signing. That's when I learned she was missing. And Daryl, too."

Tinkie nodded at me. "Let's go."

I stood up and she joined me. Clarence didn't move. He didn't even open his eyes to make sure we were leaving. I grabbed Tinkie's hand and we raced for the car just in case he came to his senses and sicced his security guys on us. We needed to be off the church campus.

34

As much as I needed to talk to Janet, it wasn't going to happen immediately. When we got to her house, we had to park half a mile away due to the number of press vehicles along the beach. I'd forgotten about the press conference, but it was the hot holiday ticket. There appeared to be media people from local and national affiliates. It was a big, big deal.

The press conference hadn't started, and Tinkie and I found Janet in her bedroom surrounded by her "team." A young woman with a wide, friendly grin gave me a thumbs-up. "You're the two detectives. So glad you could make it. We've had some inquiries about your work. We might ask you to say a word."

"No, thanks." I nipped that in the bud. Delaney Detective Agency might benefit from the exposure, but I had no desire to see my mug all over television or in print. It could also hinder future cases.

"Book sales are skyrocketing," another woman said. "We're going back for another printing and the book just hit the stores today. I've never seen anything like this."

Excitement was a fever in the room, but only Janet seemed untouched by it. She took the dress she was handed and stepped into the bathroom to change.

"Hurry, Janet. The media are all by the pool waiting. Do you have any antihistamines? The reporter from Memphis is allergic to cats."

A packet of medicine came flying out of the bathroom. The woman who'd asked for it caught it and rushed out of the room. Another woman uncorked a bottle of champagne. "This is a celebration," she said. "Grab a glass."

Tinkie stepped away from me and when I saw her face full on, I knew trouble was a'brewing, as Aunt Loulane would say. "Don't!" I said the word aloud, but Tinkie's response was a grim nod. She was going to do it no matter what I said.

She found a chair and climbed up on it. "Attention! Attention!" When everyone finally quieted down, she spoke. "I realize book sales are terrific and this is the best publicity moment in the history of publishing, but keep in mind that another writer, a childhood friend of Janet's, is missing today. Maybe temper your joy a tad."

She jumped to the floor as Janet came out of the bathroom. It was evident she'd been crying. "Thank you, Tinkie. Please, everyone. Heed what Mrs. Richmond said. Sandra O'Day and I are rivals, but we are also friends, and I am worried sick about her." She sobbed and ran back into the bathroom.

"I don't think that's an act," I whispered to Tinkie.

"I don't either."

I found Coleman waiting on the fringes of the media crowd. Tinkie opted to stay with Janet and keep an eye to make sure those representing themselves as media had the right credentials. Cece was covering the event for the *Dispatch*, and Millie had taken over organizing the catering staff Janet had hired. Drinks and fancy finger foods were madly circulating among the crowd of what I estimated to be about a hundred.

"Where's Harold?" I asked Coleman.

"He and Oscar went to the Gulfport bank. They have a contact there who's helping them sort those Capone accounts. From what I understand, it's going to take a lot of work to cut through the layers of shell companies and fake accounts."

"Harold and Oscar are the men for that job. Did either one say if Janet is due any of the money?"

Coleman shook his head. "It's complex and, until all the details are known, they have no idea. I'm wondering how this money plays into Sandra's disappearance, though. Both women are extremely wealthy. But this windfall to Janet seems like it would be the nail in the coffin of any competition or animosity. She has more money than she could burn. She could live in a different country every week of the year. It seems hard to believe that money would be a motive for her."

Coleman was right about that. "Did Harold learn anything new?"

"Not that he told me, but we didn't have a lot of time to

talk. I've been trying to put together a time line of events. If I can figure out when things happened, like the warning notes, the sightings of someone watching you and Tinkie or Janet, and how you were trapped in that mausoleum, I can at least eliminate some suspects."

"Don't forget about Mary Perkins almost getting killed in the garage."

"And someone shooting at you at Janet's parents' house. So many near misses," Coleman said. "I find that a little convenient."

"You're right. Also convenient, Janet's new book has exploded in sales, and Sandra's, too. They're the talk of the publishing world. The major network talk shows have asked Janet for bookings. Oprah called last night, according to the media gossip." I'd kept my ears open.

"I heard some company is releasing a new video game based on the disappearance," Coleman said.

"In so short a time?"

"When big money is on the line, people work nonstop to cash in on it."

I studied Coleman's open face. "You sound as if you think this is an inside job."

"I'm beginning to wonder," Coleman said. "Aren't you?"

I thought again of Janet's sudden raw emotions. "I don't know. But it seems that Janet had expected Sandra to return before now. Maybe, just maybe, this started out as one thing and turned into another."

"That could be deadly for Sandra and Daryl," Coleman said.

"I know. That's what troubles me."

We were shushed into silence as Janet took the podium. Her plea for information about the disappearance of Sandra and Daryl had me near tears. If she was pretending, she was a better actress than writer, and she was a darn good scribbler.

"She's sincere, isn't she?" Coleman asked, echoing my thoughts.

"Seems like it." I watched closely for a tell or anything that might give her away. The swollen eyes and nose, the red face, and leaking mascara were all indicators that her emotions were real. Janet wasn't someone who looked ugly, ever, if she could help it. Not even to sell her innocence.

When she finished talking about Sandra's disappearance—with exactly the details she'd given me—she opened the floor for questions. I perked up to listen for any new tidbit I may have missed in the past.

"What is your relationship with O'Day?" a young woman asked.

"We're competitors, rivals, and childhood friends," Janet answered. "Sandra and I fought. A lot. We misbehaved. A lot. We caused scenes. A lot. But never would I want anything to happen to her or to Daryl. He's been overlooked in this. He's a wonderful young man with a family who is missing him, too."

The questions went on about Daryl's relationship to Sandra and Janet, and to Janet's credit, she called in Mary Perkins to talk about Daryl. Mary looked fine. Her near asphyxiation had left her remarkably untouched. Librarians are tough birds.

Mary's description of Daryl was dead-on to what she'd told me, and what I'd learned from other sources. When I heard a sob behind me, I was astonished to find Mrs. Marcus seated in the audience. She got up and left the room. Several reporters trailed her and so did Millie, who would offer comfort but also extract any information she could.

A young male reporter in front of me raised his hand and stood when Janet acknowledged him. "Are you involved in the disappearance of Sandra O'Day?"

Caught off guard, Janet blinked. "What are you implying?"

"There's talk that you might have arranged this disappearance to impact your book sales in a positive way. I might point out that Ms. O'Day has also benefited with record-breaking sales."

"That's ludicrous." Anger crackled in Janet's eyes. "Thank you for coming." She was clearly ending the press conference.

The reporter pushed through the crowd to the front of the room. I was right behind him.

"Do you have a pact with Sandra O'Day that you will both be buried in the mausoleum on her property?"

"Where did you hear that?" Janet asked.

"My sources are confidential."

"And my answer for you is kiss my ass." Janet stalked away from the bank of microphones and disappeared in the sprawling house.

"Now her sales will really skyrocket," Tinkie said. "Nothing like planting some kind of 'Annabel Lee' sepulcher imagery and calling out the ghost of Edgar Allan Poe. It couldn't be more fitting for a writer. Bitter enemies buried together in a tomb by the sea. It's almost like that reporter was following a script."

Tinkie knew literature far better than I did, and it was many times a real bonus to the agency. She was dead-on. I remembered part of the poem, and it was a perfect fit for the Buntman mansion. "In her sepulcher there by the sea, in her tomb by the sounding sea."

A chill passed over me. I felt time slipping from my grasp. I tried to focus on the positive. "We're scheduled to go home tomorrow. We have that Christmas Eve party to attend in Zinnia, and then the Christmas play. Maylin is going to be spectacular as the star of the pageant production."

Tinkie had been flattered beyond belief when her church had asked for Maylin to rest in the manger as the Baby Jesus during the Christmas pageant. My contribution was to convince the church not to use live animals. There was always some horrific incident during the Christmas pageant, and for Maylin, I'd pulled out all the stops and convinced the church to use humans in costume. For my valiant efforts, at Coleman's insistence I was going dressed as a camel. Coleman found this endlessly amusing and kept asking if I wanted one hump or two. If he said a word during the pageant I would make sure he got two lumps—on the noggin.

"If we don't resolve this case, we can return to Bay St. Louis after the Christmas pageant," Tinkie said.

"Sandra and Daryl have been gone too long. I fear there's serious trouble." This thought had nagged me for twenty-four hours. "If someone put them somewhere without food and water, they're likely dead. There's been no ransom, and I don't think there's going to be one."

"You really think someone took them and killed them?" Tinkie looked like she might cry.

"I don't know, but it doesn't look good. We have to face reality. We can come back and keep looking, but I don't expect a good outcome."

Tinkie nodded. "This is still hard to believe. A well-known writer and her assistant abducted, never to be seen again."

"It's certainly not the case I thought I was signing up for." Delaney Detective Agency had had a few near misses, but we'd never failed to solve a case. Kidnappings weren't our specialty, and I wondered if Thibodeau should have called in the FBI on this one. It was something I'd ask him when I saw him. Truthfully, though, I didn't think FBI agents would have found any more evidence or clues than Tink and I had.

The news media began to break up, some going outside to phone in details of their stories, others scribbling notes or trying to sneak around the house, hoping to catch Janet when she was by herself to ask another question. It's exactly what I would have done, and Cece was in that cluster.

I eased up to her side. "You can ask her anything later, you know."

"I don't like to trade on friendship. I want to get my details like every other reporter."

"You noble muckraker, you," I teased her.

Her sassy grin told me she didn't care about my sarcasm. "Now stop distracting me or I'll have to grill Harold to get these details."

And if it meant a story, Cece would. I patted her shoulder and went to find Tinkie, who had disappeared. It took me a few minutes but I found her in Janet's extensive library.

"Look at this." She held up a book.

When I was closer, I realized it was the exact book I'd taken from Sandra's house. The photographs of the early movie stars were fabulous. She passed it to me.

"Check the copyright," she said.

I flipped to the front. The name stopped me. The book was written by Sandra Malone. "Malone? A cousin of Janet's?" It was a well-done book with sewn bindings. No expense had been spared to create it. The publication date was only a few years back. "This doesn't make sense."

"I know."

"Do you think Sandra and Janet collaborated on the book?"

"Check the inscription." Tinkie was too much of a lady to gloat, but she was almost there.

"To my cousin and partner, more than sisters." It was signed Sandra Malone.

"I didn't think Janet Malone had any cousins," I said.

"That's what I wondered as well."

"Then who is this?"

"Something we have to find out." I texted Cece to ask Janet about her potential cousins and the book.

Tinkie reached for the book, but I put it on a table and began to flip through it. I'd never had a chance to look at the copy in my car. "Did you find anything when you were looking?"

"No, but I didn't get far. Check to see if Helene Buntman is included."

The book was organized by years and films that were produced in those years. Photos from the movie sets, publicity shots, glamour shots, and snapshots of each actress were included. The research on each star was extensive. I could have sat on the floor and read the book right there, but I was seeking answers for a crime.

When I leafed to the middle of the book, there was a centerfold of Helene in a skimpy costume, a dancer in some Middle Eastern harem. She was incredibly beautiful, and her smile was a temptation. It was classic Hollywood, the type of photograph that made a woman a star. "Damn, she really was a beauty."

Tinkie had wedged up beside me. "Yes, she certainly was."

I went through the book, realizing that some of the photos in the book were ones I'd seen in Janet's attic. There was no doubt that Janet had been involved with creating the book, but why use Sandra's name? And Sandra was the researcher, the one who made nonfiction her forte. Janet was the one who created characters that readers loved and implausible plots that kept everyone turning the pages.

My cell phone buzzed and I read Cece's text. "Janet and Sandra are cousins. They cowrote the book."

Tinkie's expression was solemn.

I thought of Janet's tears before the press conference. She was sincerely worried about Sandra. It wasn't an act. And if Janet didn't know where Sandra was and she had hired us legitimately, then the situation was truly dire.

35

We sat around Janet's pool in the winter sunshine, seeking a bit of warmth. My skin was toasty enough but my blood was running cold at the thought of what might have happened to Sandra and Daryl.

Mary Perkins stopped by our poolside table on the way back to the library. "Thank you again for saving me, Sarah Booth."

"My pleasure. I was planning on checking up on you at the library but I got distracted. Was your car okay at the library parking lot?"

"It was. And you look none the worse for wear for ditch swimming. I heard all about it."

"I'm fine, just worried about our missing celebrities."

"Yeah, me, too. Can I look up anything in the library for you?"

"No."

"Did that redheaded reporter find you?"

My hackles rose. I wasn't afraid of redheads in general, just one in particular. "No. Who was she?"

"Didn't give a name. She was from NOLA, one of the TV stations. She was in the library this morning, looking up your PI agency."

"How old?"

"Mid-twenties, maybe. Pretty young woman."

She was way too young to be Gertrude Strom. My red alert flags faded. "No, I didn't talk to her. Was she here at the press conference?"

"I didn't see her. If I do, what should I tell her?"

"Just get a name and number and I'll give her a call. I don't especially want to be on camera."

"I hear that." Mary gave me a carefree salute and walked out with some straggling reporters.

Tinkie came to my side as I hung up. "Let's go talk to Tilly Osteller. Her husband has no spine and maybe she has a grudge going with Sandra."

We didn't have a better lead, and tonight would be our last night. After the parade tomorrow, we were due to go home. "Let's hit it. I forgot to ask Mary about the graphics from the wall in the tomb." I'd left an enlarged copy of the strange hieroglyphics with the librarian, just in case Mary had been able to find any references to the symbols as a language.

"She would have said something if she'd found anything."

"True that, Tinkie. True that."

"Let's go pick up Maylin and Pauline," Tinkie said. "The day is beautiful, a perfect time for a ride in a convertible."

"Excellent plan." My partner had selflessly been working hard, and she wanted some baby time, as did I.

Pauline, the nanny, bundled Maylin in six layers of soft and cozy clothes. Tinkie took her in her arms and secured her in the car seat. While they were getting ready, I'd called and gotten the address of Tilly's home, which was halfway between the beach and the church. I wondered why they didn't want to live on the church property, but as I thought about it, the decision was wise. Clarence would undoubtedly sell the church one day, and they would still have their home.

The day was bright and sunny with no wind, and Maylin was so excited to be in the convertible with the seagulls flying low beside the car as we drove along the beach. We found Tilly's house without issue, but Tinkie, Pauline, and Maylin waited for me in the car. I left the keys for Tinkie in case something came up.

I hadn't called Tilly to warn her I was dropping by, so when I rang the doorbell of a beautiful old creole-style cottage with sweeping front steps and a long, broad porch filled with ferns and wicker furniture, I didn't know what reception I'd receive.

"What do you want?" Tilly asked. She was well-turned out, makeup perfect, hair neatly coiffed. She worked hard at how she presented herself. She was a pretty woman. Pretty but hard-looking. Razor blade eyes and flat, thin lips. No one had to tell me she wore the pants in her marriage.

"I'd like to talk with you." I pointed toward the car. "My partner, her nanny, and her baby are in the car waiting for me. It's a little chilly—"

"Not my problem. And neither are you. I don't know

anything about those two brawling writers except Clarence thought they should donate to the church. Which they didn't. Now, excuse me." She started to close the door.

I had on my favorite boots—good solid soles. I stuck a foot in so she couldn't close it. "I just have a few questions."

"And I told you I don't have any answers. I can call the police."

"That's fine. Call them. Thibodeau can ask my questions for me. And it's illegal to lie to a police officer." That was one big lie, but it might be effective.

She sighed. "What is it?"

"When was the last time you saw Sandra O'Day?"

"You know the answer to that because you were there. At her house during the gala for the library. She was prancing about and laughing with her boy toy. Then when it came time to sign books, she was gone. I had a list of twenty people to get signed books for. She ruined my Christmas list."

Okay, then. Tilly's priorities were clear. Only her interests mattered. "I understand you come from a family with a long heritage of living on the Mississippi Gulf Coast."

"Yes, my family was well known for many generations. We helped settle the area."

"Were they a fishing family?"

"Why do you ask?"

"Background." I smiled. "Some of the stories are so exotic and adventurous. Pirates, hidden treasures, Al Capone. It's all so romantic and thrilling."

"I've heard some of the Delta families have plenty of . . . alluring gossip in their backgrounds."

"Yes, but not pirates. Not rum-runners and gangsters. Delta gossip is all about money and sex." Not exactly true, but close enough. "Was your family involved in any of that exciting stuff?"

"No, my family came from simple fishermen, and Clarence comes from a merchant background. We worked hard, saved, and built up our church from scratch. What are you implying?"

I put on an innocent face while behind my back I signaled Tinkie. Out of the corner of my eye I saw her getting out of the car with the baby in her arms and Pauline in tow. We'd outnumber and overwhelm Tilly. She'd have to invite us in—a baby in the cold. Good manners demanded it. Not for the first time I was glad I'd had a proper upbringing and knew how to apply social pressure. Tinkie was even better at it than I was.

"I'm not implying anything at all, except that your family may have had a romantic and thrilling past. The thing great novels are made of."

Tilly was a tougher nut to crack than I'd anticipated. She was naturally suspicious, with more than a pinch of paranoia. She caught Tinkie and posse coming up the walk. "Stop right there. You aren't coming inside my home. Don't bring that baby near me."

Tinkie kept coming, though Pauline fell back a few steps. She was young and inexperienced in bullying charlatan matrons. Tinkie would teach her.

"Mrs. Osteller, do you not like babies?" Tinkie asked as she climbed the steps. "Maylin is my first. She's a miracle baby. I was told I'd never conceive, and yet I did, and she is perfect. A magnificent little soul. I can't bear to be without her for even ten minutes. But it sure is cold out here. May we come in and warm up?"

The nanny's face reflected first fear, then horror, and finally appreciation. Exactly the emotions that rolled over me at Tinkie's finessing of the situation. There was no way Tilly could deny us and still claim to be a lady of the South.

"Come in." Tilly reluctantly stepped back from the doorway. "But I have to leave in a few minutes. I have an appointment."

"With whom?" I asked impertinently.

"With my hairstylist, if you must know." She was seething and it gave me immense pleasure.

"Who do you use?" Tinkie asked. "You've achieved the perfect blend of proper matron and rich dilettante."

Even I was shocked at how quickly Tinkie went for the jugular, but I hid my smile.

"Tilly says her family on the coast was earnest and downright boring. They never did anything fun or exciting. She and Clarence just worked and saved and built that big old honking church up the road."

"Too bad." Tinkie forged past Tilly and headed for the front parlor. She took a seat in an overstuffed chair, kicked off her shoes, and sighed. "Would you happen to have some coffee? I'm chilled to the bone, standing out in the cold when you wouldn't invite us in."

Tilly picked up a small silver bell and rang it. When a maid came into the room she asked for coffee for everyone. "Does the baby need anything?" she asked. I thought her lips might crack and fall off.

When we were all seated, holding bone china cups with piping hot coffee that was excellent, Tinkie walked through the forbidden door. "So your family was boring, but the word is that Clarence's family was involved with the mob in Chicago and the Dixie Mafia down here. Tell us some stories. It's all so exciting."

Tinkie held her coffee cup like a perfect lady, even with a baby in her arms. I wanted to clap, but I didn't.

"Where did you hear that?" Tilly asked with an edge in her voice.

"Why, everyone in town has told me," Tinkie said. "Is it wrong? It just sounds so thrilling."

"Clarence has nothing to do with that side of his family. His parents were merchants, as I said. Besides, they're all dead anyway."

"That's such a shame." Tinkie leaned forward. "I heard from a reliable source that Capone's money has been found in some offshore accounts. There's much discussion on who owns those accounts, and I thought perhaps it might be some of Clarence's people. But since they're all dead, that's that."

"Wait. What offshore accounts?"

Tinkie had reeled her in perfectly. "I can't say more." Tinkie sighed. "I shouldn't have mentioned that. Please don't repeat it. My husband will kill me for talking out of school."

Oscar might not kill her, but I was going to. If word got out about those accounts . . . I stopped myself. What would happen? Nothing. Absolutely nothing. If anything, a wildfire of rumors about Capone's money would only help us. It might move the kidnappers to take action. And it would certainly increase book sales for both authors. Tinkie was definitely the brains of Delaney Detective Agency.

36

Tilly's dainty little foot patted the floor with mounting fury. She was ready for us to be gone. Tinkie had asked for cookies for Maylin—which Tinkie then ate joyfully. The baby was too little to chew such things. All the while Tinkie kept up a nonstop conversation about all the scandals in the Mississippi Delta. I learned a few things and suspected she was making a lot of it up.

Tilly didn't know anyone Tinkie was talking about and didn't want to know them. She only wanted us to leave. When I felt she'd been pushed to the absolute brink of faux hospitality, I struck.

"Tilly, I haven't been completely honest about why I'm here."

"Name your amount to leave. I'll get a check instantly."

I would have felt sorry for her if she wasn't such a hypocrite. "It's not about money, or at least you giving us money. It's about Clarence. You know he's been peeping in Janet's windows."

If her lips had seemed hard and brittle before, now they looked like she could grind glass with her mouth. "You're insane, and I can tell you right now if you start spreading rumors like that we will sue you out of existence. My husband is a preacher and a man of God. He has no interest in a harlot like Janet Malone."

"Really? Perhaps you'd like to talk to Sheriff Peters. And I have photos of Clarence. I saw him."

Lying was getting easier and easier for me. I wondered if this was true of all fabricators and embellishers.

"Get out of my house." She stood up, but none of us moved at all. Pauline looked like a skittish horse. Her eyes were rolling and her breathing was short. She was ready to bolt but afraid to make the first move. I did feel for her. She was caught between two forces of nature.

"We can leave, but it won't stop the interview Tinkie is giving this afternoon in a plea for information leading to the recovery of Sandra and Daryl. It's been four days since they were seen. If they were abandoned somewhere, they are in dire circumstances. If they're dead, their families need to know and collect their bodies. It's time for this to end."

"Maybe offer a reward?" Tilly said snidely.

"Good idea." I looked at Tinkie. "I'm sure Janet would pay at least $100,000. Don't you think?"

"At least."

Something flicked in Tilly's eyes and I thought of a reptile. It was such an unpleasant association that I stood up. My body told me to get out, but I just walked behind Tinkie's chair and put a hand on her shoulder. "Did Coleman show you the photos of Clarence scouting Janet's house?" I asked my partner.

"He did. He was going to send them to Cece for media distribution this afternoon."

"Oh, stop it!" Tilly waved her hands wildly in very unladylike hysteria. "What is it you want to know?"

"In a nutshell, where Sandra and Daryl are," Tinkie said quickly.

"I honestly don't know. And neither does Clarence. He has been watching Janet, hoping for some blackmail video or something to pry some dollars from her fist. She and Sandra are so selfish. They refuse to donate to the church."

"That's their choice," Tinkie pointed out.

"They're loaded to the gills. Everyone knows that."

Tilly was of the school that what's hers was hers and what was Janet's was hers, too. "You'd better have something better than that for me or the press conference is on."

"Then you'll leave?"

"Pinkie swear." Tinkie and I performed the ritual. "Now, spill it."

"Clarence saw someone at the house the night before Sandra and Daryl disappeared. He was there hoping to get some film of Sandra and Daryl. Everyone in town knows they have an illicit relationship and he's practically a child."

I didn't want to get sidetracked defending Sandra. She could do that herself when we found her. "Who did he see?"

"He said it was Sandra's brother, Ray. The mean one."

"What was he doing?"

"Spying. He was outside the library last night at the soiree, too. I think that's who Mary was chasing."

"You've known this all along and didn't tell anyone?" I

was angry at her and also angry at myself. I'd known about the brothers. I'd done a cursory check and discovered that either of them could have been on the Gulf Coast. But I hadn't pursued it. I hadn't taken the next step to find out where the brothers actually were. I'd failed at my job. Still, I had to keep pressing Tilly to get what I could from her. "You'd better come clean or you will regret it."

"Why should I?"

"To pretend you're a decent human being?" Tinkie said with heat.

"I don't have to pretend anything. This is none of my affair. The O'Day family members are nothing but criminals. Everyone in town believed Sandra set the blast that killed her parents."

"What? Why?" I sputtered.

"For the Capone money. We knew either Sandra or Janet had it all along. Why else would Sandra buy the old Buntman mansion? It had to be on the premises, or so we thought. Now you say it's offshore."

"Janet told me that locals and treasure hunters had torn that house apart for years when it was sitting empty. If there was treasure to be found, someone would have claimed it. Or maybe they did and it's gone. It's crazy to think that Sandra magically had a way to find the treasure that no one else could locate."

"We know better than that." Tilly's nostrils flared. "There's a map on some wall. Carved into the wood or whatever. It's local legend. Didn't you notice how people were wandering around the mansion during the Christmas party? Everyone is still looking for it." She grinned with satisfaction.

"Where is Ray staying?"

Tilly shrugged. "Beats me and I don't care. But he was always mean to Sandra. Growing up he did awful things to her. Once he tried to burn her at the stake. He told everyone she was a witch and he was Cotton Mather."

"How do you know this?" I asked. Few people in the area told childhood tales on either writer unless it was happy malarkey about playing on the beach or something blissful like that. Sandra and Janet may have shown their patoots with their brawls around town, but in true small-town fashion, they belonged to the town and would be protected as a natural resource. Even their scandals were valued by many in the community. They were eccentric, awful, fabulous, famous, and native Bay St. Louisans.

She gave me the evil eye. "I made it a point to know things about those two. We needed donations from them."

Tilly had been involved in the blackmail plot. I was not shocked—among the least. I wondered if she might have played a role among the people who'd been outside the library when Mary had been knocked out, taken to the mansion, and almost asphyxiated. There had been two people and the Ostellers had been at the party. Had they left before I went outside looking for Mary? I couldn't remember. But I had an idea.

"If I hadn't fallen in that ditch, I would have caught you at the library and we might know where Sandra and Daryl are right now."

Tilly scoffed. "But you did fall in the ditch and I got away. Don't blame me because you're clum—"

I had her. She'd admitted it was her. "Mary will be filing charges against Clarence as soon as I tell her who attacked her."

Tilly pointed at the door. "Get out this instant."

Tinkie and Pauline rose to their feet. They knew as well as I did that we'd played our hand as good as we could. It was time to go. But I had one more punch to throw.

"Why were you and Clarence stalking Mary?" I honestly didn't get it. Mary had no money. Weezie was her most prized possession, along with her love and knowledge of books. What could Clarence hope to gain from harming Mary?

"Get out of my house or I'm calling the police."

"We've been through that threat, Tilly. You have more to lose from an officer asking questions than I do. But we are leaving. For the moment. If I have more questions, I'll be back and I'll bring Chief Thibodeau with me. Your husband understands what I'm capable of. Now, I think you do, too."

We took our time getting down the steps and to the car. When everyone was buckled up, I pulled away from the curb. Tilly was standing on her front stoop. She made a vulgar gesture at me and I gave her a thumbs-up. At least I knew exactly how deep the "grand lady" values ran in her. Just below the skin.

"Clarence is going to skin us if he can," Tinkie warned me in a soft voice. Maylin and the nanny were both snoozing in the back seat. The tense situation had taken it out of both of them.

"What can he do? Call Thibodeau? That should be fun."

"Why harm Mary?" Tinkie asked.

"I may have figured that out. Clarence was trying to blackmail both Sandra and Janet into making a donation. If Mary were found dead in Sandra's car and in Sandra's garage, Clarence might have some leverage to extract money from the writers."

Tinkie rubbed the place between her eyebrows with her

forefinger. "I am disgusted by that thought. And even worse, I think you may be right. It would take extraordinary greed to kill an innocent woman just for leverage."

I couldn't dispute that. "Call Mary and tell her." I wanted her to know, so she could take the necessary steps to make Clarence and Tilly pay.

"I guess when you started after Tilly, Clarence went in the other direction, hoping to get away, but Mary chased him. Tilly was lucky you fell in that ditch or you would have caught her."

I listened as she relayed what we'd just learned. I could hear Mary's squawk of outrage even though the phone wasn't on speaker.

"Don't worry," Tinkie said to her, "we're on the case. But you might want to talk to the police chief. He should know about this and move forward with what he needs to do. I'd feel better if both Ostellers were behind bars, at least until we find Daryl and Sandra."

I signaled Tinkie to put the phone on speaker, then I asked Mary a question. "Mary, what is Daryl's relationship with Sandra? I have to know the truth. It could give us a lead or a place to look for them. And also, tell me about Ray O'Day. I understand he's been in town this week."

"He has? Who told you that?" Mary asked.

"Tilly. She said he was a mean kid who bullied his sister."

"That's true. He tormented Janet, too. He was just one of those bigger boys who took pleasure in making others scared. When did he arrive in town?"

"We don't know that," Tinkie said.

"This isn't good news for Sandra," Mary said.

"We found some of Capone's financial accounts in Janet's attic. Harold and Oscar are tracking them down.

Tinkie told Tilly and it will soon be all over town. Probably by lunch. I thought you might be able to offer some information or advice."

"Fair warning to both of you. Ray never believed the treasure was gone. Never. And he means to have his share of it, no matter the cost."

"Good to know. Now, what about Daryl?"

"He is Sandra's assistant. He is like a brother or son to her, nothing more. I know that boy inside and out. When Sandra introduced him to the world of writing, researching, and publishing, Daryl might as well have been her blood. He is dedicated to her, and even to Janet. He adores books, especially their books. And he doesn't have a mean bone in his body."

"There's no romance, nothing Sandra could be blackmailed over?"

"None. And even if they were having an affair, Daryl isn't a child. No laws have been broken. There's no seed for blackmail to grow."

She had a point. "Thanks, Mary. Oh, did that reporter ever show up again?"

"Haven't seen her yet," Mary said, "but I'll call if she does show up."

37

We drove for a few minutes while I collected my thoughts. "There are two things we need ASAP. To find Ray and to check out Daryl's house in Pass Christian."

"We should have done that sooner," Tinkie said.

"True. We haven't exactly been sitting on our hands, but we can take care of it right now."

We hadn't heard from Coleman and Oscar, or Millie and Cece, which meant none of them had found anything of value. Harold was with Janet, and there was radio silence there. I didn't even want to think what the cause of that might be. Some images you couldn't ever get out of your brain.

We were almost at the coast, so we stayed on Highway 90, rising high above the bay on the new bridge as we headed east toward Pass Christian. Since we had an address for

Daryl's house, it would be the quickest to check. Tinkie also texted Thibodeau to tell him about Ray O'Day being in town and asking for help in locating him.

Thibodeau's response was, "Oink, oink, which in pig means certainly."

"I'm going to have to kill him," I said, but Tinkie was laughing so hard she didn't even hear me.

I always viewed Bay St. Louis as the artist town and Pass Christian as the wealthy people's village. Katrina's horrific damage from 2005 was still in evidence. So many of the beautiful homes, set beneath a canopy of magnificent live oaks, had been destroyed. The trees had taken a harsh battering. Those oaks had survived decades of storms without ill effect, but Katrina was different. She was the first Gulf Coast mega-storm of the global warming cycle. The oaks down the entire stretch of the coastal rim had been savaged.

The coastal cities and even private residents did everything they could to save the trees from the tidal wave of salt water that came in with the storm. Houses had been completely washed away, changing the look of the coast for almost two decades. The houses were heavy losses, but could be rebuilt. The oaks, though, caused grief for residents and visitors alike.

Some of the trees survived, but seventeen years later, they still looked tattered and weak. Sculptures had been made from the trunks of the trees that died. Incredible artwork, but never as beautiful as a living tree.

"Here's the street his house is on." Tinkie pointed at Hemingway Lane.

We turned north from the beachfront and traveled through an arch of trees. The houses were huge, old antebellum homes that captured a graciousness of a time long gone. The farther inland we drove, the smaller the houses became and the traditional Southern architecture gave way to European, Spanish, and modern influences. Each house was unique.

Daryl's was a creole-style cottage built at least fifteen feet off the ground. Double staircases swept in a curve up to a gracious front porch that was decorated in tinsel and lights. I'd heard that the staircase design was created during the floor-length skirt days to prevent men from seeing a woman's ankle as she climbed the steps. Fascinating.

Daryl had chosen a very traditional style, which was exactly what I'd expected. There was a carport beneath the house—empty. There was also a lift that took a person up the back stairs of the house, likely to the kitchen entrance. Climbing all of these steps would have gotten old fast for me.

Tinkie rode the lift up and knocked on the door. "It's locked," she called down to me as I was inspecting the ground below the house. There was storage space and tools, among other things. It reminded me of the way Daryl's parents' business was built. He was more connected to them than he thought. He'd re-created something of his childhood, if in a more elegant form.

"I'll try the front door," I called to Tinkie.

"I have a bobby pin. I'll keep trying here."

She was clever with lock picks and such, but who had bobby pins anymore? I walked out of the shadow of the house into the sun and climbed up to the front porch. I was stunned by the view, which looked out over a sliver of the gulf and several lovely estates. The house was custom designed and cost a pretty penny. Daryl had done well working with Sandra.

I knocked at the front door but got no response. When I

tried the knob, though, the door swung open. Pass Christian wasn't a high crime area, but still, only a very careless person would leave a house unlocked.

I stopped in the foyer when I saw the first sign of trouble. Books and papers were scattered over the floor in the living room. Something big had been burned in the fireplace. Being careful not to touch anything, I opened the back door for Tinkie using the bottom of my shirt to keep from leaving any fingerprints. I'd wipe the front doorknob before I left.

"Holy hell," Tinkie said, looking in the kitchen at the emptied drawers and broken plates and cups. "Either someone was pissed or they were in a real hurry to look for something."

"I wonder if they found it." I realized that better than pretending we hadn't been here would be just to call Thibodeau and confess that we walked through the open front door and found this mess. I put words into action.

The police chief was soon on his way to Daryl's home to investigate the break-in. "By the way," he said over the phone, "Ray O'Day is staying at the White House Hotel over in Biloxi. I was about to ask the Biloxi PD to pick him up."

"Give me a chance to talk to him first," I requested.

"You've got an hour. I can't risk him harming anyone if he's in town to make trouble."

"We'll be done in an hour and I'll let you know the status."

"Take that big lawman with you," Thibodeau said. "He's not as good-looking as that pig, but he'll do in a pinch."

It was official. I was never going to live down the pig ride. And I hadn't even been drunk, which made it worse.

I didn't bother to respond but hung up on the sound of Thibodeau's deep laughter. "Ray is staying at the White House Hotel," I told Tinkie. "Let's hope he's there."

Lunchtime was upon us, and the White House had a reputation for fine dining. But we weren't there to eat. The beautiful old place had been completely refurbished since Katrina hit. It had retained the old-world charm with all the modern conveniences.

In the lobby Tinkie drifted away while I asked the clerk to connect me with Ray's room on the house phone. In a moment, I was talking with Sandra's brother.

"Would you mind meeting us in the lobby?" I asked him. "Janet has hired us to find Sandra."

"Not doing a great job, are you?"

Well, the years hadn't improved his personality. "Perhaps you can help."

"I haven't spoken to my sister in a decade. I don't know a thing about her so I doubt I'll be of any help."

"Let me at least buy you a drink. I hear the Bloody Marys here are excellent."

"You've aroused my curiosity. I'll be down in ten minutes."

I hung up and saw that Tinkie was waving me over. When I got there I realized that the beautiful oil portrait she'd discovered was of Helene Buntman. She was so vibrant and alive in the painting that I stopped and gawked. "My goodness, she is glamorous."

"Yes, she is."

The male voice came from behind me and I turned to confront Ray O'Day. There was no doubt he was Sandra's brother. He favored her. And he had a chip on his shoulder almost as big as hers. "I'm Sarah Booth Delaney and this is Tinkie Richmond." I extended my hand and he ignored it. "Let's have a drink." I led the way toward a table in the bar, still a little shocked that he'd agreed to talk with us.

When we were settled, I assessed Ray. He was a handsome

man, only a few years older than me. He was athletic and confident. I got the sense he really didn't like us, or maybe it was just women in general. After all, according to the gossip, he'd bullied his sister.

"Why are you in Biloxi now?" I asked.

"Vacation," he said.

"Did you see Sandra before she went missing?"

"I have no interest in seeing her. She's so full of herself with her books and writing and bestseller lists. Besides, she's so selfish she doesn't care if she's in danger or puts anyone else in the line of fire." He waved a hand to dismiss the thought of her. "I came for the fishing."

As I recalled, the O'Day family, like so many of the old settler families, had been part of the fishing industry. The brothers, though, had given up the coast and that lifestyle for white collar jobs inland. "Is it red snapper season?" I asked.

Ray shrugged. "My trip is more for nostalgia than as a professional fisherman. I just rented a boat to get out on the water and enjoy the winter sun. I love the beaches when they're mostly empty."

So he hadn't come to fish or he'd know exactly what was running and what was legal. "If you had to guess what's happened to Sandra, what would you say?" Tinkie asked him. She batted her eyes and, for a moment, his antagonism toward us seemed to lessen.

"Sandra was always a spoiled brat. I'd say she's parked at some fine hotel somewhere not too far away, drinking White Russians and laughing about all the fools out hunting for her. She loves nothing better than being the center of attention."

"You aren't concerned for her at all?" I asked.

"Not in the least. You could throw Sandra in a pit of cottonmouth snakes and the snakes would die."

There was no love lost between the siblings. "Is your brother Ben in the area, too?"

"I don't keep up with him either. Look, once I left the Gulf Coast, I stopped trying to influence Sandra or Ben. They're both too hardheaded to help."

It was a curious way to phrase it. To help. "You tried to help Sandra?"

He grimaced. "She could never keep her trap shut. This book about the local mafia, the Capone connection, buying that dead movie star's house where everyone in town thinks the treasure is hidden. How stupid can one woman be? It's like setting a hornet's nest on fire and then standing there to watch them swarm out."

I glanced at Tinkie and she nodded. We were both shocked at how sincere Ray sounded. Contrary to what we'd been told about him, he acted as if he truly cared for his sister—albeit begrudgingly.

"You honestly think someone has taken Sandra and her assistant because of her book?" Tinkie asked.

"I'd be more inclined to believe it was because of the treasure, but the book implies she knows more about things than she possibly could. It's like a big target on her head." He cleared his throat. "I heard you found evidence of off-shore accounts Capone had set up."

My shock went deeper. Deny it or not, Ray was still connected in the community. It had only been a few hours earlier that we'd fed that information to Tilly. We were drawing closer to the knot that tangled this whole case.

38

"Do you believe Ray doesn't know where Ben is?" Tinkie asked as we followed a waitress from the bar into the dining room at the White House Hotel. I'd texted everyone to meet us there for food and a meeting. Only Harold wouldn't be with us, but he'd gotten away from Janet. He was still working on financial records from his room at the inn. Oscar had helped carry all the boxes we'd found at Janet's house over to him. Harold had borrowed a computer from somewhere and was now in business, tracking down accounts and transfers and whatever rich people did to hide their money.

Harold had decided against working on the financial issues at Janet's house. I didn't know if he was being discreet or if he wanted to give his bone marrow a chance to replenish from Janet's constant sucking at it. She was a hungry woman. I'd noticed more than once that guys often loved a woman who needed them. Janet wasn't truly needy, but she sure could make a man feel like he was the most important thing in the world. She'd carved out a superior life for herself, as had Sandra. Playing to the ego of a man was just part of the role at the socioeconomic strata they'd achieved. Thank God for Coleman and Oscar, who were just happy if Tinkie and I didn't end up injured.

"I don't know what Ray and Ben know," I said. "It's hard to find the truth about relationships around here. People cover everything up, even when it's not necessary." I felt as if my entire stay in Bay St. Louis had been filled with half-truths and deliberate misrepresentations. And, to be fair, some mighty beautiful Christmas trees, laughter, great music, and better friends.

"Are we going caroling tonight?" Tinkie asked. "We need to head home tomorrow. I don't mind missing Christmas Eve dinner, but we can't miss that church pageant. The Zinnia Beautification and Decorating Committee will kick me out if Maylin isn't swaddled appropriately and in that manger for the Christmas service."

"We'll be home in plenty of time. I promise. We can get some store-bought food since we won't have time to cook anything."

Store-bought went against every tradition I'd clung to with such intensity, but although we had come to Bay St. Louis to relax, a new case had taken over our vacation. All of my friends were missing their traditional festivities. To whine about it would be poor form. "Whatever we do, it will be wonderful because we'll be together."

"Tonight, Santa will leave Maylin toys and goodies. Her first Christmas." Tinkie leaned across the table and grasped my hands. "My daughter will have her first Christmas, Sarah Booth. It would never have happened without you."

Oh, that was taking it too far. Tinkie would have been in a hospital to have her baby if it weren't for me. Because of me she'd delivered in the Moran's backyard. "Doc and Millie saved you."

"Yes, but all of the times I was so blue about being unable to conceive, you told me I would get pregnant. You believed in my body more than I did. And you introduced me to the Harrington sisters, who cast a spell for me."

It hadn't happened exactly that way, but I let her believe what she wanted. I squeezed her hands. "And we have our perfect baby girl! Our first Christmas with Maylin. Coleman and I will be over to help get her ready for show-time."

"Coleman is a wise man, right?"

"Yes, like Oscar and Harold."

"And you're a . . . camel in the pageant?"

Why had I let Coleman talk me into being manger live-stock? I couldn't remember. "Yes, and I will be behaved and quiet so as not to wreak havoc on the nativity scene."

"A docile camel. Can't wait," Tinkie said with a twinkle in her eye.

I was about to question her further, but Coleman and Oscar showed up with Maylin and Pauline. Cece and Millie were right behind them. We ordered Poinsettias and settled back to enjoy the champagne and tart cranberry juice. The White House Hotel was beautiful at any season, but Christmas lent itself to the stellar decorations and the old-world atmosphere the hotel cultivated. A pianist tinkled out Christmas standards in the main dining room. I took a moment to acknowledge the holiday, the season, and my remarkable friends. Our stay in Bay St. Louis was coming to a close and we'd done nothing but try to find Sandra and Daryl.

We were on our second Poinsettias, with Tinkie opting for iced green tea, when Cece cleared her throat. "I may have some good news."

"Well, spill it," Tinkie said. "I'm about to slip into a depression here. We're closing out the visit without solving anything."

"Head over to the library when we finish lunch. Mary has been working on that wall art or hieroglyphics or whatever you want to call it. She thinks she may know a key to reading it."

I jumped up from that table. "I'm not hungry. I can't wait."

Tinkie, who was holding Maylin, stood up slowly. It was clear leaving her baby was tearing at her heart. "You stay, Tinkie," I told her. "If there's anything to be found. I'll call. You need to be with that angelic little girl."

Tinkie looked like she was about to cry, and Oscar stepped up. "Tinkie, I'll drive you straight to the library if Sarah Booth needs you," he said. "I think she and Coleman need some time."

"Me? I was looking forward to eating," Coleman said and made everyone laugh because they knew he was deviling me.

The bottoms of my feet were itching to move and I grabbed Coleman's hand. We were off.

Mary was waiting for us at the library. Tinkie had thoughtfully called ahead to alert her we were coming. She had all the materials laid out in her office, where Weezie rubbed against my leg and purred.

I picked Weezie up and gave her a kiss on the top of her

head. I really did believe the cat had led me to the earring, which in turn resulted in me finding Mary nearly asphyxiated. "By the way, do you think it was Clarence who did that to you?"

"I do," Mary said. "And I'm also pretty sure that red-headed reporter looking to interview you was someone from his church that he put up to it. A library patron said she saw a redheaded woman leaving Daryl's house in a hurry. I'm laying that mischief at Clarence's feet, too."

"Do you have any evidence?" I asked.

"I remember his aftershave. I caught a whiff at the party, and then when he grabbed me from behind, I smelled it again. That's not evidence, but it's enough for me. I'll take care of him in my own way, so don't even worry about it."

"Mary, let Thibodeau handle it," Coleman said. He cut his eyes at me. "I'm reasonably certain he'll get Clarence to confess."

Mary shook her head. "Clarence has been a burr under my saddle for a long time. He's not who he pretends to be, and that wife of his, Lord, she needs . . ." She didn't finish.

"Tilly isn't a very nice person," I agreed.

"She's driven by greed. But I'll have a meeting with both of them and I'll come away with a substantial donation to the library. That's better revenge than anything the law can hand me."

"That's blackmail," Coleman pointed out.

"Maybe. Or maybe I'll just appeal to their civic natures."

Weezie held up a paw to Mary as if she were giving a high five.

I had to laugh. Mary was wily, and with Weezie on her side, victory was assured. "Did you figure out what the carvings on the wall in the tomb mean?" I was eager to hear what she'd uncovered.

"Maybe. It's a wild blend of a lot of things, including characters from the Biloxi tribe of Native Americans who lived in these parts before the white settlers came and took over the land. The wall is fascinating because it also contains images from hieroglyphics, cuneiform, and rudimentary images common to children. Someone with a good education created that montage. I was able to borrow some research documents from the Library of Congress and put together what I hope is the message."

"Why would Helene or Capone blend those so very different images?"

"If it was them," Mary said. "The house was empty for a long time. I can't imagine some artist going in there to carve a tomb wall, but you can ask Janet. The Biloxi language isn't so far-fetched. Some of the early settlers married Native Americans. As to cuneiform and hieroglyphics, they look basically decorative. And I warn you, I'm not claiming I've translated this accurately at all. To be honest, it doesn't make a lot of sense to me."

"What does it say?" I was ready to jump out of my skin with anxiety.

"Let me show you."

We got behind her desk so we could look at the photo of the wall markings. Mary slowly began to sort out the different images, referring to several documents and texts to give the meaning. I saw the direction she was taking and my excitement rose. "It's a way to find Capone's treasure."

"My thoughts exactly," Mary said. "But the literal translation doesn't make sense. See here where it talks about a three-headed dog. I can't begin to figure out what that actually means."

She was in the dark only because she either hadn't been to the tomb or just didn't remember it. I had a hunch, though. "What about the three-headed dog?"

"It's like a riddle." Mary pointed out the images she was translating. "'Head one remains, head two static, head three looks at the future reward.' That's a loose translation to the best of my ability."

A statue of a goddess, likely Diana, and a three-headed dog was outside the tomb. I hadn't examined it closely, but the wall map could refer to that statue. The sculpture was stone, though. None of the dog heads could move. And to the best of my ability, I couldn't remember anything like treasure that any of the dog heads might be looking at. Mary was right. It didn't make sense.

"Is there anything else?" Coleman pressed.

"There are words, images. See here"—she pointed at a triangle floating above a wavy line—"I think this is simply what it appears to be, a sailing ship. And that one looks like a treasure chest marked with an X."

Those were the images I remembered. "But there's no other clue or text with them?"

"No." Mary shook her head. "I can't make them connect. It's just the riddle of the three-headed dog that seems to make a sentence, even though it's nonsensical."

"It sounds like one of the heads should move," I said. "But the sculpture is stone. Nothing will move."

"What sculpture?" Mary asked.

"At the mansion."

Mary's eyes widened. "Let's go now!" She turned around to get her coat and purse.

Coleman gripped my shoulder. "Now I'll put up with you riding a pig, but if you try to climb aboard a three-headed dog, it's over between us."

I almost burst out laughing, but I contained it. We rushed out of the library to Mary's car. Five minutes later we pulled up the driveway of the Buntman/O'Day mansion.

Once we parked, we ran across the yard toward the mausoleum. I still had the keys to the house and the tomb, but I was hoping we didn't have to go inside. The crime scene tape was gone, but a feeling of dread settled over me. Across the lawn I had a perfect view of the bay, and I couldn't help but recall Poe's famous poem about a dead love.

"The statue!" Mary said in a reverent tone as she approached the stone woman I took to be Diana. "And there's the three-headed dog! I've lived here all of my life and been to parties here, but I never came out to the mausoleum."

"Not a lot of people find a reason to visit a tomb," Coleman said. He walked over to the dog and felt the three heads. "Looks like a three-headed greyhound, doesn't it? Nothing moves. It's solid stone."

He was right. The dog was lean and fit. It looked ready to spring away and run for the simple joy of running. I touched the head nearest me, which was turned to the north, then the center head, which looked forward, and then the third head, which looked to the south. This dog head had a view of the bay and any ships that might be coming in. I knelt down and looked deep into the canine eyes. As far as I could tell, they were just eyes carved with holes fitted into the stone. There was no life or secret or anything else there.

Bitter disappointment flooded through me. Coleman's hand came down on my shoulder and he gently lifted me to my feet. "Is anything there?"

"Not that I see." I absolutely refused to cry. The tension and worry over Sandra and Daryl had been walled up in me and now the pressure broke. I turned to face the bay, hiding my raw emotions, fighting not to give in to tears. Coleman's arms came around my shoulders and he pulled me against him.

"Don't give up, Sarah Booth."

"I got my hopes up. I'm okay, just disappointed. I thought we were on the trail of finding them."

"Me, too," he said. "Me, too."

"Don't stop hunting them now," Mary said stoutly. "It's been a long time, but they could still be alive. Until bodies are found we can't give up hope."

"Tell me the translation again," I requested, brushing at my cheeks to flick off any stray tears.

Mary repeated what she'd transcribed and then she began feeling the dog statue. She probed and pushed and stroked, to no avail. At last she struck one dog head with her fist. "This can't be all there is to this!"

I walked around the dog and looked between its ears, following the dog's would-be line of sight to the bay. The ground sloped and dropped, and closer to the water's edge it was covered in a dense copse of trees and wild undergrowth. Nothing unusual to see, but I kept looking. "Is there something in those trees?"

"Like what?" Coleman was looking, too.

I pointed down the dog's snout with my arm. "Right there."

"What do you see?" Coleman and Mary asked together.

As the image came into better focus, I inhaled sharply. "Is that some kind of . . . grave?"

39

Without a word we all three ran across the lawn toward the woods. It was a good distance, and by the time Coleman hit the tree line, he was ahead of Mary and me. He slowed and began examining the terrain carefully. He was waiting on me to check it out. I wanted to kiss him but there was no time.

"There it is!" It was a monument of a sort. Since I was close upon it, I could see it was a dog. A beautiful little papillon, standing at attention, looked up the slope toward the mausoleum. And then I remembered the photos of Helene Buntman in her exquisite gowns and the little dog that was constantly beside her.

The gravestone was beautifully carved and listed the dog's name as Delilah. Some of the images from the wall carvings were also on the stone. I knew it was important, but I couldn't figure out how.

"I wonder why they didn't bury Delilah up near the mausoleum?" Mary said. "I'd want my dog with me, don't you think?"

I did think. And it gave me pause. "Mary, do you have a clue what these markings on the stone mean?"

She studied them. "Not really, but my best guess is something below. It seems to indicate the bay."

In for a penny, in for a pound, as Aunt Loulane would say. We continued through the woods to the bay. Someone had put in a nice bulkhead to keep the tide from eroding the slope of the property. Coleman walked beside me as we clung to the grass above the reinforcement.

"This must have cost a pretty penny to put in," Coleman said. "Even back in the day when it was built." We came to a place where the retaining wall had been washed away. The soil and grass spilled down to the sand and almost into the water.

"That'll have to be repaired," Mary said. "Left like that the tides and storms will wash a lot of this hill away."

True. I jumped down to the beach. It wasn't the beautiful white sand to be found on the barrier islands; still, it had its own allure. The damage to the bulkhead must have been done during a freak storm a few weeks ago. It required attention now. Coleman leaned down to give me a hand. I was about to step up on the fortified bank again when something shiny winked in the sunlight. "Just a minute." I bent down and dug in the dirt that had spilled from the broken wall. My fingers captured the round disk. When I brought it out of the dirt and dusted it off, I had a Liberty Gold coin.

Mary reached for it, and I handed it to her. She studied the coin. "That's worth a couple of thousand dollars today."

Coleman and Mary jumped down and we began digging. It didn't take us long to find the leather bags that had deteriorated. The coins, hundreds of them, had spilled into the dirt. Coleman put in a call to Thibodeau, explained the situation, and we sat back to wait for the lawman to bring an excavation crew.

The treasure find was a big deal, but I had hoped to find Sandra and Daryl. I couldn't help feeling deflated.

When the law arrived with a team to excavate, Mary, Coleman, and I walked back to the mausoleum on the way to the house. "I'm sorry," Mary said. "I thought we'd find them."

"Me, too." I had to pull myself out of the depression I'd fallen into. My watch showed the afternoon was drawing to a close. We could either go caroling tonight as we'd planned, or we could go home. We'd get up on Christmas Day with our families and joys of the season. We'd refresh our determination and Tinkie and I would come back to BSL to close out our case. Our first failure.

Would we ever know what had happened to Sandra O'Day and Daryl Marcus? It didn't seem possible that we'd never figure it out.

Mary put her arm around my waist. "This isn't your fault. You've looked everywhere. I heard this morning that Sandra's publisher is going to launch a full-scale search. The head of her publishing house has called the governor and the Mississippi Bureau of Investigation."

"They won't find more than Sarah Booth did," Coleman said.

I adored his support of me, but we had to face reality. "No, but they have more manpower and warrants to search places I can't. They can compel people to talk and all I can do is ask." I was thinking of Clarence and Tilly Osteller. I couldn't help but believe they knew more than they'd said.

"You snatch whomever you want to question and bring them to me," Mary said. "I'll make them talk. They'll be babbling like a brook when I finish with them."

Mary would do it, too. I smiled at her. "I don't want you to go to prison."

"Then don't give up, Sarah Booth. You look so defeated." Mary put a consoling hand on my back.

"I'm fine. It's just sad. It doesn't seem like there's family who really misses either of them. Sandra's brother didn't appear too concerned that she's been missing for days. Daryl's parents, especially his mom, want him back, but . . ." But not enough to help.

We'd reached the mausoleum and I stepped away from my friends. "I'll join you in the house in a minute."

Coleman looked concerned, but he took Mary's elbow and assisted her up the steep incline. I needed a moment alone. In a crazy way, I'd grown fond of Janet Malone, and Bay St. Louis had begun to feel like a second home. It was time to go back to Zinnia, at least for a while, but I'd never had to go home in defeat. It happened to everyone, but this had seemed like such a simple case. I couldn't bear to think of Sandra and Daryl, waiting and waiting for rescue that never came. Where in the hell were they?

I sat down by the three-headed dog. "Tell me your secrets," I said. "I found your hidden treasure." Any other day I would be jumping and screaming for joy. But the treasure was nothing to me with Sandra and Daryl still gone.

A crow flew overhead, followed by another. Then three more. They settled on the roof of the mausoleum, a regular crow festival. I listened to their cawing and watched their antics. They were smart. Why did humans always underestimate animals? These birds had complex relationships, and as far as I could tell, a sense of humor.

I put my hand on the dog to pull myself to my feet. It was time to leave the mansion and get on with the rest of the day. Then, as I looked into the mouth of the southward facing dog, I saw something in the back of its throat. I reached in and felt it was hard and cold. Dread touched me, but I kept working it until I could pull it out. To my relief, it wasn't a human bone but a carved stone object.

Nothing to write home about, but I studied it, willing it to be significant. And then it hit me. I held up the little artifact that looked like some of the carvings on the tomb wall.

I opened the door, careful to leave the stone in the door so it couldn't close and shut me inside again. I didn't have a lighter so the torches were useless, but I had my phone. I made my way to the back wall and studied the carvings until I found one that looked like the artifact.

I took the object from my pocket and pressed it into the carving. The sound of stone grinding on stone made me whip around just as the top of the empty tomb began to shift. Slowly, slowly it opened.

Paralyzed by dread, I leaned against the wall. When the grinding and shifting noise stopped, there was total silence.

I could see daylight at the door, which remained blocked by the stone placed there. Using my phone light, I inched over to the tomb and looked in. A stone stairway led down to a turn. Then blackness. If the lid of the tomb closed over me, I didn't know if Coleman would ever find me. I was about to step outside and text him to come help me when I heard a cry. It was weak and pitiful, but distinctively human.

"Help us. Please, help us."

It was Daryl! I was positive. I climbed up on the tomb and slid over the edge. In a moment I was going down the stairs, which fed into a large area. Daryl and Sandra were propped against the back wall where a portion of the stone structure had collapsed.

I rushed toward them, amazed and relieved they were still alive. Empty water bottles and food wrappers were scattered on the floor. They'd had some provisions, but they were both weak and in precarious health. "Can you walk?" I asked them.

"I can." Daryl stood shakily. We both pulled Sandra to her feet. She was unsteady, but she could walk.

"We just have to get up the stairs. Then help will come. Or I can get help."

"No!" Sandra grabbed my arm in a death grip. "Don't leave us. Don't leave."

It wasn't a great distance, but it was a journey of a thousand steps as we all three made our way up the stairs and to the tomb. I climbed out and then helped pull Sandra over the edge. Daryl made it on his own.

I knew I was pushing it, but I had to know. "Why are you in a damn tomb?"

Sandra saw the sliver of sunshine and began making her way there as quickly as she could. "Long story. Get us out of here. Please."

Daryl also stumbled toward the sunshine. "I told both of them it was a ridiculous plan."

"What was the plan?" I had a clue but it was unbelievably stupid.

They both slipped through the door and fell into the warm December sunshine. They turned their faces up to it, drinking it in with their skin.

"I thought I'd never see the sun again," Daryl said. "I'm going to learn to fish and boat and spend time with my father."

"I'm going to stop pretending that Janet and I hate each other," Sandra said. "We're sisters of the heart, and we've wasted too much time pretending to be at odds."

I wasn't about to let them off the hook so easily. "What in the heck were you thinking? Setting up something like this and not telling anyone where you were hiding?"

Sandra's head drooped. "It was my idea that no one should know our hiding place. Janet was in on the plan, but not the details. We couldn't tell anyone. If there were rumors or suspicions, our plan would fail. At first Daryl and I were running around town in the dark, leaving those notes, trying to warn you off, and making phone calls to scare you away. That part was fun and exciting." She put a hand over her eyes for a moment. "It was all like a spy game—until we decided it was time to hide. Our plan was that you PIs would find us the evening of the big tree announcement. We'd left a clear trail of bread crumbs for you and Janet to find us. We'd be rescued and there would be a big celebration. Except by then we were trapped in the tomb with no way to get out."

"Janet really didn't know where you were?" I asked.

"No one did. I'd found the way to open the tomb several months ago, and I left instructions for Janet. She would be as surprised as anyone—that part was crucial so it would play well with the media."

"And you sealed yourself in a tomb thinking someone *might* find you?" They had a lot more faith than I did.

"We weren't going to seal the tomb," Daryl said. "We were so certain of our plan I called my mother before to up the ante. I knew she'd be terribly upset. But then we'd be rescued and everyone would be happy. But before we could get out, the tomb sealed itself. We've been trapped there for what seems like an eternity."

They both looked like hell, but that was to be expected after hiding in a mausoleum. I was about to punch in Coleman's phone number when I looked up the hill and saw Ray O'Day and Mary hauling butt down the slope toward us. It was going to be something of a homecoming. I just wasn't sure whether it would be joyful or dangerous.

As it turned out, I had nothing to worry about. Ray was as relieved to see Sandra and Daryl as I was. Ray hugged Sandra and Mary pulled Daryl into a warm embrace. The prodigal writer and her assistant had returned home.

40

Ellie and Martha hosted a special Christmas Eve celebration just for Sandra and Janet. When the two writers saw each other, they couldn't even pretend they were at odds. Crying and laughing, they grabbed Daryl, too. Mr. and Mrs. Marcus arrived and the reunion was a joy to watch. Like a Christmas miracle, Ray showed up with gifts for his sister and Janet.

"I was something of a brat to both of you," he said.

"Yeah, remember the time you made parachutes and tricked us up to the roof of Mrs. Whaley's big old house? You tied the chutes on us and threw us off the roof. It's a wonder we weren't killed." Janet eyed him warily.

"I was certain the parachutes would open. They were Mama's best sheets," Ray said. "But I was wrong. About a lot of things. It's why I came down here for Christmas. Ben and I have been talking and we want to patch up the past. He'll be here tomorrow morning."

"Just in time to claim the treasure." Millie put her hands on her hips and glared at Ray.

I'd told everyone about the treasure we'd found—and that it was being excavated under the watchful eye of the BSLPD. I wondered what the brothers knew about the off-shore accounts. It wasn't my place to speak up, so my lips were sealed.

Sandra grabbed Janet's hand and held it. "If Janet agrees, whatever that treasure is worth, I want to give it all to the Bay St. Louis library in honor of Mary and Weezie."

Janet was delighted. "I totally agree. Just like always."

The two were giddy with joy at their reunion and the prospect of dropping the façade of hating each other. Old friends were the best friends, I had to admit.

Mary, who'd been spiking the punch, hugged both of them. "Thank you. Thank you so much."

"The library was a haven for me," Daryl said. He put his arms around his parents. "I love you both so much, but while I want to share the outdoors with Dad, I'll always be a bookworm."

"A very rich bookworm," Sandra said. "Our book sales are through the roof."

While they were backslapping each other, I was getting madder and madder. "We all thought you'd been kidnapped and killed. That was a mean thing to do. Janet was worried sick, and Mr. and Mrs. Marcus were in real pain."

"It was only supposed to be for a few days," Sandra said. "I did leave instructions on how to find us. They were in a kitty carrier filled with books on Janet's front porch, just as we agreed." She turned to the other writer. "Why didn't you rescue us?"

"I never got the carrier." Janet's eyes were wide. "I looked every single minute I wasn't busy. There was no carrier near the front door. I didn't know what had happened to you. I searched everywhere I could think of."

"I think you better save some of your money to repay Thibodeau and the officers for all of the overtime they've put in looking for you," Mary said to the writers. "He's been working twenty-four/seven to find you."

"So all of this was about selling books?" I asked. "You almost got yourselves killed to sell books."

"I'm ashamed to say that's true," Sandra said. "But it wasn't supposed to play out like this. We did have a rescue plan. Think about it, the hunt to save us from the tomb would have had the media eating out of Janet's palm for at least twenty-four hours. We wanted to sell a lot of books."

"And boy, did it work," Cece threw in. "You guys have been the lead news story nationally for the past few days."

"But we intended it to be just a day or so, and then we'd be rescued and we could put aside our pretend feud."

"That was honestly the goal. I was tired of the brawls and catfights," Janet said. "I love Sandra and Daryl. We work so well together. But we needed a way for that to happen that was—"

"Marketable," Cece added.

"Exactly," Sandra said. "It was never meant to be taken this far. Never. Daryl and I thought we were going to die in that tomb. Thank goodness we had each other, but we had lost hope of rescue. We were trying to figure a way to write our goodbyes, if anyone ever found us."

They'd suffered for their moronic prank, and I wasn't

one to heap coals on a hot situation. I was just glad I'd found them. And earned the Delaney Detective Agency fee. *And* saved our sterling reputation.

Tinkie's eyebrows drew together. "What happened to the instructions on how to find you?"

Thibodeau had entered the parlor and he cleared his throat. "I know. The front door camera was disabled. The last images were of a man in a hoodie sneaking up to the house with a remote device. The man was Clarence. He confessed. Clarence found the cat carrier. He didn't look in it. He thought it was another cat and he just dropped it off the bridge. Seems like Clarence is one of those men who hate cats."

"What an awful man," Janet said. "I will press charges."

"Good," I said. "Maximum sentence."

"My intentions," Thibodeau said. "And yes, there will be a bill for department overtime and use of resources for what was basically a publicity stunt. Clarence, too, will be billed for departmental expense and he'll be charged with endangering a life, trespassing, stealing, and whatever else I can come up with. If I'm lucky, he'll incriminate Tilly and I'll put both of them behind bars."

"We're happy to pay," Janet and Sandra said in unison.

"And Harold?" Coleman said. "Who knocked him out in the mansion and hauled him to the tomb?"

Daryl timidly raised his hand. "I did. And Sandra. He almost caught us having a drink upstairs. We had to do it. He would have ruined our scheme. We knew the PIs were snooping around and would find him. That's why we had to move his car, too."

Harold rubbed the knot on his head. "I wasn't hurt," he said at last. "I'm willing to let it go."

I turned to Mr. Marcus. "Were you spying on me here at the inn?"

Blood flushed his cheeks. "Yes. I apologize. I was desperate to find my son."

"And you tied me and my sister up?" Ellie asked.

He nodded. "I did. I only wanted to get away. I'll turn myself in. I realized what I was doing was so very wrong. That's why I tried to get Ms. Delaney's attention by throwing rocks at her window. I wanted her to find you. I didn't intend to hurt you, I just needed a little time to get off the property and out of town."

I held my breath to see what Thibodeau would do.

"Are you willing to accept some work on the inn and property as restitution for Mr. Marcus's trespassing?" the chief asked both ladies.

"A perfect solution," Ellie said, nodding at her sister. "Consider it resolved."

"And one more thing?" I said. This I had to know. "Who closed Tinkie and me in that creepy tomb?"

Sandra smiled. "That, Sarah Booth, was an act of God. Apparently the wiring in the tomb needs renovation. The switch triggers itself. Which is exactly what happened to Daryl and me."

And so the case was closed without any fatalities. Dusk had fallen, and outside a chorus of voices could be heard walking toward the inn. The Christmas parade wouldn't be far behind the singers, the spectacular trees lit and dazzling the onlookers.

"It's the carolers," Ellie said. "Let's greet them."

We went to the front door and saw at least twenty men and women dressed in coats, gloves, and scarves. They sang my favorite carol, "God Rest Ye Merry Gentlemen." We'd intended to be part of the chorus, but my friends and I had discussed the matter, and we were heading back to Zinnia on a cold, clear, Christmas Eve. Only Harold would remain behind with Janet, and then the two writers and Daryl would bring him to Zinnia tomorrow in time to play his role in the Christmas pageant at the church.

In no time flat, we had loaded our belongings in the cars and were driving in a caravan through the dark night toward our homes. When we entered Zinnia, Cece and Millie peeled off. They lived in town. Then Tinkie, Oscar, Maylin, and Pauline took the north fork to Hilltop. Not long after, Coleman and I pulled into Dahlia House and were greeted by the thunder of horses' hooves as the three steeds met us at the head of the drive and raced us back to the barn. I was very happy to be home.

"Do you want to exchange gifts?" Coleman asked. "Technically, it is Christmas Day."

I was too tired to really enjoy the moment. "Let's go to bed and I'll give you one of your presents. Maybe."

"I like the way you think."

I went to put hay in the stalls while Coleman brought our bags in. By the time I got in the house, he had a fire going in our bedroom and was sleeping soundly. Just as well. I fell into bed and was asleep two minutes later.

41

Something tickled my nose. I refused to open my eyes, and I swatted at my face. When I heard Coleman chuckle, I knew I'd better get up or he'd prank me. I opened one eye and found him sitting on the side of the bed, dressed in his warmest riding clothes and boots.

"The horses are saddled and waiting for you."

I sat up quickly. Sun streamed in my bedroom window, and a beautiful gift box lay on my lap. I tore into it. When I lifted the lid of the box, a bejeweled brooch winked up at me in the sunlight. I froze. The brooch was beautiful, but not in my normal line of fashion. I was more a jeans and boots kind of woman.

"It's a camera," Coleman said. "From a store in London. The latest in spyware and copied from a James Bond device."

"A camera!" I was thrilled.

"You can activate it with your phone or another remote device."

I threw my arms around him. "It's the perfect gift. Thank you."

"You're welcome, now get dressed. It's time to ride! We have to be back in time to put on our costumes for the Christmas pageant."

I'd managed to put the pageant out of my head, but I wasn't so lucky that others had forgotten. I'd have to endure it. And I was also a little worried about Jitty. Normally she would have been all over my business, but I hadn't heard so much as a peep from her. It was Christmas Day. Surely she'd show up before the pageant.

I drew on my jeans, boots, several layers of sweaters, a warm jacket, hat, and gloves and raced out the back door where Coleman held Reveler for me. He'd chosen the big black Lucifer for his ride. He gave me a leg up, and then he mounted and we were off, down the driveway and across the open, unfenced fields that were fallow since the cotton had been harvested.

The brisk morning made the horses frisky, and even as we cantered along the edge of a field, I could feel Reveler wanting to buck. He was never bad, just feeling good. I pushed harder into the saddle and lightly teased the reins to remind him I was aboard and not inclined to want to go flying into orbit. Coleman had his hands full, too.

When the horses slowed to a trot and then a walk of their own volition, we turned back toward home. We'd covered several miles, and it would be time to dress for church when we got back. Then a late brunch at Tinkie's when the pageant was done. I still had a present for Coleman, but it was one I wanted him to have plenty of time to enjoy.

Holding hands, we moved toward home at a walk. I couldn't imagine a lovelier Christmas morning. Hoarfrost covered the ground, giving the look of a snowfall, at least until the sun came out and melted it away. The sky was deep blue with a few white, fluffy clouds that settled against the brown earth on the far horizon. I knew how lucky I was in this moment in time.

"What are you smiling about?" Coleman asked.

"If I told you, I'd have to kill you."

"Oh, that's a challenge," he said.

"I promise, I'll tell you later. For right now, you'll have to settle with me telling you how much I love you."

"Good enough!"

We moved into an easy trot and covered the ground back to the barn. Our private Christmas celebration was over. It was time to join the gang.

"Where's my camel costume?" I had gone through the storage closet in the church where I'd left the costume two weeks earlier.

Tinkie was swaddling Maylin, who looked absolutely angelic. She didn't look up. "I have no idea. Do the wise men have their costumes?"

"Yes." Harold had arrived as promised, along with Oscar and Coleman, to reprise their roles as the three wise men. Tinkie looked wonderful as Mary, and Cece was the angel hovering over the crèche. She could really belt out "Hark! the Herald Angels Sing." Everyone was in their costume but me. I couldn't find the drab brown camel costume anywhere.

Mrs. Peters, the pageant director, came into the room, clapping her hands. "It's time to take your places in the crèche." She looked at me. "Camel, why aren't you in costume?"

"I can't find my costume." I felt like it was my fault, which it wasn't. I didn't want to disappoint Baby Jesus or Mrs. Peters on Christmas Day.

"The donkey has his costume," Mrs. Peters pointed out. "And even the pig." She'd added the "even" because Wilbur Redd was enacting the pig and he was always late for everything. I was lagging behind Wilbur Redd.

"I left my costume right there." I pointed to the closet. "Now it's gone. I didn't take it."

She walked to the empty closet and looked in. "What will we do? We need a camel a lot more than we need a pig!"

She was right about that. I didn't recall a pig in any nativity scene I'd ever witnessed. "Let me check the storage room off the kitchen." It was the only place I could think of to look—and it also got me out from under Mrs. Peters's scrutiny.

"Want me to come help?" Tinkie asked. She looked a little concerned.

"No. Just make sure Maylin is happy and ready to be the perfect baby. We can go on without a camel, but not without a baby."

If I couldn't find the costume, my plan was to hide in the kitchen until the pageant had started. No one would really notice I wasn't participating except my friends. The show would go on, as it must.

The hallways of the church were empty as the pews in the sanctuary were filling. There were fresh pastries and lots of goodies for after the service, but I went straight to the supply closet. It was as big as my bedroom, and I closed the door behind me so I could heave a sigh.

"Find that costume, the show must go on!" A glamorous woman dripping with jewels stood in the supply room. She smelled of gardenias, which she wore in her marcelled hair. She was so beautiful, and I knew exactly who she was. Helene Buntman, aka Jitty.

"Don't mess with me now. I'm about to disappoint my friends because someone moved that ugly costume."

"Maybe you were never intended to play a camel," Helene said. "Perhaps you needed a meatier role."

"Not." I didn't have time for this, but I did have a question. "Why didn't you marry Al Capone? He obviously loved you."

"And I him. As a friend. We were partners. I helped him create the most sophisticated booze delivery system in the nation. He did everything he could to make my dreams come true. It was so much better than romance. It was . . . family."

"Like me and Tinkie."

"Exactly," she said.

"Thanks, Helene. Now I can rest easy."

"Your mama said you would make a better jackass than camel." Helene was slowly transforming into Jitty. "If you must know, it was those terrible Hobdy boys who took your costume."

I didn't care about the costume any longer. "Mama did not say that. You said that."

"Maybe." Jitty was fully transformed—and she was wearing my camel costume!

"Give me that." I reached for it but grabbed only air.

Jitty's laughter and the scent of gardenias lingered, but my haint was gone.

"Merry Christmas, Jitty," I called to her. As I turned to go, I saw a brown costume in the corner of the room near the toilet paper supply. I grabbed it, threw it on, struggling to get my humps in place, and raced to the sanctuary entrance just in time to fall into line with the other stable animals.

"And peace to all," Tinkie whispered in my ear.

"I don't even know what kind of noise a camel makes, but I'm going to improvise."

I felt a boot to my bottom and whirled around to confront the pig. "Why did you kick me?" I demanded.

"Because the sign said to do it." He pulled something from my back and handed it to me.

"Kick me" had been printed on paper and attached to the back of my costume. Now I knew why it had disappeared. And those terrible, awful wrecking balls pretending to be humans, the Hobdy boys, had done this. My friends' faces were impassive.

"Someone will pay," I warned them just as we entered the sanctuary.

"Merry Christmas, Sarah Booth," Coleman said, taking my halter to lead me in. "We'll settle this later today. For now, peace on Earth and goodwill toward men."

"Dream on," I told him. "Dream on."

Acknowledgments

Libraries have always played a big role in my life—first as a reader and now as a writer. With the decline of so many local bookstores, libraries have become "the book place" in so many small towns. Growing up, books were my escape. They offered adventure, knowledge, exotic places, history, and so much more.

I've gone to the front desk at a library and asked for help finding the most obscure information, and I always got the help I sought. When my mother was an alderman (on the city council) in the small town where I grew up, funding the library was a key issue for her. We were always a family that recognized the many, many benefits a public library brought to a town.

I want to thank all the librarians who have looked things

up for me, sent me into the stacks with suggestions, and offered support for my writing. And I want to thank the many "friends" of the libraries who put on fundraisers and programs to keep libraries open.

I'd like to thank my agent, Marian Young. We've shared this publishing journey and a better companion could not be found.

For the editorial team at St. Martin's Press—thank you. Hannah O'Grady is fabulous. All of the editors are top drawer. They make each book better. They save me from brain slippage all the time. And the artist, art department, and book design team create the great covers and interiors that are so popular.

One person is mostly responsible for keeping me on track. Without Priya Bhakta's gentle reminders and fabulous creativity with graphics and design—plus her endless patience—nothing would ever get done.

A writer is nothing without readers, and it is so gratifying when readers ask, "When's the next Sarah Booth coming out?" A question I never tire of answering. The readers wouldn't have books without booksellers. The Haunted Bookshop is my local bookseller in Mobile, and they know and love the business of books. Visit them if you haven't. The shop has a great history.

I do write a monthly newsletter, and you can sign up at www.carolynhaines.com/subscribe.